KU-284-637

3 0012 00177900 7

WITHDRAWN FROM STOCK

FIRST STRIKE

WITHDRAWN FROM STOCK

Also by Conor Cregan

With Extreme Prejudice
House of Fire
Valkyrie
Ground Zero

FIRST STRIKE

Conor Cregan

LIMERICK COUNTY LIBRARY
G90092

Hodder & Stoughton

Copyright © 1999 by Conor Cregan

First published in Great Britain in 1999 by
Hodder and Stoughton
A division of Hodder Headline PLC

The right of Conor Cregan to be identified as the Author of
the Work has been asserted by him in accordance with the
Copyright, Designs and Patents Act 1988.

10 9 8 7 6 5 4 3 2 1

All rights reserved. No part of this publication may be
reproduced, stored in a retrieval system, or transmitted,
in any form or by any means without the prior written
permission of the publisher, nor be otherwise circulated
in any form of binding or cover other than that in which
it is published and without a similar condition being
imposed on the subsequent purchaser.

All characters in this publication are fictitious
and any resemblance to real persons, living
or dead, is purely coincidental.

British Library Cataloguing in Publication Data

A CIP catalogue record for this title
is available from the British Library

ISBN 0 340 68937 4

Printed and bound in Great Britain by
Clays Ltd, St Ives plc

Hodder and Stoughton
A division of Hodder Headline PLC
338 Euston Road
London NW1 3BH

To Hannah

COLD WAR

I

The Priest

The priest called himself Misha Girenko. He had a broken nose and colourless lips. 'I'm not who you think I am,' he said to the British intelligence officer standing in the corner of his Paris jail cell. 'I'm a murderer and even though we are almost halfway through the twentieth century, the French will cut my head off. Yes, I killed a priest and took his identity. But I am not your spy.'

Patrick Twilight stepped out of the shadow. 'I can help you,' he said. 'But I need you to admit you're Reggie Spane.'

'But I'm not,' the priest replied.

Patrick Twilight looked at his watch. In the ninth month of the Soviet blockade of West Berlin, he had more important things than chasing ghosts to occupy his time. He exhaled his frustration through his nose. 'All right,' he said, reaching into his briefcase for a photograph.

Good looking in a very simple way, with a calm maturity about him, Twilight was perhaps slightly too tall for France and too brown for the time of year. But for all that, he had a certain overriding determination in his presence and a stare that used one of his eyes to hold you firm while the other one checked you out.

He threw the photograph he had selected on the metal bed beside the wall.

'Reggie Spane,' he said. 'Disappeared from a pub in Soho, in '39, three days after the SS blew the lid off our entire Dutch operation. Body supposedly found in a decidedly overripe condition in the Thames some months later. And now, ten years on, you turn up.'

Ten years had taken the priest's hair up and streaked it with small seams of brightness which caught the sunlight pouring in from a Paris in full anticipation of spring. Ten years had weakened his skin and darkened his cheeks. Ten years had allowed a scar to blend in with the capillaried skin. But this was Reggie Spane. No matter what he called himself now.

'I can't help you and I don't want your help,' Girenko said. 'I fully expect to die. I am prepared. I know some of my friends at the monastery would like me to appeal. It's amazing how reluctant some people who profess the bounties of the afterlife are to check it out.'

The priest knelt down on his cell floor, blessed himself, said a few prayers, then picked up a newspaper. 'Stalin has cut the price of food and clothes in Moscow. Must be preparing them for war. The rituals of death, Mr Twilight. Is Berlin prepared? A tiny Western lifeboat in an ocean of communist hostility. Are you prepared?'

At that point, Twilight might have ended the interview. He stepped towards the cell door as if he were going to. But just then, as he looked like he was about to call the guard, he said something without really giving it much consideration. 'If you won't co-operate, I can have you kept alive, indefinitely, Reggie.'

What had been a routine enquiry changed at that moment.

The serenity that had dominated the priest's face dissolved and what emerged from behind it made Twilight step back against the door. 'You would deny a man paradise?' Girenko asked.

'A man who leaves pain behind in this world does not deserve paradise,' Twilight replied. 'Paradise is for those who have settled all accounts. You are still overdrawn. Now admit you're Reggie Spane.'

The pause that followed seemed eternal and Twilight was almost tempted to terminate the meeting this time, but Girenko's face kept him there. Twilight picked at one of his yellowing teeth to ease his tension. Girenko touched a small growth on his cheek.

'Okay, okay,' he said finally. Twilight, who felt he had won something of a victory but was not quite sure what kind, stopped picking at his tooth. 'Once upon a time there were two brothers,' Girenko went on, staring into space as if he were reading. 'One brother had all the brains, the other . . . well, the other had nothing particularly noticeable, except a keen survival instinct, which he did not realise for many years. They were born a year apart and might have been twins but for that. Indeed, there were people who said the second brother was just hiding in his mother's womb for another year because he did not fancy coming out that winter. Or maybe he was afraid of his brother.'

'Your brother, what happened to him?' Twilight asked.

'He went to university. Fell in with the wrong crowd. Got into some minor trouble, producing leaflets. The kind of thing that got you a jail sentence in those days. Came back with Siberian ice in his veins.'

'A Bolshevik?'

'And I joined the Okhrana,' Girenko said. 'My father threatened to disinherit me. A career in the Tsar's secret police lowered the tone. You see, we were part of that thick layer of middle aristocracy the Tsars had planted Russia with. Started as a useful crop, turned into a murderous weed. Don't you think?'

'The real rebel?' Twilight said.

Girenko nodded. 'When the revolutions came, I took one side, my brother the other. I might have seen him once during a battle in Kiev in 1919, but that could have been wishful thinking. Old Felix Dzerzhinsky decorated him later, I believe.'

'You?'

'I became just another emigre. We tried to launch a small invasion in the Caucasus in '28, but they beat us back. I spent some time in the mountains, then went to China. Made some money, lost some money.'

'But you went back to Russia again.' Twilight leaned his head back against the wall, expecting Girenko to fill in the blanks of Reggie Spane's last years.

Girenko sat down and bit his nails. 'How could you be so perceptive? A man named Dansey – quite a legend in your organisation – might have been Administrator.' The priest smiled. 'Claude Dansey asked me to go back to Russia in 1937.'

'And Dansey is conveniently dead.'

'It was the time of the great purges,' Girenko went on. 'Uncle Joe Stalin doing a bit of house cleaning. Proving he was the man of steel. Do you know he has never really liked that title. Lenin insisted on it. Stalin has always liked Georgian aliases. A mountain bandit at heart. And now he has you by the balls. Perhaps if you did keep me here long enough the Bolsheviks would get their wish and execute me themselves. He was going to be a priest, too, you know. Always spouting prayers, our little Joe.'

It was nothing more than Girenko's tone that prompted Twilight's next question.

'Our little Joe?' Twilight said. He was fiddling with the thread on one of his buttons and did not look up. 'You say it like you owned him.'

Girenko smiled slightly, not sure if Twilight was really paying attention any more. 'Sure, we did,' the priest said, as if trying to assert some authority. 'Double-cross.'

Twilight's head shot up. Girenko looked satisfied. Twilight relaxed and asked him what he meant.

'Look, you people used to run a game against the Germans during the war,' Girenko said. 'The Double-Cross programme.' Girenko tapped his nose. 'I know about Double-Cross because I met a man in the mountains near Spain, who told me about it during his confession one evening. You would be surprised what secrets I have taken into my confidence. I believe the French would like me dead for that reason alone. I see you do not deny the existence of Double-Cross. Well, we ran the same business in the Okhrana. Years before you. And Comrade Stalin was our star.'

Twilight's hand dropped the button. 'Stalin was your agent?'

'You British gave him to us.' Girenko paused to read Twilight's face.

'Go on,' Twilight insisted, trying to hide his real interest for the moment. But he had a notebook out now.

'Well, when Dansey sent me back,' Girenko said, 'I was caught and the Chekists sent my brother over here . . .'

'Forget you and your brother,' Twilight said, waving his hand. 'Tell me about Stalin and the Okhrana.'

Girenko moved in small motions around the room, going through a daily routine he had developed while in a monastery, a proportioned attempt to quantify his life for the simplest of reasons, he once told a superior.

But now his chest was tight with the asthma he had fallen victim to during freezing nights in the maquis years earlier, attending to dying men and pregnant girls, walking up goat tracks, blind in the pitch of the night, crossing ice rivers, sleeping in damp holes by shivering trees.

'He went to London in 1907. Comrade Stalin. For the Fourth Party Congress. He had escaped from a camp in Siberia, then headed home again. Into the Caucasus. Always home. Like a wounded animal. Except this one time he goes to London to see his lord and master, Lenin, who's full of praise for Stalin.

'Stalin had an eye for the ladies. Georgians and women . . .' Girenko raised one eyebrow. Its hairs were thick and pointing in different directions. 'Anyway, there was a woman. I do not remember her name. She took a shine to our Stalin. Lenin's man of steel took to that shine. I have seen it myself and I will not pass judgement on that. These things happen, rarely last, and if they were the worst thing we did to one another perhaps . . . but he raped and killed her.'

'Stalin?'

'There was an investigation. And because of the circumstances, your Special Branch were called in. They let Stalin go.

He made his way back to Russia and when he arrived, the Okhrana were waiting for him. Together with a copy of his British Special Branch file.'

'The Okhrana wanted his co-operation?'

'And they got it. Stalin knew on what side his bread was buttered, as you English say. I have never taken butter on my bread. He had a choice: work for the Okhrana or go back to London and a long drop.' Girenko placed his thick callused hands around his neck.

'He became an agent provocateur?' Twilight said.

'There were quite a few, like Malinovsky, Lenin's friend. Lenin knew he was working for the Okhrana all the time. Encouraged him. Then had him shot when the Bolsheviks came to power. Embarrassing to have a leading party member so close to the ancien regime. They found twelve agents provocateur in party ranks, then Stalin closed down the commission charged with hunting them down. The thirteenth was known only by a codename: Vasili.'

'Stalin,' Twilight said. 'There were always rumours.'

Girenko nodded. 'I was one of those waiting for him when he arrived back from London. Surprisingly co-operative, he was. Always nodding that nasty smallpoxed face. The Menshevik lobby in the party had won a ban on all armed actions. Stalin was angry at this, so we had a lever. He's a vengeful little bastard.'

'You wanted the armed actions to continue,' Twilight said.

'Sure, we did. The more they committed crime, the more we could take the gloves off with them. They were more dangerous in parliament than out robbing payrolls and organising strikes. All coups are palace coups in the long run. Infiltrate, seize, overwhelm. Nothing ever gets done from the outside, and as long as these boys were happy to exist outside, then they would be less of a threat. Our plans fell apart with the war in 1914. In the end, Lenin and his cronies only had to pick up the pieces. But Stalin did fine work for us for about ten years. You can understand how shocked I was to wake up one morning and find he was a member of the government. I knew my goose was cooked.'

'But you did nothing.'

'What was there to do? Who would believe a policeman then? And I had no evidence. I was too busy trying to save myself from Bolshevik-inspired lynch mobs. I made my way east for a time. Took up with a white unit, then wound up . . .' Girenko waved his arms. 'Well, you know the rest.'

'My heart goes out to you,' Twilight said.

Now Girenko became angry. His anger adopted a tone Twilight had seen before in men who had served lost causes. All the magnificence of futility accompanied every word and Twilight was forced to admire Girenko, something that put him on the defensive for the first time. Girenko's green eyes appeared to swell.

'I know what you think of me, Mr Twilight,' he said. 'Because I used to think it of myself. So you're way behind the times. Now, I have my conscience clear, I have made my peace with my God, and I will reach paradise.' Worn out by his own fury, the priest went over to a bucket, pulled out a damp cloth, slightly flecked with dirt, and put it to his ribbed forehead. 'We called them Reptiles. Stalin's kind. We Russians are about a metre deeper than you English, aren't we? Barbarians with souls. Perhaps that is why you resent us so much. Your Reggie Spane was my brother, Niki, Mr Twilight. Much like our man, Vasili, was Stalin.'

'I'll bet,' Twilight commented. 'Tell me more.'

Girenko thought again. 'More?' he asked. 'My brother's dead.'

'About Stalin.'

'What? If you want more, there's an Okhrana file, stamped Vasili, thick as a wine crate; even has photographs and film of Stalin executing an old Bolshevik named Genady Kirov. Kirov stumbled across Stalin's little secret, so we let Stalin administer the punishment. He liked to do things like that.'

Twilight called the guard and asked for coffee.

'My brother, Niki,' Girenko said, looking out the window, 'your Reggie Spane. I don't know why he died, but the Reds were allies of the Nazis in 1939.'

'Tell me about Stalin's Okhrana file,' Twilight said.

2

The File

'I was in a camp in the western Urals in 1938,' Girenko
continued. And Twilight had the feeling he was listening to a
deathbed confession. 'Near a small glacier between two
mountains that looked like the broken teeth of a dead animal,
a very blue place where even the snow ached with the cold.
The rock was a sharp volcanic petrified lava, and very loose.
See this?' He pointed to a scar on his arm. 'I got this from
trying to dig a hole in it. I saw men lose eyes that froze over
and fingers that broke off. Only the cold kept them from
bleeding to death. There is a special kind of pain in cold
places. I don't suppose you have ever experienced it.'

'I once rode a convoy to Murmansk,' Twilight commented.

'Luxury cruise. There was a man in this camp, Ivan Pyotr. A
former policeman I had known in St Petersburg. We used to
call him Ivan the Terrible there. He was a big heavy man from
beyond the Urals. Very Tartarish looks. The kind of fellow
who made people stop talking when he entered a room.
Strong, physically, bright enough to play the great game
but not clever enough to save himself. A bit like me. But
he had the eyes of a hungry wolf. Mine are artistic. Like yours,

Mr Twilight. Anyway, when I arrived in the camp in 1938, this fellow Ivan was not so terrible any more. And thin as a gardening implement. Rather frightening to those of us who were new. A glimpse of the future.'

Twilight nodded with a serenity that defied his excitement.

'Don't feel sorry for this fellow, Mr Twilight. I have seen him hang men over his back on occasion. And worse. Why the Bolsheviks kept him alive, I couldn't understand, until one day when we were sitting in the corner of a quarry, during a break in work. And he showed me a letter.

'His kid was sick. I don't remember what it was. I think it was something to do with the lungs. The boy was weak. Well, Ivan wanted to get his kid out of Russia – the Soviet Union – so he writes to the dwarf, Yezhov, Stalin's chief butcher. It was a time of purges and people were being shot for looking the wrong way, and yet this Ivan writes to the head of the secret police. Can you believe it?

'Well, I thought it would be a bullet for him as soon as the letter landed on the commandant's desk, let alone the poisoned dwarf's at the Lubyanka. And that made me scared because if Ivan got it I would, too. I feared death then, I'll tell you. But what do you think happened? Yezhov wrote back to Ivan. At first, I though this was insane. Yezhov writing to a number in the Gulags. A zek.

'"You can get my kid out," Ivan says to me then. "You can see he makes it to Berlin or Paris. Gets the right treatment. I have money. And you can do it, Misha." That was the first time he called me by my name. It was a threat. There we were in the middle of a glacier, freezing by degrees and starving by numbers and this fellow, this stupid monster, tells me I have to escape, find his child and get us both out of Russia. I laughed.'

'How did you get out?' Twilight asked.

Girenko wagged a finger. 'You're ahead of yourself. I had to witness the weekly executions. Slow hangings on bad gallows, shootings in shallow pits. Bodies never decayed and months after a shooting you would see limbs emerging from the ground or torsos forcing themselves out of shallow graves – sitting up, like this.' Girenko demonstrated. 'Then the wolves would get them. And slowly men would be picked clean by them and anything else that needed a meal. And I mean anything.' He looked at Twilight with a mixture of horror and superiority. 'I have seen things, Mr Twilight. There was one man and he had a jawbone hidden in his mattress for months. And each night he would suck on it; it was his brother. Ivan Pyotr offered me a way out.

'Suddenly, this man seemed to think he could arrange escapes. Other people's anyway. I see you are not surprised. Yes, the line between guards and prisoners in such a place is vague and a community develops that has pretty much nothing to do with events in the outside world. Some prisoners were more powerful than the guards and many guards were worse off than prisoners. People who could make things happen had value. And Ivan had a few tricks up his sleeve.

'You see, Ivan knew things about everyone. He had worked in the Okhrana's file section. And very few files were found after the Bolshevik coup. Okhrana records seemed to vanish with the last snows of winter. But they had not, they had been moved to places where winter could keep them frozen. For posterity.'

'So why did the Bolsheviks not just have your friend, Ivan, shot? Or why did he not buy his way to freedom?'

'You have heard the term Mexican standoff? That was our Ivan. He had them under threat and they had him at the point of a gun. And Yezhov wanted Stalin's file.

'Ivan told me Lenin had called for him once. He wanted all the Reptile files. But our Ivan, who knew what colour socks Lenin wore, would not budge. Then Lenin said something curious: "I want Vasili." A few weeks later he was dead. This man of steel, this Stalin, he is a powerful man, but not powerful enough to wipe out all of his past. No one is that powerful. I hope. I have very little faith in humanity and hope hell is worse than we can imagine, Mr Twilight. I want those bastards with no faith to suffer. I want to hear their agonies.' Girenko paused to recover his composure. 'And now I am being unchristian,' he said.

'So where is Stalin's file?' Twilight asked.

'Helsinki, perhaps. Switzerland. Pick your place. Ask Ivan Pyotr. If he's still alive. Yezhov was shot in '39. When I got out, I headed straight for China. I heard his kid died later. I wasn't going risk another term in that camp for the sake of Ivan's brat. I had my priorities.'

When he returned from Paris that Friday, Twilight was irritated if not surprised to find no one in London interested in his discovery. Josef Stalin had just removed Vyacheslav Molotov from his position as Soviet Foreign Minister and all eyes were on the Kremlin to see what effect it would have on the Berlin situation. Molotov had been in favour of a softer line than his master, Stalin. In the end, the old bespectacled foreign minister's departure seemed to have no effect on the situation. None visible, anyway.

Then, three days later, Twilight was woken from a piecemeal sleep in his London flat and summoned to his Administrator's office on the fourth floor of Broadway Buildings, opposite St James's Park tube station.

It was well past midnight when Twilight met the Administrator in his small fourth-floor room. Rationesque, someone down the corridor had dubbed the mean style of the place. Perhaps just fashionless, Twilight thought. Designed to give a sense of permanence and continuity. Twilight just found it cold.

The Administrator, who had now visibly aged since the beginning of the Berlin blockade the summer before, resembled an old oak tree, in that he was slightly lumpy and twisted, with brittle limbs and a thin foliage. The contents of his room appeared to enhance the effect. The starkness, combined with the cold, just made Patrick Twilight shiver.

'I was on a break in the country, you know, Patrick,' the Administrator said. 'Just so you realise you're not the only one inconvenienced.' He paused to allow Twilight's reserved face time to acknowledge the sacrifice. Twilight pushed one of his long locks of hair back over his ear. 'Anyway, we'd like to do something about this Okhrana file on Stalin,' the Administrator said then.

'What did you have in mind?'

In his late thirties, Patrick Twilight perhaps lacked the pedigree to warrant comparisons to an ancient tree, and was definitely too intelligent to need them. He always remembered being told when recruited from photo reconnaissance in 1940, that being right was not everything. So he cut his wisdom to suit the circumstances from there on, but occasionally it came through.

He was what the firm called a might-have boy: might have

finished school if his folks had had the cash; might have done a double first if he had finished school; might have done better quicker if he had had the familial requisites. The only thing he could work on without money was an accent. Which now had the same reserve as his face.

'If it's at all possible, we'd like to persuade Colonel Ivan Pyotr to come west,' the Administrator said. 'Tell us about his files.' His spartan surroundings only emphasised his privilege. With a private income and competence in too many languages for his own good, he had performed all the necessary field tasks before a job in Whitehall took him away from the sordid basics of their trade to the rarefied heights of hypothetical strategic planning. Twilight could imagine him lecturing already.

The Administrator could only focus on Twilight's taste for suits he probably could not afford and handkerchiefs that drooped in his top pocket. And a hairstyle that was too long.

'And Reggie Spane?' Twilight asked.

'You know, I remember when professionalism was confined to a separate dressing room in any respectable sport, Patrick. I think Reggie reminds people of those days. Except he's become a bit of a byword for betrayal and duplicity, you see. I'd like to feel Girenko has closed the book on Spane. And we are all professionals.'

'Do we grant Girenko his wish?' Twilight asked.

'We keep Girenko alive but in our custody.'

He indicated that Twilight should pass him his case notes.

Twilight placed the sheets of paper he was carrying on the desk in front of him. The Administrator read the pages very slowly, pausing now and then to correct spelling errors with a pencil. The correction markings were very faint in the margin, and Twilight struggled to read them while talking, his eyes failing him now.

'You know, Surgical's department dissected Spane,' the Administrator said. A degree of distance in his voice told Twilight someone was in for a bollocking. 'The enquiry came to the conclusion he had committed suicide while the balance of his mind was disturbed. There is a body. People helped identify it as far as was possible.'

'I wasn't in the firm's employ at the time,' Twilight replied. 'I never met Spane.'

'Me neither, actually,' the Administrator said. 'He was one of those shadows Claude Dansey had moving all around Europe just before the war. More people wanted to know Reggie Spane than ever did. You see the problem?'

'That why I was sent to interview him?'

'You Huntergatherers have a facility for discretion.'

'And now you want me to find a prisoner who has been in the gulags for three decades.'

The pause that followed showed the Administrator's capacity for calculation and Twilight's for patience. More figures, small notes and a rearranging of his desk.

'We're going to want someone who knows this camp Girenko says Pyotr is in,' the Administrator said.

'Was in,' Twilight said.

'We're predicating all this on the notion he still is. Worth a try, given our circumstances.'

'I take it Girenko is not a candidate for guide?' Twilight said.

'I don't think we can risk that,' the Administrator said.

Twilight felt a degree of tightening in his stomach. 'I couldn't get our Special Branch file on Stalin,' he said then.

'That's because I have it,' the Administrator said. 'Useless up till now.' He noticed Twilight's frustration. 'Heading Huntergatherers is not a licence to know everything, Patrick.' The Administrator paused again.

Twilight was at the door, pushing his hand through his long hair, licking his heavy lips, when the Administrator spoke again.

'By the by, you'll be liaising with CIA Strangers on this one, Patrick. Joint operation, as they say. They have so much more in the way of resources nowadays. Particularly in Russia. And they can twist French arms. Indo-China is costing our continental neighbours a fortune.' The Administrator almost smiled. 'You don't mind?'

Twilight did mind but he let it go.

3

Brytenn

All that winter the mild weather had drawn the wolves towards Finland. And three miles inside the Soviet Union, Cooper Brytenn listened to them howl at the moon from the other side of the frontier.

The yellow moon sprinkled drops of golden light along the branches of the conifers, and a hard frost coated the ground, throwing most of the moon's light back at the sky. The sky looked sick as a result. Brytenn's companion looked worse.

'One . . . two hours,' Brytenn said. 'Can you hang on?'

Swell Johnson nodded his pale boyish face and stayed true to his name. 'Swell,' he said. *G-90092*

Brytenn, a sharp-featured man with polished skin, a movie star moustache, a cleft chin and worried eyes, took another look at Johnson's wound. The small mine had punctured his left side with a dozen or more little holes, and blood was beginning to flow from some of them again. Brytenn re-adjusted the bandages under Johnson's field jacket and tried to pick a few of the more prominent pieces of metal from his flesh. Johnson let out a broken cry. Brytenn covered his friend's mouth.

LIMERICK COUNTY LIBRARY

'You won't leave me, Coop?' Johnson said then. 'You won't leave me? Remember, put a bullet in me but don't leave me.'

'I won't leave you.' Brytenn's hard upper lip was covered by his lower one.

'Swell.'

Brytenn checked the magazine in his submachine-gun and then reloaded his pistol. Both weapons were Russian, and the submachine-gun had a silencer.

'If I didn't know you, I'd say you tripped that mine deliberately,' Johnson said. 'To get out of your card debts.' He tried to laugh but could not.

Brytenn pulled out some chocolate, broke a piece off, fed it to Johnson and listened to the temperature drop and the arctic winds check in for the night. 'We'll get there,' he said to Johnson. He took back whatever chocolate the wounded man could not eat but refused to eat it himself. And the moonlight gave Brytenn's face a sort of porcelain vanity.

'Bit of a fucking mess, eh, Cooper!' Johnson whispered. 'I think I'll give this stuff up and take a swell job lecturing for the Agency in Washington about the dangers of landmines.' He opened his mouth and closed his eyes at the same time, and Brytenn was forced to cover his friend's mouth again.

'Coulda happened to anyone,' he whispered into Johnson's ear. The cubic Minnesotan football jock passed out. 'I'm sorry,' Brytenn added. 'Central Intelligence Agency SNAFU.'

It might have happened to anyone but it had happened to them. It was always the simple, straight tasks that threw up the bad angles. A few photographs of shipping from Murmansk; a two-day job now become a week. Cooper Brytenn rubbed the stubble on his face and listened to the noises and felt the last resources of his strength begin to slip away.

The snow started again just after midnight and Brytenn lifted Johnson while the wounded man was still unconscious, and propped him up against a tree. Then he slapped him awake. 'I'm going on ahead,' he said to Johnson. 'See what's up there.'

'You're not leaving me, Cooper?' Johnson grabbed Brytenn's jacket.

Brytenn smiled. 'Back in fifteen minutes.'

'Swell.'

Brytenn pulled himself up from the small depression and tried to get the blood circulating in his legs before moving off. He failed, and it was a painful climb up a steep gradient after that. The howls around him forced him to stop about a hundred metres up the slope in a small clearing where the ground had escaped the permafrost and gave way beneath his feet till the water was almost over his boots. He could hear the babble of a river. But the howls were getting closer.

Shadows moved around the boughs of trees and small night creatures, woken from the winter sleep by the mild weather and now trapped by the return of the cold, scurried around in the sparse undergrowth looking for food and warmth while the snowflakes settled on the sharp rocks which broke the surface of the drifts left over from the last fall. Brytenn heard a crack.

Three flashlight beams converged out of the darkness and twice that many shots followed. Bullets hit the trees around him and the bullets were followed by shouts and more flashlight beams and then the dogs.

Brytenn fired, emptied a magazine, reloaded and fired in the opposite direction. A fat Russian soldier with a balaclava under his helmet appeared on top of the ridge above him. The man's face was bathed in reflected moonlight, which made him look sick, too. He shook as he raised his rifle and Cooper Brytenn killed him with two shots to the chest.

'Cooper . . . !'

Brytenn moved back towards Swell Johnson, hesitated, fired in separate directions and then turned away and ran to the top of the ridge. Again he stopped in soft ground. Again Swell Johnson cried his name. Brytenn hesitated, looked towards the river, looked back to where Johnson was shouting from, fired a long burst into the trees, ran forward and then threw himself into the river.

After that the cold took over and he was grateful.

'So you saw Johnson killed?'

Sitting in a Finnish log cabin, Brytenn was still shaking, smoking and shaking, but beginning to feel the warmth of the log fire bring back whatever life had been taken from him the night before. And with the life came the memories and the last sounds of Swell Johnson. Brytenn nodded. 'Yeah, I saw him shot.'

'And nothing was left?' The interrogator was a lawyer from Boston who wore glasses and smoked a pipe and insisted on asking every question a dozen times. Cooper Brytenn did not know if he could tell the same story a dozen times, did not know if anyone could tell the same story the same way a dozen times. Time changes even the truth.

'We got your pictures,' Brytenn said. He looked up at his tormentor slowly. 'Didn't we?'

'I'm sorry, Cooper, but with the way things are in Berlin, we have to be sure. Can't have them using a thing like this to hit us over the head with. Agency has to have plausible deniability. And Strangers have to be so deniable, it's unreal.'

'It's over,' Brytenn said. Then he waved his hand as if he were letting something down again. 'He's dead.'

The older man paced around the room and rearranged things. 'How many trips have you done the last couple of years, Cooper?'

'Maybe too many. Maybe they're on to me. Maybe I'm the liability. I should stay training.'

'Yeah, well, you're wanted back in Munich, pretty damn ASAP. You go to Helsinki tomorrow.'

'For what?'

The older man's look said it all.

'Oh, Jesus, no,' Brytenn muttered. 'Not through the curtain again.'

'I didn't hear that, Cooper. I know you're tired, old boy, but if you want to make your way in our organisation you gotta put cold time in.'

Brytenn regained himself quickly. 'Of course, of course.'

'Hey, the way things are with Uncle Joe Stalin right now, I wouldn't be surprised if they wanted you to punch a mile-wide tunnel all the way to Berlin. Hey, that's not a bad idea.' The older man paused to look at Brytenn for a while. 'You did fine, Cooper. Swell . . . well, that's the way of it.'

After that both men sat down.

The next day, while they prepared the car, Brytenn sat on a balcony, rocking in a chair, looking towards Russia, while a flock of birds flew in formation overhead. In the distance he could hear howls.

4

Central Intelligence

Patrick Twilight still shook slightly whenever he heard foot-steps behind him, still jerked his neck whenever his name was called with a certain tone, still found more than an hour's continuous sleep difficult, still wondered why they had asked him to head Huntergatherers after the war. Twilight let that pass with a small breath of wind. Maybe they just wanted to see him drown.

They said on the fourth floor of Broadway Buildings that you could tell a drowner by the way he held his head: slightly tilted as if treading water. Now, every day, when he had finished his routine Twilight spent a few minutes in front of a mirror examining the angle of his head.

But the firm had rescued him from a life he still feared returning to, and the series of dour buildings masquerading as industrial concerns in Pullach outside Munich was enough to bring back memories of a year spent in a paper mill in northern England and make him forget the indignities of an intelligence career.

'We need to find an SS man named Anatoli Beshov,' he said to the little German general sitting opposite him.

While Patrick Twilight waited for a reply and a top-heavy woman with hazelnut eyes and very white skin began to pour the coffee, from outside the smell of burning tar slipped in through a vent and made everyone at the table sniff at the same time.

'Why?' General Reinhard Gehlen, Hitler's former eastern front intelligence chief, stared out at a party of men in the courtyard below, who were beginning to shovel the tar into a hole.

'Because we're asking, General.' Cooper Brytenn had a sharp migraine which made one half of his face redden and tighten at the expense of the other. 'And that should be enough for you.'

'Gentlemen, would either of you respect me if I gave out your names to anyone who asked for them?' Gehlen had not changed in the four years since Patrick Twilight had first met him, even with the switch to civilian clothes. He was still a spare figure, almost as mean in his countenance as the Administrator's office was in appearance, as if so miserly with his own self he was weary of sharing even his presence with anyone he did not have to. And those blue eyes still gave Twilight cause for concern. But then so did Cooper Brytenn.

The ambition Twilight had seen in Brytenn during earlier meetings was now tinged with a determination that appeared to border on the obsessive. Something Twilight envied and distrusted in equal amounts. Brytenn just seemed to be trying too hard.

'Patrick and I are together on this one, General,' Brytenn said to Gehlen, 'so don't try the divide and conquer thing. Please. Patrick . . . ?' Brytenn's manners were pure Ivy League, though his headache was undermining his usual confident veneer.

Twilight handed Gehlen two sheets of paper. 'We want to break into a gulag in Russia,' he said.

Gehlen read the two sheets.

'It's quite feasible, General,' Brytenn said.

'Then why not take the priest, Girenko?' Gehlen asked. 'Why my man?'

'We'd rather Girenko did not know what we were up to,' Brytenn said. 'Need-to-know . . .'

'Then you don't fully trust him?' Gehlen said.

Brytenn felt he had been outflanked and held his tongue.

'When a man loses the critical faculty he loses himself,' Twilight said for no reason. 'Claude Dansey told me that.'

'Yes, you were one of the last of Claude's bright-eyeds, before he went abroad for the last time.'

'We're aware of the risks of what's being undertaken,' Twilight said.

'We feel they're worth it,' Brytenn added in a tone that said at least part of him did not exactly share the sentiments he expressed. His headache was undermining him more than he thought and for a moment it sounded like he was trying to convince himself. 'Given the circumstances,' he threw in.

Gehlen, who could read strength and weakness the way most people could the weather, looked at Brytenn. 'Then I take it you're leading this escapade, Mr Brytenn. If you people had supported us instead of Stalin during the last war, we would not be in this situation.'

'The CIA is very anxious you co-operate to the fullest extent,' Brytenn said, trying to cover himself and be more diplomatic at the same time. 'Now we could go over every mistake that has let communism thrive, but I do not think that would serve our situation, General.'

'Mr Brytenn, please tell me you're not one of those terribly educated Americans who find solace and depth in other people's troubles,' Gehlen replied.

'Cooper's just back from some difficult business on the other side of the curtain,' Twilight said. 'I don't think discourtesy is called for, General.'

Brytenn, cursed with an imagination he did not need and a sophistication he could not always use, just coughed. And the cough allowed a high forehead and thin eyebrows to combine to reveal a degree of frailty he knew Gehlen and Twilight would notice.

'We don't have a lot of time,' he said then.

'You're very new here, Mr Brytenn,' Gehlen said, 'a fresh face among the stale visages of the Iron Curtain war. You have ambitions you reveal too easily and strengths you are unaware of.'

'Just cut out the cheap psychoanalysis, General,' Brytenn snapped, the pain in his head now overriding his diplomacy. He resented the degree of contempt Europeans held his nation in. He could not understand how they could take American money and spit on the hand doling it out. We ask for nothing in return, he had once said, believing it at the time. Now he knew better but still could not cope with the residual spite. 'What's been decided's been decided.'

'I have been fighting communists since the thirties,' Gehlen said. 'Mr Twilight's organisation tried to kill the Bolsheviks at birth. You should listen to what we have to say.'

'I was in Italy during the war, working with the partisans — most of them communists,' Brytenn replied in a death-sentence tone, 'and we had a box full of Mussolini's men in a kitchen. So the great debate started and each man talked about the rights and wrongs of executing them.'

'You were for shooting them.'

'No. When we came to a decision, four of them were gone.' Brytenn looked up at the ceiling. 'Those four came back with some SS the next day and killed most of our group.'

'And now you're here. What is it you do at CIA Strangers, Mr Brytenn?'

'I train men to drop over the curtain; to stay alive; to report to me. Strangers for strange lands. I train animals to live outside their natural habitat, if you like.'

'Well, you want to meet a real animal in Anatoli Beshov,' Gehlen said. 'Look, if I give you what you seek, gentlemen, what will you give me?'

Brytenn knew his reply was the wrong one as soon as he made it. 'What more do you need, General? We're asking for your co-operation in something that can prevent your worst nightmare coming true. How do you think your little set-up is going to fare if we lose Germany? And if we go to war over Berlin, then even if we do not lose Germany, it may well become an atomic battleground. And you will lose it anyway.'

Twilight preferred to drink his coffee and wait for the worst of the tar smell to pass. He had known Cooper Brytenn a little over a year and despite his best efforts could not bring himself to be anything but suspicious of the American. Like a driver whose car has stalled watching one whose beautiful new vehicle is gaining speed coming towards him, he thought.

'I once heard a tale that you planned to explode an atomic weapon on the Russians before they took Berlin, General,' Twilight said.

Gehlen stopped what he was doing, then looked out the window again. 'It might have saved us the bother we have now,

Mr Twilight. If it were true. Germany's atomic programme was destroyed in Norway.'

'Beshov,' Brytenn snapped again, finding his migraine very difficult to control now.

Gehlen raised his hands. 'I can arrange an introduction, but I cannot guarantee he will not bite your head off. Mr Brytenn, if you have a wife, you should have her iron your suits; it does you no service to be perceived as Mr Twilight's henchman. How much does that suit you're wearing cost, Mr Twilight?'

Outside, before they got into their car, Twilight turned to Brytenn with a frown that resembled a desert landscape before a storm. 'You should have just kept quiet in there, Cooper,' he said. 'Instead of indulging him. That fellow relies on you for everything he is. But he's still Hitler's old henchman.'

'And we rely on him for everything we know. You know the old joke about the inmates taking over the asylum, Patrick?' The small slide into wit released some of Brytenn's tension and his headache began to ease slightly.

'You're too clever for me, Cooper,' Twilight said.

'The benefits of a Harvard education.' Brytenn resented saying that, but it helped his headache some more. 'But you do dress better than I do.'

'I never went to university, myself,' Twilight said. 'I'm not much of an academic. I used to take pictures.' He touched his temple as if it were a shutter button. 'I have a photographic memory.'

'If you're trying to impress me,' Brytenn said with that honesty that Europeans find embarrassing, 'then forget it. I graduated cum laude. If you're trying to scare me, then remember that I'm gonna be Agency Director one day. What's your excuse for what you do?'

'I obey orders,' Twilight said. 'Do what I'm told.'

Brytenn could not even admit to having such thoughts. 'Let's go catch an animal,' he said.

Two hours later, Twilight and Brytenn were across the Swiss border and checking into a small chalet.

5

The Beast

As a child, Anatoli Beshov had been bullied once too often for an even temperament. Consequently, he always carried himself as if the sky might be just about to fall, and treated the world like he wished it would. Beshov sometimes resembled the remains of something solid eroded by constant heavy wind or a plinth minus the statue that once gave it meaning. And he rubbed his hands in time with the escaping-steam wheeze which sounded like a warning whistle to those who had the misfortune to be around Beshov while he was exercising his desires.

Beshov had begun what the Russians like to call the Great Patriotic War in a detention cell near the Bug River, on a charge of embezzlement and contracting venereal disease. He was due to be court-martialled and sentenced on Monday, 23 June 1941, and might well have faced a bullet in the back of the head or a trip to Siberia if several million Germans had not come to his rescue on the Sunday before his date with Soviet justice.

In return for their help, Beshov volunteered to serve the Germans almost immediately and joined Einsatzgruppe D in

Ukraine in the first weeks of July. After eighteen months murdering thousands of Jews, Beshov again fell foul of the military authorities, this time for raping a minor while on leave in Germany. Since he had been raping and killing minors with impunity all over Ukraine for over a year now, he was somewhat taken aback to find himself before a court of enquiry, and promptly escaped and offered himself back to the Russians, complete with a stolen German order of battle for the area around Kharkov.

The Russians launched a counter-attack based on the plan but unfortunately for Beshov, they ran right into a new German commander and three fresh panzer divisions. Beshov was thrown into a labour camp, awaiting Josef Stalin's pleasure.

Given the choice of reinfiltrating German lines or being shot, Beshov opted to be dropped by parachute near Kiev in 1943. Back with his German masters, complete with bogus intelligence and a cover story that involved his kidnap and escape, he avoided his earlier rape and desertion difficulties by volunteering for a Waffen-SS anti-partisan formation composed of Russian deserters and other turncoats, and failed completely to contact Soviet intelligence again.

By 1944, Beshov had his own SS unit, composed mainly of the men the SS could not handle any more. The Kampfgruppe Beshov earned its reputation for viciousness first in the mountains of Yugoslavia and then on the streets of Warsaw during the autumn uprising of that year. Later, in lower Silesia, retreating from the Russians, they took their vengeance on a column of 5000 civilians of all nationalities, trapped in the little village of Zvg by the advance of the Red Army. Those who saw the results never spoke of it again, and all that is left of the village is a small plaque in the forest. It was said the Red

Army unit that found the bodies had to be relieved on the spot and some of them went mad.

Beshov's mental condition was never in doubt. He was awarded the Knight's Cross with oak leaves and put in charge of a suburb of eastern Berlin during the Russian assault on the city. His men fought like cornered animals, either spurred on by their own sense of invincibility or the thought of what the Russians would do to them. However, before they were overrun, Beshov ordered one last atrocity. His men went through the buildings of his area and dragged out every male between the age of sixteen and seventy and hanged them from lampposts and balconies. Those of Beshov's men unlucky enough to be captured were burned alive by the Red Army, with the bodies of their victims.

Beshov was believed to have died defending the Reich Chancellery, so when he turned up in Zurich in 1947, selling chocolate and secrets in equal amounts, Reinhard Gehlen made immediate contact and signed him on for his new American-sponsored spying organisation.

The fact that he was now a vicious man forced to be civilised did something to Anatoli Beshov: it instilled a degree of self-discipline in him that bordered on the monastic. Only in the areas of sex and survival did the old turncoat lose none of his untamed zeal. In fact, the more disciplined he became outside the bedroom, the more uncontrolled he let himself be inside it. Mistresses complained of near-death experiences and payoffs. Never did a woman who succumbed to his charms last more than a night with him; often they had to be hospitalised, sometimes they were found on the side of the road, drugged, unable to remember what had happened to them. And Beshov had enough money to buy whomever needed purchasing.

So on a sharp spring night in Zurich in 1949, he displayed the same hungry look that always accompanied his dalliances as he left a casino with several thousand francs in winnings and a tall debutante clinging to his arm. They did not talk in the car to his hotel. As the girl prepared herself for the pleasure she believed was coming, Beshov allowed his control to slip away gradually. It had a pattern and anyone who might have seen him in those days with the various women he courted could have timed him by the pattern, and anyone who might have been interested in his safety might have pointed out to him that such a pattern and such a lifestyle were not conducive to a long and happy life.

Beshov had already beaten the girl across the large Louis XIV room, and was enjoying her screams and the various angles on her agony supplied by the large mirrors on every wall and on the ceiling, when he finally divested himself of any semblance of the civilisation he used to keep his chocolate-manufacturer front up in daylight hours. Now, he might have been back in a village in Russia or Poland, in a street where the women were lined along the walls awaiting his pleasure, where the beatings he had received as a child found their outlet.

The girl, a bored youngest daughter from South Kensington in London, who had come to Switzerland the previous winter to escape the drabness of her home, to find romance on the ski slopes, to enjoy what she felt she deserved to enjoy, was face to face with something most people do not even know exists, and never have the misfortune to meet in their lives: the pure hatred of mankind, the pure hatred of having been born, and the desire for revenge against the species that had made it happen. Beshov took her from behind and sodomised her with the handle of a bullwhip. She bit him, drawing blood from his fingers. He bit her ear off, threw her off the bed and slipped a large signet ring on to his right index finger.

'Please!' she begged.

When Patrick Twilight had examined the girl, he eased his gun from Anatoli Beshov's head, while Cooper Brytenn searched the Russian's pockets. Beshov lay across the period bed with one leg of his pinstriped trousers still on, and a large gash across his chest. The girl was naked and cold.

'She dead?' Brytenn asked.

Twilight nodded. There were times when it was easier to accept things than say anything. Cooper Brytenn punched Beshov in the stomach and shoved his pistol into the Russian's mouth.

'Cooper!' Twilight said.

For a few seconds, the anger and frustration in the American fought a losing battle with the sense of compromise he had developed since joining the CIA two years earlier. 'Yes, of course,' he said to Twilight. Then he stared back at Beshov. 'At any other time,' he said. He pulled the gun from the Russian's mouth and then punched him again, splitting his lip.

Beshov raised his hands and then wiped his mouth before looking at the body of his companion. He began to regain his calm, gave a false name, and explained that the girl had been alive when they had gone to sleep. 'I like to see them in pain, for God's sake,' he said after some time without a response. 'What the hell's the use in killing them?'

'Don't speak unless spoken to.' Cooper Brytenn hit Beshov again, this time with his gun. And Beshov, who could see a terrible sense of righteousness in the American's eyes, something that puzzled more than shocked him, crawled back to the centre of the bed and tried to explain himself again, his own narrow eyes all the time looking for an opening.

'Don't talk, Herr Sturmbannführer,' Twilight said. 'For your own health.'

Twilight continued to search the room but Beshov kept his eyes on Brytenn, still unsure if he would be shot.

'You're not police,' Beshov said, more by way of enquiry than statement of fact.

Brytenn shook his head slowly. 'You should wish we were,' he said. And he hit Beshov again. Beshov almost retaliated, but he had enough of the survivor in him to know when resistance was futile.

'Reinhard Gehlen told us where to find you,' Twilight said.

Beshov now lost some of his gathering composure and began to sweat at the temple and above his lip. He instinctively placed his hands on his head, then spread his fingers. One of his fingers was disfigured, and between the hairs on his head Brytenn noticed several very large scars.

'So what do you want?' Beshov asked.

'You'll be deported, you know,' Brytenn said. He had shifted down a gear, from outrage to necessary indifference, in the change of an expression. 'Swiss don't mind taking in old Nazis, but like all amoral people they hate scandal. Bad for the banking trade, bad for the watch trade, bad for the chocolate trade. You can commit any crime you like as far as the Swiss are concerned but you must do it outside their patch. This is a country attached to an army and you know how armies run themselves. Never go sick after roll call, never shit inside your own country. Outside, they can claim all sorts of extenuating circumstances and there'll always be people to believe them; at home there's always a nosy crowd who cause trouble.'

'So the Swiss are fucking bastards with the moral sense of a pimp,' Beshov said. 'Tell me a country that is any different. Tell me a country that makes chocolate like they do. I'll tell you, a country that makes such good chocolate should be allowed a few indiscretions.'

Brytenn hit him again. Again Beshov crawled away, this time reaching for a monogrammed towel to wipe his face. He looked to Twilight for some sign of support.

'You shouldn't speak out of turn,' Twilight said, opening a massive white wardrobe.

'You're British, yes?' Beshov asked.

Twilight nodded. 'Supposed to be.'

'And you, sir?'

'None of your fucking business,' Brytenn said. And he hit Beshov again.

'Jesus, stop him, will you,' Beshov said to Twilight.

'Shut up.' Twilight went through Beshov's suits.

But Beshov could not shut up. 'Okay, okay, I killed her. I'm a son of a bitch. I have people to blame for it. What's your excuse? Apple pie? Toad in the hole? Fish and chips? You Yanks ever paid for the Indians? You British killed more people in one famine in India in 1942 than we did in Auschwitz. Oh, yeah, I'm not one of those bastards who say it didn't happen. I'm one who's sorry we failed. Now we'll have nothing but trouble from those Yids. You mark my words. So, do you wanna kill me or what?'

Brytenn, who was now fully in control of himself again, lowered his gun and went over to a bowl of fruit on a marble table. 'No. We want a reason not to bring this to the attention of the Swiss and have you sent back to Moscow.'

'You piece of fuck,' Beshov said.

'And you an officer and a gentleman,' Brytenn replied.

'Who the hell is he?' Beshov asked Twilight.

'He's your worst nightmare, Mr Beshov,' Twilight said. 'He's a man who thinks he knows what's wrong with the world and how to fix it. I'm a man who knows the world doesn't need fixing, just replacement. Now, you have about ten minutes to listen to us and make up your mind about your future.'

'Judging by your previous history, I think you'll make the right decisions,' Cooper Brytenn said. 'In a minute there is time for decisions and revisions which a minute will reverse.' He had once tried writing and was prone to quoting passages from well-known poems and novels of his youth in an effort to appease his sense of failure in that area, as if by quoting them they became his. He had qualified as an architect to be able to tell people he had a profession and worked as a fisherman to satisfy his own need to prove his courage, but literature had been Cooper Brytenn's aim.

'Tell me what you want,' Beshov said.

'We want to get into a gulag. Number Thirty-Six in the Urals, Anatoli. We believe you stayed there for a time some years ago.'

Beshov deflated immediately.

6

The Camp

It was that same day that Camp Thirty-Six in the Urals witnessed an execution. There was nothing special about the execution and most of those assembled at the gallows looked sadder than the emaciated victim. The victim was made to stand on a small stool, which proceeded to sink into the mud of the compound before the guards could get the rope around his shaved neck. The victim fell off and slammed face first into the mud, breaking his nose.

The guards lifted him back on to the stool, while two prisoners held the stool firm. The victim cried out when the rope was placed around his neck. Then the stool sank again.

The guards kicked at the two prisoners who were supposed to be holding the stool firm. They let go and the stool fell over. The victim began to hang, legs kicking out in different directions, one of his feet catching one of the prisoners beneath him in the mouth. The guards grabbed the victim and held him up, shouting at the two prisoners thrashing around in the mud to steady the stool.

The guards placed the victim back on the stool, readjusted the rope between his strangulated coughs, listened while another guard announced the crime and punishment, then kicked the stool beneath the victim. But this time it would not move. So they pushed the prisoner, but the rope was too tight around his neck and he was wedged between the rope and the stool. The guards began shouting at the two prisoners beneath the victim to pull the stool away, then started punching the victim to force him off the stool. He spat blood.

Ivan Pyotr was tempted to look at his old friend's agony but Mikhail Kevenko had passed beyond the boundaries of comradeship to a place where he was past sharing, where he had become a bad omen to those who had liked him and an irrelevance to those who had not. The solitary dance, the prisoners called it.

Several minutes later, Pyotr caught a slight glimpse of Kevenko's old leather boots before familiarising himself with the patterns the rain was making in the mud.

'I wanted those boots, Mikhail,' he whispered to himself. Around him they were already organising the work parties and various men were starting to trade.

The early morning market lasted until the work parties reached their destinations. Sometimes those headed higher up on the glacier, to one of the open-cast mines, or along a rock face, would sell everything they had for some small pleasure, convinced they would not be returning that day. Nine out of ten times when a man did that he did not return, if only out of courtesy to the others and respect for his own dignity. Often men petrified in the cold, only to be found melting like waterlogged papier-mache in the spring. Once or twice, Pyotr had seen men disintegrate in the hands of those sent to retrieve their bodies, and float away in the melting streams running down the mountain sides. The freedom flow, they called that.

But Ivan Pyotr had things other than freedom on his mind. There was a man from Moscow in the commandant's office, a very burned man with the flat skull and deep-set features of a mountain eagle, or a Georgian. The same man who had come at the same time for so many years now, Pyotr had grown to view him as a good omen.

'Quite an ugly business, Ivan.'

Vladimir Romanovili was a distant relative of the murdered Russian royal family and therefore always anxious to prove himself more of a Chekist than your average secret policeman. Somewhere in the deep distant past his branch of the family had been exiled to the Caucasus, for what reason no one now knew, and so the Russian Romanovs became the Caucasian Romanovilis. Intermarriage and the mountains did the rest, and now only the first three syllables of his name and a few over-studious geneaologists could cause his mountain face to change or lose its colour altogether.

'Can you get me his boots?' Pyotr asked.

Romanovili wore the uniform of a colonel but did not carry himself with the confidence of anything more than a captain, and was far less intimidating to Ivan Pyotr than Pyotr had been to Romanovili's comrades before the Bolshevik coup, when they called him Ivan the Terrible. Now he was Ivan the old policeman, who could buy and sell the weather if he so chose. Only Romanovili knew all of Pyotr's past.

The routine of these meetings had been established a long time ago, and each man played his part, knowing what the outcome would be. Pyotr's teeth were beginning to fall out, though, and it was becoming harder and harder for his interrogator to believe the stories he had heard about this man.

'The answer is still no,' Pyotr said.

Usually, they would have chatted for a bit, but Romanovili was in a different mood today, more upset than frustrated. Pyotr recognised traces of extra pressure on the intelligence officer's face.

'What would you do if Comrade Stalin died?' he asked Pyotr. 'After all, he's just about seventy now. How much longer do you think he might have? And when he dies, what use is your file?'

'Does he know I'm still alive?' Pyotr asked.

'It is not for you to know what happens outside here,' Romanovili insisted. 'And, believe me, it is better you do not. Do you remember a man named Girenko?'

'He escaped from here. Years ago. One of the guards was shot for letting it happen. Then the others were shot for letting him let it happen. Then the commandant was shot. I suppose it was neater that way. One day we had a whole new set of guards. Girenko was one of those men who drift into a particularly important position without knowing why, and get carried away by the tide of history while others, desperate to play a part, get left behind. I often wonder if God plays tricks with our ambitions for his own amusement or to some greater end.'

'Yes. Do you think of escape, Ivan? Is that why you refuse to co-operate?'

'How little you know of prison,' Pyotr replied.

Romanovili, who had a dread of ending in a gulag he barely kept concealed on these visits, drew breath and offered Pyotr some tea.

Pyotr drank the first cup and took the leaves of the second. 'I can trade them with whoever gets Kevenko's boots.'

'Comrade Beria wishes an outcome,' Romanovili said then. 'This little game of yours has gone on long enough. There are events taking place . . .'

'Lavrenti Beria is not even head of the secret police any more,' Pyotr said. 'He's in charge of nuclear weapons. So why is he still sending you?' Pyotr's smile exposed his bloodied gums. 'We are remarkably well informed in here, you know.'

'Let's just say Vasili is his great unfinished business.'

'Just like it was Yezhov's before Stalin had him shot.'

'Comrade Beria hopes to be restored to his security position after his current assignment is completed.'

'And Vasili might just be the mechanism to do it with.'

'Don't be too smart, Colonel Pyotr.'

'Finding the thirteenth Okhrana agent provocateur within the Party would be quite a coup. Perhaps he should just ask Stalin. After all, Stalin knows everything, doesn't he?'

Romanovili appeared distinctly uncomfortable with the direction the conversation was taking. 'You should know there are events taking place now that may negate the importance of what you conceal.'

'You mean Stalin's stranglehold around the western sectors of Berlin,' Pyotr said. 'I try to keep up with world events. The Americans will not abandon Berlin. And that will mean war. Atomic war. Are we ready for that?'

'We are this close to having an atomic bomb,' Romanovili said. 'Six months at the outside.'

'Dangerous times. Perhaps this camp is the safest place for me to be. I am an old man.'

Romanovili thought for a while. He had grown to like the old Tsarist policeman, something that he did not wish to show.

'Stalin ordered your death, Ivan. Years ago. I have the order, signed, in my pocket. It is undated. Your only sure way out of here is in a box. Unless you co-operate.'

Romanovili pulled a small envelope from his pocket and showed it to Pyotr. Ivan Pyotr just stared at the wall.

7

The Team

In 1938 Cooper Brytenn had been on a friend's yacht, off the coast of North Carolina when it sank in the remains of a hurricane. He was washed ashore, alone, in a lifeboat. He never told anyone what happened and, as with such events, people were willing enough to invest all their horror and admiration in the survivor who had cheated nature. Brytenn's migraines dated from that time.

Eleven years later, the sheer simplicity of his proposal to snatch Ivan Pyotr from Camp Thirty-Six might well have caused Patrick Twilight's heartburn, something he had never had before. Twice he went over to the map, lying on the plain table in Brytenn's dusty, oversized Munich office, and examined the drop zone. Twice he queried every detail of every step of the route from the drop zone, though the taiga to Camp Thirty-Six in the western Urals. Twice he went over every problem and added more problems to them. Then he rang his wife from a public telephone and wallowed in the longing he felt for her until his money ran out and her patience snapped. Dorothy Twilight was a wife in the way bank managers and accountants are confidants, devoted to her client but more aware of his duty than he sometimes was.

There was something about being happily married that concerned Twilight. He had seen so many marriages just vanish into the black hole of overwork and long-distance operators.

'My wife still loves me,' he said to Cooper Brytenn later that day.

It had begun to snow again, and the Bavarian Alps around them were now obscured by long lines of twisting snowflakes and a huge black cloud spraying the thinnest mist Twilight had ever seen. He felt the car get cold the moment the engine stopped.

'Oh, bad luck,' Brytenn replied in a fake British accent. 'I almost got married once. One of those things where you wonder forever if you missed the train. Still have the ticket but she's gone. You have to make so many choices that seem easy at the time and then soon as you're settled into what you're doing they come back and they're the size of the Empire State. You ever been up the Empire State?'

'I don't like heights,' Twilight said. 'Do you trust Beshov not to sell you out?'

'He fears capture more than anything. Success is his only escape.'

'Is that not true for all of us?' With that, Twilight was prepared to let it go.

Brytenn, though, seemed to want to elaborate on his own personal philosophy of good and evil, and from there reach into the depths of what they were doing. 'Look, I appreciate you Britishers would rather be taking care of this yourselves, Patrick. And I know the way you must sometimes feel about me. But we need each other to win this one, just like we need Beshov.' Brytenn almost stopped. 'Just so long as we win,' he said.

Twilight had the feeling the American was looking for approval but the Englishman just could not approve of someone who seemed so certain of himself. 'A predecessor of mine used to say we were the disinfectant by which humanity avoids succumbing to its own disease.'

'Don't worry, Patrick, I wash my hands a lot these days, too.' He showed Twilight his manicured hands.

'When will you go?' Twilight asked.

Brytenn thought seriously before answering. His possessiveness wanted to exclude Twilight, but his basic desire to be liked wanted to share every detail of his ideas with the Englishman. And his growing fear of the work he did now needed some kind of outlet. In the end, his New England sense of security told him to hold his tongue, and that held his fear in, too, for the moment. 'You know you should take that wife of yours on vacation, Patrick,' he said. Which was a ridiculous arrogance since the two men did not know each other that well and Brytenn had never met Twilight's wife.

'So what the hell are we going to do with Stalin's file if we get it?' Twilight asked the American then.

'Give it to the man himself, I suppose,' Brytenn replied. 'Wrapped in ribbons.'

It struck Twilight that despite his suspicions about Brytenn, the two of them shared something that would keep them together. 'And hope he'll respond by calling off the dogs around Berlin?'

Brytenn slapped his colleague's shoulder and grinned like he was in pain. 'Could be. Need to know basis, Patrick. And your need is coming to an end for the moment, old boy. Anyway, my job is to get Ivan Pyotr out, nothing more.'

'And if Ivan is not even there?'

'Are you against this, Patrick?'

'I'm asking the questions I think you should ask, Cooper. Remember, I'm not going.'

'All my life I've been pushing myself,' Brytenn said, as if he were quoting from a book again. 'We have to believe he's there, Patrick.' He went on to make a very measured speech about the situation in Berlin, the prospect of war against the Soviet Union and China, the chances of success in such a conflict, and the consequences of failure. It was very appealing except for the fact that Twilight found he did not care about any of it. His mind was on the priest who called himself Misha Girenko, in the Paris jail cell.

'I wish you luck, Cooper,' Twilight said. 'I mean it.'

'Hitler used to live around here,' Brytenn said then. His desire to impress unnerved Twilight, and yet there was something very basic there, almost naive in its simplicity. Twilight allowed Brytenn to lecture him on Hitler's mountain retreat and then subverted the whole thing with the subtle insertion of a piece of information Brytenn could never have imagined.

'One of our men shot Hitler, you know.'

Brytenn had enough sense not to give his ignorance too much rope. Britishers who knew too much had a ruthlessness that hid beneath the modesty of their words. So this was a major attack.

'They called him Valkyrie,' Twilight said. 'He was a German, actually. We caught him in London. Some Jews hired him. He didn't kill Hitler.' Twilight let the matter drop, right when Brytenn was getting so interested he let all the well-formulated facial expressions he usually relied on drop to the floor.

'What happened?' Brytenn hated himself for asking.

'There were strategic considerations,' was all Twilight said. 'Need-to-know . . .'

'We're moving Girenko over this way, under Gehlen's cover,' Brytenn said, by way of revenge. He was not proud of it. Twilight was angry.

Cooper Brytenn went through a series of checks that afternoon, rather like a pilot before takeoff, or an obsessive. Simple routines that reinforced his sense of his own ability and helped him get over the fear he now felt about what he had proposed. His pride was now making all his decisions and stamping hard on any cautious rebellion from within. Brytenn was fully aware of the several personalities fighting for control of him at any one time and laid them off against one another to avoid the crushing pressure of reality forcing him to confront his own deficiencies. At any other time, in any other place, he might have commented about himself: 'There's a man whose reaching the level of his own incompetence.' But there are truths that for the greater good dare not speak out for fear of destroying not just the individual but the things he is part of. Leaving his Munich office to meet Anatoli Beshov again, Brytenn felt a headache coming on.

He met Beshov in a small brick cafe near the Marienplatz, a high-ceilinged vault of a place peopled by insipid creatures with profiteer faces and collaborationist movements, who mostly dined alone and overate. Beshov looked nervous.

'There's no need to be nervous of me any more,' Brytenn

said to the SS officer. 'We're on the same side for the moment. And I'm a man of my word.'

Beshov touched his slightly swollen lip, smiled and nodded and examined the faces in the restaurant. 'Others are not so honourable,' he said.

They had a light lunch of sausage, potato salad and sauerkraut, washed down with a beer brewed by monks from a thousand-year-old recipe. Beshov felt the American either looked like a civilian who wanted to be a soldier or a soldier trying to look like a civilian. He could not make up his mind which, but either way it unnerved him.

'Cut that moustache off,' he said to Brytenn. 'You'll never grow it heavy enough to be effective and unless you have a weak upper lip, who'll know?'

'I'm trying to look Slavic,' Brytenn said.

Beshov shook his head and then smiled in case Brytenn might be offended. 'Just look poor,' he said.

Brytenn didn't understand. Anyway, he had other things on his mind. He envied Europeans. Even a monster like Beshov. Their depth and traditions were a fancier costume to wear, he had said to an old girlfriend before being shipped out years earlier. But there was more to it.

'The States does not provide enough reward,' he said to Beshov when the latter asked him what made him come to Europe. 'Know what I mean?'

'You must be rich,' Beshov replied. 'I have always wanted to visit America and taste its rewards.' He said it with such charm that Brytenn was almost moved to invite him, but chose instead to down another portion of his beer, the proof of which was beginning to loosen whatever bonds kept his revelations and viewpoints tied down. And ease his headache.

'Americans seek respectability more than reward,' Brytenn said.

'That's because they're rich. After rich comes respectable.'

'Respectability strangled the British Empire.'

'You seek empires?'

'There is a certain glory in it.' Brytenn did not believe himself but the beer made him continue. 'You know what they say we did when we beat Hitler – we destroyed the last vestiges of heroic man, and replaced him with that most boring of creatures, economic man. Economic man has hobbies. Heroic man builds empires.'

'Just keep talking like that, Brytenn, that'll convince everyone you're Russian.' Beshov downed a larger portion of his beer and looked around him as if he expected to be arrested at any moment. And yet he was willing to sit there and eat simply for the sheer pleasure of doing it. His kind of courage made Brytenn jealous.

'I told you you're safe with me,' Brytenn said in order to demonstrate his own strength. 'No one can touch you. No matter what.'

'I'll hold you to that, Mr Brytenn,' Beshov said.

Brytenn's loathing of Beshov made that statement frightening, and when the American's mind drifted back to the hotel room in Switzerland he almost wanted to stand up and shout Beshov's name and career to the world. Except that he was in Munich. 'Anyway, you're among friends, here,' Brytenn said. 'Right?'

'There are people who know me, Mr Brytenn,' Beshov said, 'who for whatever reason would slit my throat. Have you considered that I might not have your best interests at heart?'

'You have your own at heart, Herr Sturmbannführer.'

'There was a time when that title would have made waiters click their heels and young ladies amuse me with their favours. Tell me, do you like the human race?'

Cooper Brytenn preferred to drink than answer that question and his drinking made his eyes roll as he began to check for possible difficulties with the local population or the police.

'I'll bet they still remember you in Berlin,' he said to Beshov.

'I hope they do. I have little to recommend me in any way in the world, Mr Brytenn, little but my reputation. I did not go to a fine university, I did not have the benefit of money or social standing. I believe Winston Churchill recommends a polo handicap for that. Do you have one?'

Brytenn had to admit he did, even though he did not, but secretly he knew that Beshov could see through his lie. Brytenn hated most of his lies and often went into a rage after he had told them, but he could not stop himself telling them any more; they were his addiction and the creature he had manufactured was his life's servant, without which he could not survive any more.

'We'll be out before they realise we're in,' Brytenn said, holding his chest out and allowing the alcohol to boost his confidence. His headache finally went when a gentle breeze entered the cafe and his thinning hair parted in the middle revealing a smooth scalp. He ran a freckled hand through his hair and touched the moustache which curved towards his lip.

Beshov felt Brytenn was making up for what was deserting him elsewhere with what he could grow on his face. The Russian had met many Americans during his time in the SS and felt he could easily tell what was inside from what was on the surface, that they were walking advertising salesmen, but

Brytenn was so obvious Beshov did not trust his own judgement and kept looking for something more.

'I wish I had your confidence in military operations, Mr Brytenn. You were in Italy?'

Brytenn seemed like he might like to talk about it but held himself back for some reason. 'We should discuss Camp Thirty-Six.'

'Let's move,' Beshov said. 'I'm full and beginning to feel vulnerable.'

They walked north, past the Hauptbahnhof, to an area destroyed by bombing, to the old barracks where Brytenn's office was. Most of the buildings around were still shattered, still cloaked in clouds of dust whipped up by the afternoon winds. Brytenn's office was full of useless furniture, but very neat.

Brytenn was more singular and definite and workmanlike here, as if he had set aside all the covers he used and was relying on something more basic, which could still perform given the right environment. He pulled out various aerial photographs. 'Camp Thirty-Six,' he said. 'Not terrific but they'll do for a start.'

'Where did you get these?' Beshov asked.

'The Luftwaffe.' Brytenn's skin puffed slightly. And his chest swelled.

'How the hell do we know Ivan Pyotr will co-operate with us when we get in?' Beshov demanded. 'Assuming he's even there.'

'Let's assume he's there,' Brytenn said.

'So, what the hell happens if he refuses to go? I've seen it with prisoners, they get so institutionalised they fear escape more than death.'

'That's where you will have to use your charm, Anatoli,' Brytenn said. 'To persuade him. Otherwise we stay with him and take notes. You're protected now but I haven't forgotten what you did to that girl in Switzerland.'

'Nor I. I think you're a little crazy, Mr Brytenn. Or trying to prove something. Tell me you're not trying to prove something.'

Brytenn felt the need to put some distance beween himself and Beshov. 'Just concentrate on getting Pyotr out of this camp. That's all you're here for.'

'I think you're a bastard, Brytenn,' Beshov said, 'a bastard as much as I am. So what makes Ivan Pyotr so special?'

'None of your business.'

Beshov gave up. 'Okay, what about this help you promised?'

'You're not the only one who took up arms against the Union of Soviet Socialist Republics,' Brytenn said. He smiled and changed his whole demeanour. 'Don't worry, Anatoli, we'll succeed. A few days on the ground, straight in, straight out. Even the weather's with us.'

'What, only a few degrees below freezing?' Beshov allowed himself a little amusement. Until Brytenn raised his eyebrows again. Everything on the outside looked fine, Beshov thought, but as soon as a window on Cooper Brytenn let any light into his soul, what you saw was disconcerting and not a little frightening.

'So who are these people who will meet us?' Beshov asked, more to take his mind off what he was thinking about Brytenn than because he was interested in the subject.

'Small group we managed to infiltrate a few years back. Our people, disaffected Russians and a few people from penal battalions, victims of the Kremlin of one sort or another. They sabotage railways, pick off officials, provide intelligence, that kind of thing. There are outfits like them all over the place. Even in Siberia. God knows how long they can last, but they have quite a network of sympathisers. We drop supplies when we can. It's difficult work. Planes go in from the Arctic or Turkey. Fly low. We've lost a couple. Don't fret, Herr Sturmbannführer, you and I will freefall from a great height: Halo – high altitude, low opening. Should work perfectly.'

Beshov did not react the way he should have. He had a fear of flying he could not conceal any longer and the last time he had been dropped from an aircraft over Russia he had cracked a rib.

'They tell me Heinrich Muller is in Russia,' he said. 'Is that true? Is the head of the Gestapo living in Moscow? Was he Moscow's man all the time?'

'I have heard he's in Switzerland,' Brytenn said.

'I suppose you can't believe all you hear,' Beshov said. 'I hope your friends have the red carpet waiting for us.'

In a forest in the foothills of the western Urals, several hundred kilometres north of Perm, the following morning, the sun warmed the few spring flowers on the carpet of moss which dominated a small clearing in the trees, before a sharp morning breeze brought a reminder of the reappearing winter.

An animal jumped out between two trees and toppled over into a hole, and the breeze whipped up a cloud of decaying leaves and pine needles to reveal the remains of a corduroy road made of thick silver-barked trees stretched out like an arm towards the east.

Jack Summer examined the lice in his clothes with a degree of almost scientific curiosity before taking a fine-tooth comb and digging them out one by one from along the seams of his jacket. He moved his lips each time he did it.

'You want me to do your hair?'

The boyish woman sitting beside him wore knee-high hobnailed jackboots, and smoked unfiltered cigarettes. She took Summer's slender head and began examining it. Summer closed his eyes while she plucked a louse from his hair.

'I should shave it again,' he said.

'Like me, Mr Central Intelligence Agent?'

He pulled the scarf she wore from her head and ran his hand across her scalp, feeling the short spikes of hair, the lumps, the scars, the protruding veins, and then running his fingers down between her ears and her skull and down the back of her neck. She closed her eyes this time. When he had finished, he put her scarf back on and she plucked another louse from his head. He took half a dozen from his jacket.

'They'll be back tonight,' he said. 'It's as pointless as all this.' He looked around at the dew-soaked, cobwebbed camp. 'How would you like to take a boat to Hawaii with me?'

'You don't mean that.' She kissed his very blue eyes. Then he kissed her cherry lips. She put her hand between his legs. He pulled away, his strong body moving faster than her hand. He might have been an athlete, she thought.

'I just wanted to show you . . .' She caressed his face.

His face was tight to the bones and rough like tree bark but his blue eyes were very bloodshot and this gave them a sensitivity she knew they did not deserve.

Summer took the cigarette from her mouth and began to smoke it. He pulled a grey blanket over his shoulders and two lice hopped from his hair and down the blue line of the blanket. 'I'm sorry,' he said. His bloodshot eyes watered and the blue in them turned a shade of green she could see around their edges. 'Some things maybe don't work so well in the cold.'

Olga Sharankova kissed him on the cheek. She touched a cobweb with her nose while withdrawing her small cherry mouth from his face and wiped the cobweb away with her hand. Then she returned to the business of cleaning his hair.

'What time do they arrive?' Summer asked her. He knew already but she played along, her serious expression and heavy forehead made more so by the deep tone of her voice.

'We'll be contacted fifteen minutes beforehand. I'll cut your hair.' She had that matter of factness and strength of will Summer felt was given out to East European women with their mother's milk, a harsh belief that it can get worse and a sense that it will. That was what fired her smile, too, that and her pointed cheeks and dark eyes. He had to put his arms around her.

'You think they'll bring weapons?' he asked her.

'I don't know. You should have the doctor look at your head, Jack. Those bites you have will go septic and if they do I will not like you any more. Please, let him have a look.'

'He doesn't even clean himself,' he replied. 'How can I expect him to clean me?'

'You're an American at heart, Jack. That will give you away to them in the end, you know. One day you will be some-where, well disguised, with that perfect Russian accent and those wonderful Slavic looks, and you will see something ordinary that offends your American sensibilities and they will have you. You should not be here. You endanger all of us.'

'Thank you for the vote of encouragement, Olga. I will radio my masters in Washington and tell them to promote me.

Anyway, the doctor's miles away. And we haven't the time. So you'll just have to look after me. You're a medical student anyway.'

'Was.' She dug into his scalp with the comb and he drew back from her. He swore before she did. They sat looking at one another.

'You know it is only a matter of time,' she said, returning to his head. 'The Interior troops will find us one day, find us and smash us. That is our fate. It is the fate of the world to be communist.'

'Then why do you fight?'

'Where do you suggest I go?'

Summer felt a mosquito touch his cheek. He waited, fascinated by the tenderest tickle of the insect's feet, for it to strike. But it flew away.

'I didn't think it was warm enough yet,' he said to Olga.

'It isn't. He probably could not get through that frozen leather you call skin.' She squashed the mosquito between her palms and showed the remains to Summer.

He kissed her.

Then a branch broke and several birds took to the air in formation. Every head in the little makeshift camp behind Summer's head turned. Two hands reached for nearby rifles, and a man in a vest and trousers came out of a camouflaged bivouac holding a revolver. He was shivering and could not place his shells in the weapon.

A single Interior Ministry soldier came out of a wiry thicket, through a long twisting thorn bush and fired a burst from an automatic rifle at the man in the vest. He toppled over. Then the mortar rounds landed.

Olga ordered the dispersal and when Summer looked

around for her again she was gone, replaced only by a wall of dirt and smoke.

Summer reached his rifle in front of two mortar shells. A young man with a pale face and hard nose, who had only been with the group a month, fell down. Another, a relative, tried to lift him but was hit from behind by two more Interior Ministry troops. Summer shot one Interior soldier in the face then disappeared into the camouflaged bivouac behind him.

He found the tunnel instinctively, dropped into it, set the booby trap and sealed the entrance behind him.

Inside the tunnel, his claustrophobia squeezed his mind into the darkness of a nightmare where he was being digested alive in the belly of a beast. He scrambled along the narrow corridor for perhaps several hundred metres, probably much more – two or three of these tunnels went on for a few kilometres – spitting clay from his mouth, swearing to himself, the frozen earth tearing small strips from his exposed skin, the wriggling life of the underworld slithering across his hands, almost in sequence, the cold sucking the remaining warmth in his body until he could not feel his extremities any longer.

A sharp dart of pain brought back the feeling. Then another. Then another. Suddenly, little legs were crawling on his and teeth were biting at him. He cried out, called Olga's name, tried to fight them off, but there were more than he could fight and they were at his face, biting and scratching at him, an impossible swarm, cold and wet, squeaking, the occasional flash of a rodentine tooth in the slivers of light which were now coming to him from the end of the tunnel.

'Oh, Jesus!'

He fought and screamed and crawled and lashed out with

his hands and legs in the tiny space. 'Jesus, they're all over me!' He was being eaten. And he could feel it. Every single bite, every piece of flesh, every creeping piece of wet fur under his clothes. Then they went for his eyes.

He gave up when they went for his eyes. The horror of being eaten alive was as nothing compared with the horror of having his eyes eaten out. You could not find heaven without your eyes, they said.

Then there was something on his head, tearing at his hair, pulling at it. Summer tried to swipe at it, but his hand was caught and he was helpless against what had him now. The sound of distant shooting brought him back.

He rolled over to see the sun above him and a cloud overhead to the right and Olga's face checking his. 'What the hell were you doing there?'

Summer took his arm from his face and she helped him up. 'They were eating me alive.'

'Nonsense,' she said. 'We had more sharing our bedroom when I was a girl. You probably frightened them. How would you react if a big animal came crawling through your home without warning. I told you to carry fire with you down there.'

'I didn't have time.' Summer swung round to the sound of the firing to his right. 'How the hell did they find us?'

'I don't know,' she replied. 'Come on, we have to go.' She led him down a ditch and through a thick growth of flowering trees. Several more men and women joined them as they went, and all afternoon stragglers came into the meeting place with stories of how they had escaped the ambush.

By nightfall Summer and Olga had half their original group with them, and some of them were on the verge of deserting.

'We have a Gravedigger among us.'

The man who said this was a small bearded Ukrainian who had been a cavalry officer in the White armies during the Russian Civil War, and a volunteer for the Vlassov army of exile and anti-communists during the German invasion. He had so much hair on him that people claimed whole animal species lived on his body.

'Every time this happens, you claim we have a Gravedigger among us, Sasha,' Summer replied. 'Now one day you may indeed be right, one of those devils may infilitrate us, but if there is then who can we trust?'

Sasha looked at Olga. 'Trust is not a word I know, Summer. Trust is what is written on American dollar bills. And the only people you Americans trust is God. I will follow your good example. We'll have to cancel the drop. There is no way we can accept whatever it is they wish us to take.'

'No!' Olga insisted. 'And forget Gravediggers, Sasha, they're GRU – army people – not Interiors. Army doesn't much like Interiors; Interiors don't much like army. If we ever have a Gravedigger here, he'll be working for us.'

'Well, it is useless staying where we are, Olga,' Sasha said. 'They will find us by Friday and exterminate us by Sunday. We must move. Perhaps further into the mountains. Winter is clearing fast in the east.'

'Siberia?' Summer said.

'The taiga over there is the only place to begin to hide from these bastards,' Sasha said. 'Even they can't catch us there.'

Summer sat back and examined the wounds caused by the rats who had eaten at him during the afternoon. 'I need a doctor.'

Olga Sharankova brushed him aside with a degree of coolness he found difficult to take, and Summer shut up.

'Maybe you should leave on the next aircraft out of here. We need a drop zone by tonight,' Olga said then.

'I wonder what they're coming for,' Sasha said.

'To start a revolution,' Olga said, 'to march on Moscow. To kill Stalin.' She began to laugh, the emotion of having escaped capture taking her over.

Sasha and Olga left Summer with his thoughts. Those around him took care of the small wounds and the cares of the survivors and made little reference to those they had left behind. Summer went to the edge of the new camp and watched the darkness drop.

8

Tsar

Because the winter had been mild up to that point in Moscow, now that spring was coming, the cold weather was beginning to feel it had missed out and seemed to be anxious for one last explosion of power. Four years after the end of his Great Patriotic War, the thorn of western Berlin in his body politic, the thought of Tsar Alexander I's triumph in Paris, after the first defeat of Napoleon, still playing on his ageing brain, Josef Stalin felt seventy might be a good time to achieve new ambitions. Maybe the last time.

Stalin was staring out the window at the various people in the park below when Nikita Khrushchev lumbered his pneumatic body through two doors leading to a small room in the Kremlin's Poteshny Palace. From somewhere to the right the music of Johann Sebastian Bach caught his ear before the doors were closed and Khrushchev found himself standing, waiting for his boss to acknowledge him, marvelling at the beauty of the music, examining the minutiae of the day.

It was a split day, the kind that threatens terrible winter but winds up pleasing you with brittle sunshine, leaving a relaxed bronze colour to everything around the Kremlin. In Red

Square small wild flowers poked their noses through the cracks in the paving and slipped their petals out of fissures in walls, testing the temperature of spring's welcome, ready to fold back up if the promise became threat once more, ready to blossom if the brittle sunshine tickled a waking yawn from their heightened expectation. While beyond the spires, in the east, the sun's rays stood like stalks in a wheat field, ripening with the day and swaying in the gentle wind.

The small bending frame of the first among equals of the Soviet empire turned round slowly, the blank expression of the lower part of his axehead face hanging from the handles of a rusting moustache, sharp features above the tip of the nose focusing on furiously energetic yet impassive eyes, grey hair high above his forehead as if reluctant to rest too comfortably on the frown that had launched a thousand purges. And the whole body and personality held together by the permanent sense of paranoia that surrounded one who had spent a life reinventing himself to suit the moment.

'I was reading my own account of the action around Tsaritsyn during the war against counter-revolution, Nikita. I had forgotten how Trotsky had almost thrown away the whole front there to the Whites. I came down and saved the day.'

Khrushchev knew not to interrupt. Just as he knew when to laugh and when to drink himself senseless and when to be sick. He may have spent the first thirty years of his life illiterate but he had learned lessons that just could not be found in books.

'That was why I knew we could beat the Hitlerite fascists there in 1942,' Stalin continued. 'That is why Tsaritsyn now has my name. It is the rock of the union. Control Stalingrad and you control the Volga; control that and you have the union. Like Berlin.'

'The rock of our continental security,' Khrushchev said.

'Or a stone in our collective shoe,' Stalin replied. The humour was probably intended but Stalin did not display any sign of amusement. 'Stones can cause infection,' he said. 'Berlin could become an open sore. But that's not why you're here, Nikita.'

'What do you want of me, Josef?' Khrushchev asked.

Stalin smiled as if in delayed reaction. 'There's some business I want dealt with. But I don't want Beria's cronies involved.'

'Difficult,' Khrushchev replied.

'He still has too many people in the intelligence services working for him. He gets their information before me. I split intelligence after the war to limit Beria's ambition, not enhance it. Now he has all the power without any of the responsibility.'

'I see.'

'Do you? Beria has the perfect buffer. Molotov failed me there, you know. He was supposed to get between Beria and Intelligence, not between me and Beria. I blame that bloody wife of his. Perhaps she's in Beria's pocket.'

'So no Foreign Ministry people either,' Khrushchev said.

'No.'

'Army intelligence, then,' Khrushchev said.

'You know people in the GRU, Nikita, reliable people from the Stalingrad days. Have them work through you.'

Stalin paced across the plain room with its single table, wall-panelling and obligatory picture of Lenin at work, to the pile of papers lying on one corner of the table. He picked up a sheet of paper and held it up for Khrushchev to read. 'From Beria.' Stalin never let go of it. 'He is advising a first strike into

Germany, as soon as we are ready with our atomic bomb in the autumn.'

'It's his pet project,' Khrushchev said. 'Our atomic bomb.'

'He's like a proud father. Is he right? Should we wait for the Americans to bite, or bite first?'

'Depends on your point of view, I suppose.'

'And what's yours?' Stalin asked.

Khrushchev watched his leader fold Beria's missive and lean back against one of the chairs around the table. A keen sense of survival made him hold eye contact with Stalin and smile right as the Georgian did. 'I am above all things your comrade, Josef.'

'So let's get to business, Nikita. Give me some reliable GRU names.'

UNION OF SOVIET SOCIALIST REPUBLICS

9

Dogs

Two days after Josef Stalin's meeting with Nikita Khrushchev, the West Mark became legal tender in the blockaded western sectors of Berlin, while on a bald patch of ground between Syktyvkar and Perm, deep in east European Russia, Anatoli Beshov cut the straps of Cooper Brytenn's parachute harness and pulled him into the cover of some trees.

The two men watched Brytenn's silk canopy billow in the wind and begin to float across the field. Then Beshov grabbed a loose strap and brought the parachute under control, drawing it in around his arms, slowly deflating the bubble, throwing his head around in all directions, watching the small flickering lights making their way towards him through the veil of a gathering dawn.

'Can you move?' he asked Brytenn.

Brytenn touched his ankle and winced. Then he cast his eyes across the low rise and down to the toothpick forest where the lights were. 'Maybe they're our welcoming committee,' he said.

'Somehow, I don't think they're friendly,' Beshov said. 'Friendly people never bring their dogs. It's bad manners.'

Brytenn pulled on a backpack, stood up despite the pain and began to walk.

Two hours later, Cooper Brytenn sat opposite Beshov, examining a gash across the back of his hand and attempting to stem the blood with ice, muck and leaves. Twice, the wind lifted the forest floor and threw it into his eyes. The wind brought the howls of the dogs, too, and Beshov tried to judge their distance while he drew oxygen from the moist forest air.

'We have to move again, now.'

Brytenn just looked at his ankle. 'It doesn't look broken,' he said. 'It just feels like it.' Then he pulled himself up on one leg and slowly pressed his other foot into the soil. The blood drained from his face so fast Beshov thought he would drop right there. 'Jesus!'

The Russian shook his head. 'What a way to come home!'

'Help me strap it up!' Brytenn barked. If he was as distressed as he looked, then he was holding it back from his voice, Beshov thought.

'We have time,' Brytenn insisted. 'Move quickly and we have time.'

'Are you a fool, or something?' Beshov drew a bandage from a canvas field pouch. 'We should call in the pick-up aircraft,' he said then. 'Get you out now.'

Brytenn shook his head. 'We're staying.'

'God, that Englishman was right in everything he said about you,' Beshov said. 'Shit!' When Beshov had finished bandaging him, Brytenn tied his jump boot up so tight it felt like all the circulation in his lower leg had been stopped and a weird numbness took over until he put the injured foot down again. Brytenn swore, more in anger than pain this time.

'You want morphine now?' Beshov asked.

'No, no morphine!' Any fear Brytenn felt was overwhelmed by his other emotions. 'If I can't move, shoot me,' he added. But he did not mean it.

'And then what?' Beshov asked. 'Me stay here? I have a past. These people do not forget. And their memories are vengeful. But you couldn't give a shit about me, could you?'

If Brytenn meant to answer his mind was distracted by the distant sound of dogs barking. 'We have to lose them.'

'Where the hell are your group?' Beshov demanded. 'These people you said would be here to meet us. Jesus, are you sure they are yours? I mean, we used to run groups like that during the war, people the Russians thought were working for them, but were really ours. All you need is a radio. I have this feeling that causes me to sweat just below the hairline.'

He lifted himself from behind the tree and broke his way through a series of bushes and broken branches, before sliding down a small embankment to a snaking stream which disappeared into the undergrowth about a hundred metres away.

'I see ten men with dogs!' he shouted back to Brytenn.

'Police? Interior troops?'

'Can't tell. Might even be hunters. They're headed this way. And if they find us it will not matter who they are. You . . .' Beshov looked around to see Brytenn supported by a long stick he had whittled from a branch, carrying a map and compass.

'Take the radio, Anatoli. Let's move into the water and try and lose those dogs.'

'It's freezing.'

'Freeze or have your throat torn out.'

Beshov was forced into a quiet almost disbelieving

admiration for the American's performance. He shook his head and chuckled to himself. 'You should have been in the SS.'

It began to rain.

The stream caught the occasional daggers of sunlight that managed to make their way through the covering foliage, while the rain rebounded off the new leaves and ran down Beshov's face. His face was scarred and bruised, and the water numbed it, while the cold air froze his breath and the bottom of the stream gave way to his feet. He sank to just above his ankles. When he reached the undergrowth, he fell to his knees and began crawling through the freezing water. Once or twice he looked behind to see Cooper Brytenn. Brytenn always grinned that annoying masochistic cat smirk that Beshov was beginning to hate.

'Scared, Herr Sturmbannführer?' Brytenn asked once.

'Fucking sure I am.' The Russian began to laugh to himself.

There was a certain thrill about it all, a grotesque drumbeat fear, all trembling fingers and a tremulous tingling tickle down his spine, a synthesis of physique and thought, a symbiosis of body and spirit, struggling for survival . . . and the air. The air was cold and fresh and it carried sounds for miles.

'Shit, they're still there. The dogs.'

The two men broke free of the water when they could no longer feel their fingers, dragged themselves up a bank and through a drift of filthy hardening snow, then over stony ground up a solid hill, across tree root obstacles. The pain caused Brytenn to stop and draw bellyfuls of breath but he refused help, which made Beshov curse him.

'You want to put a bullet in me?' Brytenn asked him again. Inside he was desperate to stay alive, but he could not help himself issuing the challenge.

'You're my ticket out of here, Brytenn.'

Then a dog barked somewhere nearby. And another.

'Shit!' Brytenn said. 'Move, Herr Sturmbannführer.'

And Beshov moved further ahead. The top of the hill gave them another small hill and after that there were more hills, more than Brytenn had breaths in his lungs. His lungs reacted in a sharp protest, and in a minute his spirit lost the support of his body. In these moments, Cooper Brytenn hated himself.

'Beshov!' he cried finally. It was a weak cry, barely audible against the sound of the wind and the dogs behind them. Brytenn fell to his knees in a thicket of trees and rolled into a small hollow.

When Anatoli Beshov paused to look back at him, the first dog caught him from behind. Beshov rolled with it, punched the dog and threw his backpack off at the same time, pulled a knife and drove the weapon into the animal's stomach. He was trying to get up from under it when two more dogs caught him.

The tall, thin man standing in front of Beshov had a youthful charm and that slow breathing which characterises the genuine sadist from the part-timer. His eyes shone as he touched the dog Beshov had killed while the two other dogs held Beshov's arms apart. His fourth hound was standing off to the right, waiting for an order to tear Beshov apart.

'You didn't have to kill him,' the dog-handler said.

'An animal, they say, knows when it is the right time to die,' Beshov said. 'A human being never does.'

'Why is that?' The dog-handler's uniform said he was a lieutenant in the Interior Ministry's troops, his demeanour said he thought he was something more important. The fact that he was not looking for Brytenn told Beshov he was not.

'Because there's always more of us,' Beshov said in reply to his question. The SS man's look of raw savagery made the lieutenant call out loud for his comrades, who were still a good kilometre back in the woods. The dog-handler had been an athlete before being taken into the Vnutrenniye Voyska.

'Which one am I talking to now?' he asked Beshov. 'I chased you across eight kilometres. You are fit. But I am fitter and now their time of reckoning. Who are you?'

'Fuck you.'

'My name is Grigori.' The lieutenant drew a pistol, pulled out the magazine and flicked each of the rounds out until he reached the last one. Then he snapped the magazine back in and handed the pistol to Beshov. 'And yours is?'

Beshov took the pistol, shrugged and moved his head.

'Anatoli.'

'If you kill me,' Grigori said, 'they'll tear you apart. If you kill one of them, the others will tear you apart. If you kill yourself then you won't know if you could ever have escaped. If you talk, I'll call them off. You choose.'

Beshov smiled and studied the face of the Rottweiler in front of him, the lifeless eyes of the animal reflected in the sunlight coming through the trees, with single drops of sleet beginning to float along the corridors of trees from a black cloud settling on the hill above them. 'I suppose you have them trained to eat my balls off first.'

'I've seen them trained to kill blond men and women with field grey skirts and children with blue eyes and square heads and this size of face and that kind of boot. How much do you want to live?' Whatever confidence the lieutenant had momentarily lost, he was regaining.

'You're a sweetheart,' Beshov said. 'I bet your friends won't approve.'

'They'll never know. And I'll get back to civilisation for a few days. Tell me who you are and what you're doing and I'll put a bullet in you.'

'I wish you luck.' Beshov put the pistol to his own head.

Brytenn shot the Interior lieutenant in the back and the dog holding Beshov's left hand through the head. Beshov shot the dog in front of him and Brytenn shot the third dog as it launched itself at Beshov.

'I could have taken him, made him crack,' Beshov argued.

'You could have, if there had been more time,' Brytenn said. 'But to what point?'

Beshov fired twice into the dog handler's eyes. 'Let him find heaven now,' he said.

Rain and then snow, and then darkness, cloaked them from the remainder of their pursuers and they followed a zigzag course by compass, circling round the area in which they had landed. The moon was frozen stiff.

'I suppose you want me to thank you,' Beshov said to Brytenn once. He was so cold the argument was the only thing that might keep him going. For a moment he wished he had shot himself, but only for a moment.

'Look, I have no stomach for fatuous arguments, Beshov, and little energy,' Brytenn said. He was sweating profusely and shivering. 'There is a part of me would like to see you torn apart by dogs. So shut up and keep moving.'

'You have to talk to me,' Beshov insisted. 'Look at you. Talk to me, you bastard.'

Brytenn nodded. 'He probably wouldn't have had them tear you apart anyway. Prisoners are better than corpses.'

'No. I know him. We come from the same crop, you know, he and I. Just harvested by different machines. I would not have killed me. Yet. That is the one advantage a prisoner has.'

'I'll bear that in mind when we reach our destination.'

'You won't make it with that ankle,' Beshov insisted. 'And if you do not, I won't.' He tripped and regained himself. 'I have to say I rather liked that fellow back there. Of course, I have SS training and there is something special about that. Live firing exercises across open ground. Minefield clearances with the fingers. You earn your SS pips.'

'The SS is an illegal formation,' Brytenn said. He was bored with the conversation already.

'I forgot. I figured that now you boys in the CIA have realised who the real enemy is, you might have seen your way clear to allowing us to come out of the shadows. My God, you use us in such quantities, what would be the problem?'

Brytenn had many smart answers but if he was honest they were pointless and humiliating against the truth of what Beshov had said. Sometimes, often when he believed himself to be at his strongest, the mask of Cooper Brytenn slipped and revealed what only he knew. Except this time Anatoli Beshov had seen it and Beshov was not a man to forget an incident like that.

'So what about our friends? Where are they? Did they send that committee?' Beshov asked.

Brytenn pulled out a map and a small torch. 'I don't know.'

'And if they don't come? If they're gone?'

'We go alone. You and me.'

Beshov let out a string of curses. 'We won't last the fucking night out here.'

'I warn you now, Beshov, if you in any way jeopardise this operation, I will have a dog rip your throat out.'

Beshov remained impassive and suddenly Brytenn was facing something only the dead now knew. 'I had a mistress once,' Beshov said. 'Nice Latvian girl. She served me until the day I decided I needed another. I killed her with my bare hands. I killed her and seven members of her family with my bare hands. Because I had no need of them. Do you understand what I mean? You are on my territory, Mr Brytenn, and the world you know has turned upside down. So treat me with some respect.'

Cooper Brytenn counted the cost of his decision to jump from a transport aircraft in pure despair and tried to recount his way to the ground in the darkness. He was still wrong by three seconds, and the thought of it winded him again.

He sat down. Everything was soft and wet, and Brytenn felt his body beginning to sink into the ground as he wrestled with his pack. The cold gave him such a headache it took time for him to register the blade of the knife dug into his back.

'Stay still.' The voice was calm.

Brytenn expelled air. Beshov went for his pistol. Jack Summer kicked it from his hand and pointed an automatic rifle at him. 'I said, stay still,' he said in English.

He looked at the two men, dressed in winter combat suits, weighed down with backpacks, streaked with camouflage, nearly blue with the cold, and shook his head.

'This place is crawling with Interior troops. You should have saved them the trouble and dropped right in the courtyard of the Lubyanka in Moscow.'

Brytenn put out his hand. 'Jack, I thought we'd lost you.'

'We couldn't get near you. You caused a stir back there.'

Summer helped Brytenn to stand up and stared for a moment at Beshov. 'Do I know you?'

'I don't believe we have had the pleasure,' Beshov replied. He unbuttoned a canvas holster at his side and replaced his pistol. 'My friend is wounded.'

Olga Sharankova arrived with two men and whispered into Summer's ear. Then she grinned at Brytenn, who was still having difficulty unhooking himself from a bag of equipment. 'Allow me,' she said. She drew a long machete and sliced the straps from Brytenn's waist.

'Nice girl,' Beshov said to Summer.

Summer did not answer.

Five minutes later, they were in a narrow ravine in the woods. Brytenn's ankle was on fire but he told no one.

10

Defectors

The small swarthy man who turned up in the Russian sector of Berlin the same day, wearing a new suit and a personality refit, was Yuri Podvoysky, a major in the GRU, Russian military intelligence. People who met him said later that he seemed depressed, and that he was drinking. The GRU chief in Berlin, a colonel with political ambition, offered to put him back on a train to Warsaw, where he might rest, but Podvoysky just swung at him and disappeared.

Two days later Podvoysky appeared at the apartment of an old wartime friend, Jacob Pelnakov, an unimaginative man, who had risen to his position in the Soviet secret service by virtue of his skill as an executioner. Jobs other men found distasteful, Pelnakov would do while downing the last of a heavy meal. Killing was as natural to him as breathing and he never lost a wink of sleep over it.

No one was quite sure how someone like Podvoysky, who had a master's degree in political science, could be friends with a semi-literate thug like Pelnakov. Perhaps it was because they were both orphans, both bordering on the ugly and both fond of the kind of carousing frowned on by Party zealots. Or perhaps there was more. Hard men often need one good friend.

Pelnakov took charge of his old friend, put two men on to Podvoysky round the clock and sent an urgent message to Moscow.

'You know you will be arrested, Yuri,' he told Podvoysky.

It was late at night in a small apartment near the Brandenburg Gate, between the Wilhelmstrasse and the Unter Den Linden, and the sound of aircraft from the south of the city was constant.

'They fly round the clock,' Podvoysky said. He could sense Pelnakov's tiny sympathy and drew more of it out with every sentence. 'Do you ever think about that?'

'What's wrong, Yuri?' Pelnakov asked finally.

'I want to defect, Jacob. Go west.'

This should have made Pelnakov pull his gun and arrest Podvoysky but the latter knew that his companion could not do that now without seriously undermining himself. Pelnakov grinned.

'Just walk up to the Brandenburg Gate; it's the large area beyond that,' he said. 'We may be blocking land routes to the west from this city, but people are free to move around. They come over here all the time. So off you go, Yuri.'

'And get a bullet in the back?' Podvoysky said.

'The down side of our profession,' Pelnakov said.

'I'll bet there are other ways.'

This time Pelnakov laughed.

When they found Pelnakov he was sitting up in an armchair, stiff as an east wind, slightly grinning, one eye slightly open, but glazed like a fake gemstone, the eye turned out to the left as if trying to look at the bruising on the side of his neck.

Yuri Podvoysky crossed the ideological frontier between the Russian and western sectors of Berlin through one of Pelnakov's tunnels, between a lake and a forest to the south, then in and out of leftover bomb craters filled with refugee refuse, down a waterlogged trench and through the visceral remains of someone's home.

Overhead, the American and British transports kept coming and going, threading their way along the filamental corridors still left open to them, the gentle throbbing of their engines a reliable guide to the right direction.

By lunchtime, Podvoysky sat on a bench in the Tiergarten, redressed, reading a paper. At two thirty, according to an American intelligence record, he strolled towards the zoo where he met a woman.

Trudi Weiss had the dubious honour of being employed in the two oldest professions in the world at the same time and often with the same clientele. Beautiful, with petal lips and that high Germanic forehead so admired by fashion magazines, and supported by legs that appeared to go on forever, Trudi was, in fact, part Croatian Muslim, with just enough Jewish blood to have made her a candidate for the gas chambers. But nobody had bothered to check when she arrived in Berlin in 1944 with a German intelligence officer husband and a suitcase full of forged documents.

Her husband was killed fighting in the mountains of Bosnia a few months later, and Trudi, whose real name had been shredded in the sharp wind of a Balkan winter, began attaching herself to other suitable men with the reckless abandon of one dislocated from everything they have known and driven by a desire to survive so intense it caused her to break into sweats.

'I have to get through to Wiesbaden tomorrow,' Podvoysky said to her. 'Unnoticed.' When she had first met Podvoysky, he was in control and she was frightened. Now she was in control and Podvoysky appeared to be frightened.

'I can get you on a flight,' she said. 'But it will cost. Come, I'll make you dinner and arrange things.'

There was an air of quiet desperation about the western sectors of Berlin during the ninth month of the blockade. People had expressionless faces and walked with the mechanical movements of prisoners and the uncertainty of the condemned. And still the aircraft flew in, one by one, relentless carriers of hope, like messengers bringing news of the possibility of something else.

'I've defected,' Podvoysky explained to Trudi when they were safe in her tiny dull apartment north of the Tiergarten. 'You're the only one I can trust here.'

'I see.'

Rationed food often leads to rations elsewhere. People ration their movements and their speech and their emotions. They even ration their space. Trudi stood closer to him and asked him functional questions, nothing more than a query or two on how much money he was carrying and what did he think he could get with the cash and where might he go.

'Don't wear anything conspicuous when you're boarding the plane,' she said to him then. 'They look out for small things: new clothes, nice hands, well-combed hair. And your eyes are all wrong. Stay a few days and learn the stare. You have to look as if you have seen the end and cannot talk about it. Very important here.'

She made love with the same spirit of shortage that she applied to the rest of her life. She had learned to issue her sexual favours with small amounts of added-on value, increasing their return, and even Podvoysky, who had once spent a week in bed with her in the summer of 1945, could not make her return to her old ways.

'You could make money by selling me out,' he said.

'I'm a whore, Yuri. Not a traitor. Why don't you just go to the Americans now?'

'I told you, it's a matter of trust.'

They spent the next hour or so doing the pedantic deals that were their trade, small exchanges of detail, queries that repeated themselves over and over again, reluctant admissions, rationed parcels of information, skeletal reports, small figures scribbled in pencil on the backs of cigarette packs and old postcards. 'The people at Moscow Centre will kill you if they ever find out,' Podvoysky said when they were finished.

Trudi Weiss closed her eyes.

Almost two thousand miles east of her, in the vastness of the east European Russia, Anatoli Beshov opened one eye to see Olga Sharankova standing over him, holding a revolver. He could see the rounds in each of the visible chambers. Her grip tightened and the veins on the backs of her hands pulsated in anticipation. 'I should kill you now.'

'If you're expecting me to agree with you because you are pointing that at me, then forget it. Perhaps if you sat down and we took some tea from that samovar over there, we could discuss this. Do we know one another? My heart is a careless instrument.'

Olga's face, a simple sketch then, took on more shape. She

had anticipated more from him. Almost demanded it. 'You piece of shit,' she said as if to encourage what she had expected. It was not easy for her, swear words did not come naturally to her, she was uncomfortable with them in the same way she disliked too much intimacy in conversations with people she did not know well. Her face narrowed and she began to squeeze on the trigger.

Jack Summer placed his hand on her shoulder. 'It will be heard,' he said. 'If you're going to commit murder, then do us the favour of using a silencer. Or a knife.'

'I couldn't find one,' she replied.

'The silencers are in my bag.'

Beshov relaxed his breathing and sat up. She was not going to kill him. He lowered his hands very slowly and watched Olga's hand ease on the revolver. Jack Summer took his hand away from her shoulder and held it out. Olga Sharankova put her thumb to the hammer and depressed it slowly.

'You know who he is?' she asked Summer. Then she passed him the revolver.

Summer breathed out very slowly through his nostrils, opened the revolver and tipped the bullets into his hand. 'I don't care,' he said. Summer had a disconnectedness that, when it dominated his actions, disgusted Olga. Her pinched face reddened and a tiny twig settled on the down below her temple. It looked like a scar.

'I am to assume then we have met before.' Beshov raised one hand in an act of peace. 'And not in love. I fought communism. I make no apologies.'

Olga was about to reply when Cooper Brytenn came out of a small cave above them, a shallow mouth in the rock, shored up with planking and covered with freshly cut branches. They had hollowed out the cavern inside and driven small boreholes into the rocks to diffuse the smoke from their fires. Still, Brytenn had a brown blanket draped over his shoulders, and the pain in his ankle was now visible in the taut muscles of his face and the slight stoop his body had adopted.

'Trouble?' he asked.

He might have been enquiring into the lack of hot dogs at a barbeque, Olga thought. Her natural colour began to return.

'I think my past is catching up with me,' Beshov said. 'I told you, Russians have such long memories.' He looked at each of the men now gathered on the rocks and tree stumps above him, faces he had seen in a hundred places liked this during his time in the SS, faces he had executed, faces he had stepped over, faces he had betrayed. Beshov was moved in a way only men who have betrayed everything they were supposed to have believed in can be, a liberation and an imprisonment. He dipped his eyes.

'We don't have time for personal feuds,' Brytenn said to Jack Summer. 'You control your people.'

'It's controlled,' Summer snapped.

Beshov stood up without permission and backed off to where he might have a chance of escape if he moved quickly enough. Except that escape might mean running into the hands of the Interior Ministry troops looking for them, and with his reputation, that was a worse prospect than dying of a single wound here. 'You were a communist, then?' he asked Olga.

She walked up to him, slapped him across the face and walked away.

For a few seconds, Summer's eyes followed her, until she disappeared into the twisted trees above him. 'You are a lucky man, Mr Beshov. Olga was married to a Polish officer. They both joined the underground when the Germans marched in. Her husband was killed by the Germans. Your men, I believe.'

'So how the hell did she end up here?'

'She got little better treatment from the Red Army when they liberated Lublin. Fifteen of her family were taken out and shot by the secret police. They tortured her, raped her. She went back into the forests. The rest is none of your concern.'

Beshov took the revolver Summer still held and examined it. 'It's British,' he said. He looked at Brytenn. 'You know, gentlemen, you should not believe all the stories you hear about me. I was just a minor functionary, obeying orders.' He smiled and handed the revolver back to Summer.

'Gentlemen,' Brytenn said, 'get to work. I want to move as soon as the sun starts to die. We're behind time.'

Brytenn found Olga sitting on rock, watching a bird struggle with a snare in the slush at her feet. 'You could kill it,' he said. There was a nervousness in his voice he wished he could lose.

'If I interfere, I will only get hurt,' she said. 'You should remember that.' She looked up at him and because his head was directly in the way of the sun, she had to squint when he moved slightly. 'The more it struggles, the tighter the snare becomes. It will kill itself for me, so I don't have to do anything.' She grinned but her eyes stayed sad. 'And we will have meat to eat. You should take morphine, you know. You look like shit.'

'I came to . . .' Brytenn nodded instead of saying any more.

'Don't worry, I'm over whatever it was.' Olga scratched her head and then her arms. 'I feel so damn dirty,' she said. 'You know?'

'I think I do.' Brytenn examined every piece of her, from the tiny lobeless ears to the sharp nose and the bristled scalp. But nothing in her looks could compete with the fact that she was Summer's girl. Brytenn could feel excited and slightly ashamed at the same time.

'No, I mean filthy,' Olga continued. 'Unwashed. Do you know what I would give for a wash? A real wash? And I'm lousy, too. Just to feel clean, and maybe wear a dress. Sounds stupid, yes?' She paused to watch the bird again. It was shaking now, twitching. 'You're too clean, Mr Brytenn.'

'Cooper . . .'

'You smell like a soap factory. You'll have to get dirty like the rest of us. Your smell is strong enough to bring dogs from Moscow. You should roll around in the mud here for a few hours, get all that soap and whatever out of your pores. Get some of the taiga into you.'

'Which particular bit of mud did you have in mind?' he asked her. It allowed his nerves to ease and his body to relax. And she played along.

'Oh, that one there is mine, so you can't have that, and that one over there is Jack's, and he's very particular about his mud, but you can have any other piece you like, people are usually generous. Look, sit down, I don't like talking up to you.'

'I'd prefer to stand.'

'You should not be here then.'

'I don't think it's broken.'

She showed concern for a couple of seconds and then stamped on the bird's neck. 'See, it's dead now. I'd like to be able to dance,' she added suddenly, 'wear a dress and dance for a few hours. Do you dance well? I'll bet you do.'

'Not at this particular moment.' For the first time he felt comfortable with her.

'No. Look, just keep that SS dog on a leash, Brytenn, keep him away from me, and I will think about eating meat and breaking the necks of birds.'

'He's essential to what we're doing,' Brytenn said.

'They always are. Once in a while, though, I'd like to know what we're doing.'

'You've been having a bad time here,' Brytenn said.

'They're on to us, Brytenn, the Interiors. I've seen it happen, when your friend and his SS people came into the Ukraine. They get on to you and then they keep coming until they wear you down. It takes time but they have time. Irregulars do not have time. Each time we escape from them it's with a little less space. One day we will not escape them. I think I worry too much. I think I'm a mother at heart. People say I have good child-bearing hips and good breasts for feeding. What do you think?'

Brytenn was so embarrassed he just went red and was only saved from further discomfort by the arrival of Summer, whose mouth showed immediately that he was not happy with what he saw. Brytenn tried to calm his colleague by smiling but it did not work.

'I've located some horses,' Summer said. 'Only a few and it'll mean a day's walk.'

'We need horses,' Brytenn said. 'We've a hundred and fifty kilometres to travel. And no morphine, Olga.'

That evening they left the bulk of Jack Summer's group behind and began the move towards Camp Thirty-Six, north first, then east. They marched for over a day through the forest, Cooper Brytenn out in front so no one would see the pain on his face. It was raining when they finally came out of the forest, on to a small dirt road. And Brytenn did not know how much further he could go. He led his party to the edge of what appeared to be a small hamlet in a hollow, by a trickling stream. The sugar frost of the late evening was dissolved by the rain which turned to lumpen ice, while the owls announced their decision to hunt.

'These people help us for money,' Summer explained. 'But they're usually good for their word and they know that if we go down, it's just possible they'll go down too.'

'Money and fear,' Brytenn said.

'Don't you just love humanity?' Beshov whispered.

Summer tapped Olga and the two of them walked up a stone path and knocked on the low door of a wooden house with intricate carvings around the windows.

'Of course, if they think it's in their interest they'll tell the police when we're gone,' Sasha said to Brytenn. He nodded at the house and picked at his whiskers. 'This collective has had three bad harvests. We bring things they can buy and sell with. The police used only to come here once a year. So they could afford to be brave. Now, with these Interior sweeps . . .'

Brytenn acknowledged the information but his concentration was on his ankle and the elements. A silver sheen gradually spread across the landscape, thin trees in early creeping foliage bending slowly in the sharp breeze, small drops of rain beating the noise of spring on the leaves while the wind whipped up what remained of the hardened snow and carried it away to melt.

'Will they give us shelter?' Beshov asked Sasha.

'Maybe . . .'

Beshov and Brytenn wiped tiny flecks of ice from their faces and watched the moon's beam illuminate the long spread of field to their right. A cow made a noise in a nearby shed, and the shed creaked in the wind and the rain rolled down the shed's roof and spilled at the feet of the cow. The cow turned inside and dropped its load at the door of the shed. The rain began to spread the load.

'If we have to stay here much longer we will all die of pneumonia,' Beshov said to Brytenn. 'I know now why I fought for the Germans. I hate this fucking country. Know what I mean, Brytenn?'

Brytenn could not answer. The pain in his ankle was just too much now. He shook his head and listened. The collective was a series of stone and wood silhouettes, occasionally lit by the moon and tiny flickers of yellow, the low moan of animals breaking the gathering growl of the elements, the peppered shouts of children a reminder of things that were beginning to escape his memory.

'Are you all right?' Beshov asked him.

Brytenn thought it strange that when he looked at the Russian in the moonlight, it seemed like he should be asking the same question. 'Yes.'

Beshov went to examine his ankle but Brytenn shoved him away.

'You'll have to have someone look at it,' Beshov said. 'Where we're going you'll never make it, and if you do not make it, then I am in serious trouble, Brytenn. So, please, let me have a look at it. I need something to do, this place gives me the creeps.'

'Memories?' Brytenn asked.

'Too far east,' Beshov said. 'It's always so easy for you, isn't it?'

Olga Sharankova came up the road with her hands in her pockets, a gentle swagger in her movements that caught Brytenn's attention. She sent a man back into the darkness and told two more to go to the house. 'Security police and Interior Ministry troops were here three hours ago. They took two men away. Let's hope it snows again. Jesus, you look like death, Brytenn.'

'He needs morphine,' Beshov said.

She agreed.

I I

The Man From Berlin

Yuri Podvoysky had once stood to attention for twenty-six hours during a training exercise, but as he looked out the window at the quilted landscape of the area around the German frontier, for a few moments the uniform nature of the topography made him doubt himself. He could see no divides, no differences. Perhaps that was why pilots were very unreliable political warriors, he thought. He had learned to fly in his spare time and was going through the cockpit routines in his head, which killed his doubt. His doubt killed off, he began to imagine the differences between the eastern and western portions of Germany.

Later, the aircraft banked slowly to the right and they crossed a river before Podvoysky felt the undercarriage coming down beneath him. He was closer to the ground now and all his indelible prejudices were reactivated. The differences reappeared. A column of tanks and several checkpoints and unfamiliar roadsigns woke him to the sights and sounds of the West.

The man he wanted was sitting in a jeep, reading a copy of Pravda, trying to pick holes in the syntax of an article about projected grain harvests for the coming summer. He was dressed in American army uniform, with the rank of captain, hair oiled down on his scalp, face coloured by the fresh sunshine which had burst upon the day without warning several hours earlier, a strong sense of ambivalence in his eyes.

'Captain Pell?'

The captain did not shake Podvoysky's hand.

'Major . . . we could have brought you out ourselves.'

Podvoysky nodded, then glanced around the airfield. 'I like to work alone.' The aircraft he had come in on was being reloaded with food while other planes were moving towards the runway and taking off. It was a continuous process and reminded Podvoysky of an ant hill.

The two men drove through the north Bavarian countryside without speaking. Once, the captain offered Podvoysky the copy of Pravda but the Russian refused.

'Have they mentioned Pelnakov?' he asked.

'Nothing,' Pell said. 'But then what would you expect?'

The small house in southern Bavaria was guarded by ranks of pines. It was a two-storey structure with a wooden front and spring flowers in the window boxes. And there were large stones on the roof to break up snowfalls.

'When do I get to meet Gehlen?' Podvoysky asked.

'Nothing's come through,' Pell replied.

He struck Podvoysky as a man who had actually passed the limits of his capabilities and was relying on the situation to save him from his own ignorance and incapacity. He seemed to use the strength of the furniture around them to back him up.

'True to form,' Podvoysky said. 'They say the General can keep a man waiting for two years.'

'You Chekists are often true to form,' Pell said. 'Defector or not, we have to check you out. And the General will not give the all clear till you are checked out. We have heard of Smersh – Death to Spies – and Moscow Centre would like nothing better than to have the General out of the way.' He began to prepare coffee and arrange an armchair so that it was away from a window and place logs in the fire. The fire was weak and neither man sought warmth from it. Pell produced a bottle of vodka and placed it on a small table, while Podvoysky examined very cliched photographs of Bavaria on the walls around him.

'And I'm a GRU officer,' Podvoysky said. 'Not a Chekist.' He made a facial expression which confused his minder. 'What did the Irishman, Collins, say? Kill a soldier and he can be replaced in a day, kill a spy and all he knows dies with him. Irreplaceable. I should like something to eat.'

Pell's face showed that he did not like being corrected. He listed a series of irrelevant facts about the Berlin airlift, the way Americans sometimes do when they suspect they are about to be upstaged in any area. Podvoysky felt he was talking to an advertising executive as the captain listed his own achievements with those of his country.

'You worked long for Gehlen?' Podvoysky asked.

'I don't work for him. I'm his liaison with Uncle Sam. I get to see everything that comes in from the other side. See if we can do anything with it. This is American property. Gehlen works for Uncle Sam, Major, not the other way round.'

'What do you know about me?' Podvoysky poured himself a drink, then looked at Pell the way a veteran in any profession does to a beginner. Pell had killed men himself, but never with his hands. There was a special excitement about looking at a man who had killed with his hands.

'Tell me about Pelnakov,' Pell said.

'I'll tell you about me first,' Podvoysky said. 'I was fourteen when I killed my first man. He was a banker who lived down the street from us. I was not born privileged. My mother worked in the kitchen of a bourgeois's house, my father drove a limousine. My father was killed at the front in 1916, my mother got typhoid. I decided to change my circumstances.'

'Pelnakov, please.'

Podvoysky laughed and downed another drink. 'Irrelevant. Are we alone?'

'This place is secure. We were told you had something for us. Something special.'

'You might say that.'

Patrick Twilight flew back to London from Germany the following Wednesday, for a meeting with the Administrator. Before going to his office he went to a public house in Elephant and Castle and drank until he had to vomit it all up against the wall of an alley around the corner from Waterloo train station. Then he began drinking again.

He telephoned his wife half an hour later to say he was working into the small hours. She accepted with the usual concern for his health and a soft whisper of affection before he hung up. He had met his wife at a party during the war, a small gathering when he was lonely. She was very keen and he was too tired to resist her. Then they were married and Twilight found he liked it. But he could not get it out of his mind that he might not love his wife. That problem was one of many that dogged him in the spring of 1949, and that was why he went with other women.

The other woman that night was not particularly beautiful.

But she had the telltale signs. It takes one to know one, Twilight said to himself. He could tell a lonely woman from five hundred yards, like a lion selecting the weakest of a herd of wildebeest. Twilight had done a few months in South Africa before the war and always promised himself he would buy a farm out there if he ever gave up the trade.

The woman wore tweed and a serge coat, and had that pasty pallor so common in the war, with small dark crescents under her eyes from overwork or lack of sleep or whatever. She held herself in the same hunch that the Administrator did, but she did not have his relaxed distance, that amiable detached ingratiating face that caused Twilight to pick at his teeth and fingernails during their meetings. 'My name is Patrick.'

He held her hand before she could decide to take his. His handshake was comforting, the way he had practised it, hers felt unsure, the way it should, the way the thousand and one thoughts and questions that were flowing through her brain should make it. Her eyes darted around the public house like those of an animal cornered by its only predator, a sudden awareness that being alone in a bar said more about her than any response she might give. She almost told him she was waiting for someone. 'I missed my bus,' she settled for.

'I missed mine, too,' he said. 'You'll be more comfortable over there.' He pointed to where he had been sitting, and she nodded and picked up her handbag and drink and followed him over to the corner of the room. Several less courageous eyes followed him with envy and bitterness and one or two men passed a remark until Twilight caught their eyes and shut their mouths.

Her flat was in Bayswater, down a street that shuddered from the underground trains, near a cafe which offered chips and gravy at a special price. For some reason Twilight recalled eating an orange for the first time after the war.

'Deborah . . .'

He brushed her hair with his fingers and she shoved herself into his stomach and moved her lips. 'I'm asleep,' she said.

She smelled of cheap perfume and mothballs, and Twilight rolled on to his back and watched the shadows of the outside world on the ceiling. He had about an hour before he should go home. He wondered if her smell would stay with him, if he should have a bath, if he should just stay there.

'I hope you respect me,' he said while getting dressed.

She smiled like a tart, and the rouge on her cheeks cheapened the effect in the yellow light.

Twilight, now aware of his own imperfections, hurried his movements, struggling with his tie. 'Should I leave you some coupons?' he asked.

She looked pleased rather than offended but refused his offer. Then she started talking about herself. Her Essex chatter bored him but he replied at all the right times.

'I have to go away,' he said.

She began to talk about her work and her family and then her figure. 'My mum says I've got a big bum. Do you think I've got a big bum?'

'I like it.'

'Will I see you again?'

'I told you, I have to go away.'

When he reached his home in Dulwich, Twilight went straight upstairs. His wife was asleep. He did not wake her, just washed his face, took a leak, washed his hands, then slipped into his children's room. His sons were sleeping in two beds at right angles to one another. He looked at them for a while, watching the shadows from outside play with their faces, then he kissed them both. As he was going to the door, his younger boy, Paul, called him.

Later, Twilight left the room with sadness in his eyes.

Downstairs, he found the note his wife had left for him and telephoned the Administrator in Broadway Buildings.

'Where the hell have you been?' the Administrator said. 'Girenko's gone.' After that, the conversation was short.

Twilight went into his study and unlocked a small safe. He took a shoulder holster and an automatic pistol wrapped in oiled linament from the safe, and then three magazine clips for the weapon. When he had closed the safe, he placed the weapon and the magazines in a bag and examined his clothes. Then he placed them in the bag, too, and went over to Reggie Spane's file.

The Administrator was shuffling his own files when Twilight arrived. This time he leaned back in his chair as if distancing himself from Twilight. Twilight in turn leaned back and the gap between them was swallowed up by the jaundiced light from the Administrator's desk-lamp.

'You know sometimes I have the creeping feeling someone very senior in this firm is Moscow's man,' the Administrator said. And when he had said that, he dropped his papers on the desk and put his hands behind his head, as if he had divested himself of a great burden. 'But then I tell myself, it was the Americans who took Girenko under their protective wing, and it was the Americans who lost him. Well, Gehlen, anyway, and he's bought and paid for by Washington, despite what he thinks. Yuri Podvoysky, you know of him?'

'GRU agent,' Twilight said after some thought. 'Once

attached to Smersh – Death To Spies. Now with the Grave-diggers, the Red Army's answer to my Huntergatherers. Though I like to think we're better, despite the legends that attach to Gravediggers. How did they know Gehlen was minding Girenko?'

'Probably the French,' the Administrator said. 'Riddled with Reds, they are.'

'Or Gehlen's organisation,' Twilight said. 'We could have problems there.'

'Our immediate problem is friend Girenko. If he's not face down in a ditch, which is unlikely, then he's on his way to the Lubyanka or wherever to have his nails torn out while being asked embarrassing questions about us; while Podvoysky enjoys the benefits of his success in a Black Sea Dacha. I think if they'd just meant to kill him, then Girenko would be lying on the floor of his cell in Bavaria.'

'Should we abort Brytenn's operation?' Twilight asked.

The Administrator, who seemed almost to flower at that moment, picked up a sheet of paper and began writing on it, as if what he were writing would negate in some way what they were discussing. 'No,' he said, and Twilight knew the decision had been made before he arrived. 'What does Girenko know? We questioned him. They must know that, too. And he'll try and keep as much of that to himself as possible. About Ivan Pyotr and the Vasili file? Well, they probably know something about that anyway. If Pyotr is still alive in Camp Thirty-Six, then people in Moscow know his importance. And if they manage to extract Girenko's knowledge, then they'll know we know. But Girenko doesn't know anything of our plans. So we still have an edge. Risks, Patrick. We are awfully anxious to get hold of that file. You look puzzled, Patrick.'

'We're assuming Girenko was kidnapped.'

The Administrator took his glasses off and breathed on each lens before rubbing them, a habit that irritated Twilight, who had a thing about germs that only surfaced when he was deep in thought. Not something he could explain, or indeed wanted to explain.

'That vista has presented itself to those of us who make decisions here, Patrick,' the Administrator said.

'Perhaps they were banking on us sending Brytenn in,' Twilight said.

'Then why blow it all by springing Girenko?'

'The die is cast.'

'No. They wouldn't jeopardise such an operation by doing something like this.'

'So it's a kidnap or a killing?' Twilight said.

'Let's just say we'd like to have this priest back before he gets where he's going, whether he's going voluntarily or not.'

Twilight found himself wiping his own hands on the legs of his trousers. He thought for a while before speaking again. 'How much are you going to tell Brytenn?' he asked.

'As much as is necessary. Patrick, just leave it with me. I want you chase Podvoysky and Girenko. If there's a chance they're still around, I want them back. If only to make sure this is what we think.'

'And what do we think?' Twilight asked.

12

The Village

Aktjabrj in the last snows of winter looked for all the world like a frozen cadaver, half-eaten by animals. At one end, on the highest ground overlooking the river behind it, an abandoned church dominated the landscape, and as the village moved away from the church and down the hill the buildings became smaller, until they were virtually indistinguishable from the small hills in the thin birch forest that surrounded them on three sides. Only the rolling fields to the north showed the log houses for what they were, crouched among the high banks of snow, and in the ice mist which followed a cold night, even the fields seemed to vanish.

Nestled in the foothills of the Urals, surrounded by rivers, forests and marshes, a day's march from anywhere, at the end of a dirt road made virtually impassable by the winter snows and the spring thaw, it was said that Aktjabrj had escaped the Time of the Troubles in the sixteenth century because an army sent to reduce the area around it could not find the place.

The fur trade provided any living the land could not, and the isolation provided security no amount of wealth could buy. In 1812, while Moscow burned under French occupation, the family of Tsar Alexander I stayed in the village for a few nights, which was one of the reasons it took the White side during the civil war that followed the Bolshevik coup in 1917. The Bolsheviks took their revenge by executing every male they could find between the ages of sixteen and sixty. Aktjabrj never forgot the lesson.

The reception Cooper Brytenn's party received when they rode in was very different from the naked mistrust they had endured at the collective farm where they bought their horses a few days earlier. One old Aktjabrj woman came out with bread and salt and a man who may or may not have been her husband played a tune that sounded something like Yankee Doodle on his violin. For a few moments, when someone threw flowers at them, Cooper Brytenn felt like a conquering general and, except for the colour of his face, it showed.

'There's nothing like a little brutality for recruiting sympathy,' Jack Summer said to Brytenn, more as a means of re-establishing some of his own status than anything else. His youthful face, burned by the elements, tried to bolster his ego, but Brytenn was not interested. 'These people hate the Bolsheviks,' Summer said then. But now his tone changed and this time Brytenn did pay attention.

'They think we're coming any day now to liberate them,' Brytenn said. 'And they must believe it.'

'Do you believe it, Alexander?' Summer said to the man standing beside his horse.

A short suspicious man with deep furrows in his face and small hands, Alexander Trepper was the main contact in Aktjabrj. He had been hired for money and his nerve fought with his greed every day of his life.

'I never thought I'd see his face again,' he said, staring at

Anatoli Beshov. For two years, Trepper had served with Beshov, but had managed to escape deportation and execution with the help of American Intelligence, who sent him back to Russia with another man's name. He wound up in Aktjabrj, by design, and found he had to work some fields at the edge of the village.

'What goes round, comes round, Djedooshka,' Beshov replied. People in Aktjabrj called Trepper Grandfather because he looked older than his years. In Beshov's unit the term had had quite a different meaning, and had involved under-age boys. Trepper lived alone now, in a small log house in among the trees. When the welcome was over, that is where Brytenn told Summer to establish their billet.

'I should call the authorities, that's what I should do,' Trepper kept saying. He checked every door and window of the house twice over and stopped Beshov fiddling with every piece of furniture around him.

'Then you would never live to see the liberation,' Brytenn said to him.

Trepper, unsure of just who Brytenn was, turned to Summer. 'Touch nothing,' he said.

His house was rich in animal skins, utensils and farm implements, as if it doubled as a workshop, but short on the basic comforts, and it was obvious Trepper lived in only one room.

'We need a fire,' Brytenn said to Summer, who just nodded, happy to let Brytenn conduct business with Trepper.

'You'll have to pay for it,' Trepper replied when told about the fire. This time he looked at Brytenn when he spoke. 'You know you shouldn't come here when there's a drive on. The security police, the Interiors, they are everywhere these days.

They say the Dzerzhinsky Division is nearby.' Trepper marched around the house, checking the cupboards. In the kitchen he opened every door and counted everything he owned. 'Yes, I'll need money,' he added. 'A lot of money.'

Summer pulled out enough money to wipe away whatever fear Trepper had. But when Trepper had counted it he looked at Cooper Brytenn, who was leaning back against a wall, to give his ankle some rest and try and prevent a headache coming on. Trepper recognised symptoms of authority the way most people do disease. 'So who're you?' he demanded.

'A friend,' Brytenn said.

'He's from the West. Can't you tell?' Olga Sharankova said. She went to a window, rubbed the frost and looked out. Then she turned to Cooper Brytenn. 'That's the way to your camp,' she said. She nodded up the road, where the houses were low wooden hunched lumps, made of darkened planks, and the chimneys had thin streamers of grey smoke bending in the wind above them. 'We've come to visit Camp Thirty-Six, Alexander,' she said.

Trepper swore.

'Just two or three nights,' Brytenn said to Trepper. His face was now slightly blanched, and he was having trouble holding himself up without support. And the headache was coming on, regardless of his efforts to prevent it. 'That's all we ask.' He held his hand out for Trepper to shake and almost fell over.

'I'll have to look at that ankle,' Olga said. She looked at Summer, as if to ask permission, but did not wait for him to give it. Summer busied himself with the details of unloading the horses.

'I have a pain, too,' Beshov joked, touching his neck.

'When was the last security patrol?' Summer asked Trepper.

'Five, six days ago. How far have you come?'

'Far enough. We left some of our people behind, so you only have a few to look after.' Summer joined Olga at the window, which she was rubbing to allow more light in. He touched her, as if to cement something. She went back to Brytenn and crouched down at his leg. Looking up, she could see Brytenn's face had lost most of its colour again.

'You're going to have to let me give you something, Brytenn,' she said. 'Sit down, please.'

'I think I'm gonna need to take something for the ankle, Jack,' Cooper Brytenn said quietly to Summer.

Summer did not react immediately. Instead, he let Brytenn sit down while he watched a man pass the house on a cart pulled by a horse. The horse was old and dark and bent under the weight of the cart, and two small sparrows were feeding off its back. The sparrows were joined by other small birds until the driver flicked his whip and the birds took to the air, hovering over the horse, flapping their tiny wings until they felt it was safe to land again and pick at the insects in the horse's hair.

'So give him something,' Summer said to Olga then. 'You should have done this days ago.'

'I apologise,' Brytenn joked.

Olga took something from her pocket, slipped into a corner and examined it. And Summer began to examine Brytenn's leg.

While he did it, Brytenn sat down and talked to Beshov and Trepper. Trepper looked like he was in a dentist's waiting room and drank vodka as if he were, watching all the time as Beshov helped Sasha and two men from the village bring in equipment, dripping snow and water.

When she had administered the phial of morphine to

Brytenn, Olga touched his wound. 'Your ankle's beginning to bend out of shape,' she said.

The morphine flowing through his veins was beginning to dull his pain. He watched her undo his boot with a detached fascination and a certain longing.

'I think it must be broken,' she said.

'Then splint it,' he said.

'If it is broken and you continue to walk on it, your ankle will knit badly. Maybe worse. Poisoning.'

'Just do it,' he snapped at her. Then he apologised. 'I guess I'm a little edgy,' he added. 'Give me time. Any sign of a real problem yet?'

'There are no smells if that is what you mean,' she said. She prodded the ankle when Brytenn was issuing an instruction to Sasha, and he cried out. 'Sorry,' she said, 'I guess I'm a little clumsy.'

All Brytenn could think of was how many shots could he have before Summer might replace him? All he could concentrate on was how weak it made him in the eyes of the others.

'It's just bigger from being in a stirrup, Olga,' he said. 'We need some ice.' He smiled at her. 'Just a couple of days. That's all I need.' She smiled back. Summer noticed and made a face that forced her back to the wound. The scowl on her face that followed drove Summer back to work.

'How come you know so much about ankles, sweetheart?' Beshov asked then. He was carrying two boxes and winking at Trepper, who reacted like his worst nightmare had made an appointment for dinner.

'She was a medical student,' Summer said. He snapped a rifle bolt into position, then placed the rifle on a table, grabbed some bread and checked two more rifles.

'Hey, don't worry, Brytenn,' Beshov said, 'I'll keep you going, if I have to carry you, myself. Hey, Trepper, you remember Baldy? The Lithuanian. Bastard was covered in hair. They have a name for the condition. Anyway, he caught one in the stomach, walked for three weeks with this thing in his guts, all the way to our lines. Jesus, he was a tough bastard. Ugly, too. Hated Poles.' Beshov grinned at Olga. She noticed nothing else other than he had perfect teeth.

'You'll tell me he's living in Switzerland next,' Brytenn said, slightly high now and trying to re-establish a rapport he felt he had lost.

'No.' Beshov's tone changed. 'Some fucking drunk surgeon tore one of his arteries. He bled to death on the operating table.'

Trepper nodded and drank more.

That night, Sasha arrived back at the house with two boys who were on the run from the army. One was intelligent but not completely reliable; the other, a big boy of about sixteen, looked like being with Brytenn's team just about matched the Red Army for discomfort. But he was related to Sasha and reliable. Both boys shuffled about the house nervously, contenting themselves with keeping the fire going.

After a supper that involved too many potatoes for his digestive system, Brytenn asked Olga for another shot of morphine and brought Summer and Beshov into a small annex full of hunting implements and went over the diagrams of Camp Thirty-Six. Trepper and Olga played cards and drank vodka. Sometimes, when there was a lull in the conversation between the planners, Brytenn caught Olga looking at them through the half-open door, with an animal stare. It upset him enough for Summer to notice.

'Jack,' Brytenn said later, when Anatoli Beshov got up to fetch some tea from the kitchen. 'I know you resent my intrusion. I know you believe you should have command here, but I think we should try to reach an accommodation.' And then Brytenn did something that had more to do with the morphine in his system than anything else, and certainly embarrassed him. He put his hand on Summer's shoulder. 'I need you, Jack,' he said. And he shut the door of the annex very deliberately.

'You all right, Cooper?' Summer asked.

'Look, what I'm telling you now is for your ears only,' Brytenn said. And he told Summer about the Vasili file like he was giving a coded message.

Summer did not know whether to be pleased or disturbed. But he did relax for the first time in days, feeling he had regained something. 'Jesus, they must have someone high up in the Kremlin on the Agency's books for this one to come off.'

Brytenn shrugged. 'I know only what I know.'

'Okay, Cooper. But keep him' – he nodded towards the kitchen and Beshov – 'on a leash.'

'And Olga?'

Only much later did Summer wonder if he had answered the same question Brytenn had asked. But by then it was too late. 'I can take care of Olga,' he said. He put his feet up on a chair.

'Let's see about that tea,' Brytenn said. He opened the annex door a little more, in time to see Olga Sharankova put her foot out and trip Anatoli Beshov as he returned with the tea. He fell forward over a chair and spilled tea on his arms. 'You bitch!'

She pulled a pistol from her belt. 'Just give me a reason,' she said.

Beshov returned the smile to his face, bared his teeth and licked the tea from the scalded area of his arms. 'It doesn't hurt, you know.'

Later, when the meeting had broken up for a few minutes, and Jack Summer was outside with Trepper, Beshov left Olga and Brytenn alone.

'I realise you cannot be expected to forget what happened during the war,' Brytenn said to her, 'but there are things at stake here. If you might just understand.'

Whatever she had been thinking, she stopped it and blinked and sniffed and agreed with him. 'You wouldn't have a shit like that if he was not necessary, I guess.'

'Deal,' Brytenn said.

She nodded, then thought for a moment. 'You should make sure Jack goes back with you, Brytenn,' she said.

'And you?'

'I'm needed here.'

That evening dragged on laboriously and Cooper Brytenn's realisation of his own limitations forced him to dominate discussions as much as possible, even though the morphine in his system impaired his ability to concentrate so much sometimes that he had to stop what he was saying and collect his thoughts. Occasionally, he would pick an argument or go over something again for no reason. And once he shouted something pointless at Sasha, who was cleaning the weapons and smoking a pipe in the corner, just to divert attention from himself. Sasha just swore under his breath.

When they had examined Camp Thirty-Six from all angles,

Summer placed a drink on the table in front of them. 'So who goes to look this place over?' he asked.

'We three,' Brytenn replied without thought.

'You're not going anywhere,' Summer insisted.

'You're a liability,' Beshov argued.

Brytenn did not want to go out but felt he should offer and would have been willing if the others had agreed. Now that they had argued against it, he felt his authority was undermined and, because they both suspected his motives, his credibility too.

'I would appreciate it if you would agree with me, Jack,' he said to Summer afterwards. 'Don't consider Beshov completely onside. He knows who we're here for but not why.'

'What made you volunteer for this, Cooper?' Summer asked him. 'Are you hoping to make a name or just plain stupid?'

'I think you need a rest, Jack. Perhaps you should come with us when the plane arrives. I think that would be the right thing.' Brytenn was a man who knew how to use authority given the right situation, and his considered logic angered Jack Summer. Who walked off.

'He was caught in a tunnel,' Olga explained to Brytenn. 'He's a little scared.' She gripped her head with her hands to demonstrate.

When she helped Summer with his equipment an hour after the sun had gone down the following day, he frowned at her. 'What did you say to him?' he asked. 'He's being polite to me all the time. Men like Brytenn are at their worst when they're polite. It has to do with class.'

'I just said you were tired.'

'Well, I'm not.'

'You could go out when the plane arrives, you know. You've done enough here.'

'You want me to leave?' he asked.

She shook her head. 'I used to think you'd become one of us, Jack, but you're still American. Enough makeup to perform the part but if they sent you somewhere else, you'd just change costumes. Were we always just a diversion for a bored soldier?'

Summer wanted to argue but it was time to go.

13

Surgical

Yuri Podvoysky was expecting more than just argument, he was expecting resistance, but as he pushed Misha Girenko down a narrow path of fine moistened gravel, between small stalks of golden sunlight, the old priest just would not provide it. Perhaps it was the day, perhaps too much time locked away. Girenko had his own answer.

'Let's just say I take exception to being knocked unconscious and bundled into the boot of a car, Comrade,' he said. 'So where are we?'

'Never mind,' Podvoysky said. 'Down here, please.'

Podvoysky gestured towards a small cottage, wedged between two blunt summits, a dark dwelling, squat and damp and dripping brown water from a gutter. It might have been Austria or Germany, or even Switzerland. Girenko studied the minutiae for pointers and watched the mountain birds circle overhead on the rising thermals.

'Where the hell did you get this place?' Girenko asked when they reached the cottage. 'I had thought my final minutes would be spent in more splendid surroundings.'

'You're quite a smartarse, Misha. Very sure of yourself.'

'And you take yourself too seriously, Yuri. Why didn't you just kill me back in Pullach?'

'You seem intent on dying.'

'Aren't those your orders?'

Podvoysky made Girenko open the door and then kneel down when he entered the cottage. 'Tell me, what have you done to make them so angry at you in Moscow?'

'I used to be with the Okhrana.'

'They say you looked for death in Paris, too,' Podvoysky said.

'I'm a priest. Yes, officially ordained now. But I had killed a priest. So I was ready to die.'

'I hope you're as strong as you make out.'

'The Americans are going to be livid, you know. I'm their guest. Well, prisoner really. And the British . . .'

'I take my orders from Moscow.'

Girenko turned his head. 'Whatever you do, Yuri, you're a dead man. Why do you think you were sent after me?'

'Not my concern. I do what I'm told.'

'You were sent after me because I know about something people in Russia would give their souls for. I know the name of the thirteenth Okhrana agent provocateur in the Party. Josef Stalin.'

Podvoysky lowered the silenced pistol he was holding and bit on a piece of chocolate he had kept in his pocket.

'You don't believe me?' Girenko said. 'Why send you here for a priest?' The serenity of his face, pale from too much time indoors, told Podvoysky more than any more words Girenko could speak.

'Shit,' Podvoysky said. 'You know I had a feeling. We used to call it the winter feeling in the war. When you thought the weather would get better and it only got worse.'

'Who sent you?'

'Guess?'

'Well, now you know why. And all you've succeeded in doing is breaking me out of jail and signing your own death warrant.'

Almost at the same time in London, Patrick Twilight walked across a wet street between struggling street lights and a pearl-tinged daylight pushing through low clouds and industrial smog. He had two things on his mind. Joe Louis had decided to retire. A decade previously, the Brown Bomber had torn Max Schmelling, the best Germany could throw at him, apart. At exactly the same time Reggie Spane had been the centre of the firm's Continental shadow stations. Claude Dansey's mister fixit. The great contender, they said.

After his encounter with Joe Louis, Max Schmelling joined the German paratroopers, was dropped on Crete and became a hero of the Third Reich. The heavyweight champion of the world was not allowed to join his country's paratroops because he was black, and had to content himself with public relations exercises, urging black men to join up. Some accused him of playing Uncle Tom. By that time Reggie Spane's ambitions had washed up with his corpse in the Thames, like used toilet paper, most of his head missing and the rest of him virtually unidentifiable, except for his teeth.

'His teeth were perfect,' Twilight said to himself. Perhaps Schmelling would return to the ring now that Louis was gone, he thought. Twilight laughed at that. Schmelling was too smart and the ring too far away now. So why would Spane return? Sometimes it felt that the distance between 1939 and 1949 was centuries.

Surgical looked like a country parson, acted like a grave robber and spoke like a man for whom passion was an easily dissectable part of the human anatomy. Surgical's department did not so much exist as appear, and once they were gone getting them back usually took an executive order.

'You don't have any minders?' Twilight asked Surgical inside the latter's flat. The place had a Victorian feel, as if Surgical had laid it out from a Conan Doyle story. Surgical had his own ambitions, they said. Some people said he was writing. Others maintained that was not possible, Surgical had been dead for years. His complexion spoke death, but in a refined artistic way.

'Who?' he asked, looking out of his window.

'Couple of fairies across the street.'

'Ask head office,' Surgical replied. He poured the drinks with the precision of a lab scientist measuring out an experiment. Twilight took the drink and tried to wipe his own fingerprints from the glass. 'Rather not,' he said.

'Unofficial visit?' Surgical asked.

'Reggie Spane,' Twilight said.

Surgical did not respond any more than Twilight would have expected. 'He's in a cemetery in Watford.'

'I'm not interested in the body.'

'That man of the cloth in Germany still missing?' Surgical asked. He waited for a suitable pause to elapse. 'We do hear things, Patrick.'

'I'm looking for Reggie Spane,' Twilight said. 'I need what you have on him.'

They both looked at each other for some time, waiting for the telltale blink.

'It would require an Administrator's request,' Surgical said.

'Why bother him with something so trivial?'

Surgical gave a schoolboy chuckle and picked at the hairs in his ears. 'I do love your ridiculous inability to leave well enough alone, Patrick. Reminds me of Claude Dansey. You finding people giving you a wide berth at Broadway?'

'Failure is contagious.'

Twilight sat up all night, reading what Surgical had given him, sipping weak tea, occasionally breaking off small morsels of burnt toast and placing them on his tongue until they disintegrated, then sipping more tea to wash the toast down.

Reggie Spane reappeared in small pieces of typed paper, ringed in red pencil, underlined in crayon: expense sheets with question marks, applications for bank accounts, enquiries about pension rights, and a few personal letters to people Twilight had never heard of.

'You don't expect a man with a secret life to keep secrets from that secret life,' Twilight said to himself. He was in the habit of speaking to himself in these night sessions when he was sure he was alone, and then after he had spoken he would remain quiet for five or ten minutes, just listening, in case someone was there. Once he had discovered his younger boy, standing at the door, crying, the quietest tears Twilight had ever seen, and when he had asked the boy how long he had been there, his son just shook his head. But his skin was frozen. For a moment, Twilight had judged his son.

That night, his son appeared at four, when the dog across the park began barking and some of the early rising birds began to stretch their wings to the rising sun. The chill of morning lay over the tops of the trees on the heath, a pale white glow caught on the stillness of the hour. Twilight put his son on his lap and threw a rug over both of them.

He rang Surgical after breakfast.

'Spane had a woman in Cambridge,' Twilight said.

'She ran a boarding house near the Cam,' Surgical replied. 'Tall dwelling, covered in ivy, with oak doors and a view of the river. He wrote rather nervous letters he never sent to her, in very reserved handwriting. As if trying to solicit affection.'

'The kind of thing a man not writing in his native tongue would attempt if he was very sure of himself,' Twilight said.

There was a pause at the other end of the line. Surgical had dropped something. 'Yes,' he said then.

'Why save them up?' Twilight asked.

'Who knows? Have you never written letters with the intention of sending them?'

'And they all definitely came from his hand?' Twilight asked.

'We're very thorough. No bone unturned is our motto.' Surgical laughed. 'We checked the woman out. Nothing to speak of. Husband was in the services. She knew less about Spane than we did. There were others but she was the only regular. Bit of a ladies' man, our Reggie.'

'But no links to anyone else?'

'Nothing. He was the kind of orphan the firm loved in those days. One of Claude Dansey's secrets, when Claude was running his parallel game in Europe before the war. I do miss Claude. Things just aren't the same without him.'

'I bet they met in hotels, this woman and Spane.'

'You Huntergatherers have a sickly sense of life, Patrick. There's no evidence they ever met like that. Perhaps it was a platonic thing. Perhaps Reggie had a decent side to him. I suspect you'll want a chat with her now, and then I'll have the Administrator on my back.'

Twilight put the phone down.

When Twilight turned up at Broadway Buildings the same day, he was summoned by the Administrator. Mrs Ackland, who handled the Administrator's summonses, dealt with this one in a quiet cavernous way, directing Twilight through the labyrinth of his superior's mood.

'I hear you were talking to Surgical yesterday,' the Administrator said.

Twilight could do nothing but admit his guilt. 'I'm not convinced about Spane.'

'You're supposed to be looking for Podvoysky and Girenko, Patrick. How not convinced?'

'There's just too much detail. Addresses, tastes in clothing, favourite films and books he meant to read and friends he sent gifts to at Christmas. I've never seen a file so big with so little, on anyone. Then there were the personal effects. Just about everything you had ever heard of was found in his apartment by the time Surgical had finished, heaps of things he would never have used, tickets for this, programmes for that, old newspapers dating back years. This is a legend. The only problem now is figuring out whose.'

'What are you thinking, Patrick?'

'That Girenko is Spane. That there's no brother Niki.'

'And what would that suggest?'

'I'm not sure. But he gave us the information on Ivan Pyotr and the Vasili file. And now he's gone. Pinched from under our noses.'

The Administrator scratched his head. 'Then why is

Brytenn still active? Look, Girenko was one of life's pieces of refuse. Perhaps the relevant refuse collectors just swept him up and dumped him where he belonged. You just have to make sure of it.'

Twilight could not tell if his master was telling him a truth or speculating a hypothesis. 'He's no longer on Foreign Office files,' Twilight said. 'Spane.'

'As I understand it, he was never officially F.O. For God's sake, Patrick, the man was one of Claude Dansey's hirelings. And a bloody pointless embarrassment now. Look, once we have Pyotr, who or what Girenko is or is not will not matter. I thought we'd closed the book on Spane.'

'They say that if you look into a mirror, at a mirror behind you, then the repetition of reflections over a period of time would mean that the further away the reflection was coming from the younger you would be. Conceivably you might see yourself in the immediate reflections as you are and yourself years younger in the deeper reflections. You are not going back in time, time is merely trying to catch up with you.'

'Do you need a rest, Patrick?' the Administrator asked.

'We could be stepping into the world of the mirrors, sir, waiting for the last one to catch up,' Twilight replied. 'It never will.'

The Administrator told him to take the rest of the day off.

Twilight caught a train to Cambridge at lunchtime, eating a sandwich and doing the Telegraph crossword while the vehicle steamed its way through the serrated countryside. Spring flowers dominated his thoughts, colours he could recall from a childhood immersed in poppies and grapes, neat rolling countryside, the folds of a fat man or a lazy animal, or the twists and bends of a porkish pasteurised land, layer upon layer of which gave only goodness and freedom.

'Mrs Mary Malty?'

The woman was far younger than Twilight had expected. Perhaps in her mid-thirties, quite pretty in a way women who choose domesticity or have it thrust upon them often are, except for the tiredness inherent in keeping a boarding house and feeding two medical students and three prospective engineers.

'I read history myself,' Twilight lied. He could tell them with such conviction now he almost believed them himself. But they were functional, expedient lies, designed to solicit information, not bolster his own sense of himself. He allowed himself to feel some sympathy for Cooper Brytenn.

They sat in a parlour eating cakes and drinking a tea so weak Twilight felt it would simply vanish when he put the cup to his mouth. The cup was a perfect bone china, but less expensive than that behind the glass case. Mrs Malty had a hierarchy of display which she applied to everyone who came to her house. The students would never have been given the cups but only her friends received anything in the bone china behind the glass.

'I prefer technologists,' she said. 'My husband was a technologist. He was killed . . . over Berlin, I think.' She gestured to his photograph. He wore a DFC and bar above his left chest pocket and that perpetual weary fear Twilight had noticed on all combat pilots.

'I'm interested in a man named Spane,' Twilight said.

She remained impassive.

'I found this in his personal effects. It's a postcard you sent to him. He wrote you letters, you sent him postcards.'

She examined the postcard in a way one might do a piece of evidence in a trail, reading the words to herself, nodding her head slightly, changing facial expressions as memories flooded into her consciousness. If she had said nothing after that Twilight would have known what she was thinking.

'I had almost forgotten about this.'

'I know it's been a very long time since you were with him,' Twilight said, expecting her to cry or something. Sometimes he felt there was not a reaction he could not predict or had not seen. And for a moment his mind ventured into the alleys around Half Moon Street and a girl leaning into his car the previous morning. 'Joe Louis had beaten Max Schmelling to become heavyweight boxing champion.'

'No,' Mary Malty said. 'Reggie came to me last August. Yes, it was August and he came to talk about my husband. Victor. They were friends, you see.'

'We are talking about the same man?' Twilight enquired, shoving a mugshot of Spane into her eyes.

'He always looked on the verge of something awful, I felt, and I knew he would vanish some day. He just stopped writing. I thought that was what you were here for. He had been abroad, he said. Perhaps, that's what's happened again. Always a gentleman, Reggie. Nothing ever happened between us. Nothing.'

Twilight felt the rush of life enter his body. He tried not to show his excitement, but his constant glancing at his watch gave him away. She offered him more tea.

'Please, tell me about your husband,' he said.

14

Missing Presumed Killed

Not long after that, Victor Malty poked a dead rodent with a small stick and watched a line of white grubs emerge from under the animal's tail. Malty, whose own bulldog face and heavy dark eyes had endured remarkably well given his circumstances, wiped his nose and looked at the sallow, pencil-sketch faces around him. 'Even the maggots are leaving,' he said.

The big man beside him, whose lips were a series of loosely connected sores, adopted a grin Malty had often seen during his time in captivity, a feline exposure of teeth and gums, tongue pressed hard up against the roof of the mouth, muscles, or what remained of them, stretched to disfigurement on the skeletal frame, pulsating blue lines swelling beneath the margarine complexion, all held together by lines of stubble rivets and a limitless desire to survive.

'I'll have the head,' he said to Malty. Then he reached out through the frozen air, huge hands clouded in the condensed breath of his fellow prisoners, a kind of semi-permanent dung steam rising from the barrack floor as if to curtain off the rat from those who would benefit from it, and touched the still-warm body of the dead animal with the tips of his fingers.

'Squeeze it,' another man said. He was very tall and bent like a piece of fuse wire. He turned his yellow eyes to Malty. Malty nodded once. His companion lifted the animal and began to put pressure on its body. Very slowly, a visceral ooze began to leak from the back, dropping in large tears to the stone floor.

'Jesus, we'll lose it all.'

Malty stopped two men to his right from interfering. Then he pulled a small penknife and shoved it into the rat's belly.

'Anyone want the stomach?'

A man to his left raised his hand, then checked with his companions, then cupped his hands. Malty emptied the contents of the rodent's stomach into the makeshift cup.

Victor Malty watched him eat it with envy. 'Breakfast time at Camp Thirty-Six,' he said. A strong Ural wind blew the hut door open.

Two hours later, when his work party stopped at the edge of a ravine two miles from the camp, Victor Malty passed a cigarette to a thin old Russian man with a Tartar's face and a lifer's ritual. The snow had returned and the guards were trying to decide where they should sit to avoid freezing. One of them was arguing that they had to work.

'Otherwise they will freeze,' Ivan Pyotr said to Malty. 'Sometimes being a guard is more dangerous than being a prisoner.'

'Have you heard anything about food?' Malty asked.

'The roads are blocked again. We are very isolated here. So a few of us die before the thaw. The police just make some raids in Moscow and we are replaced by better specimens. That's how it happens, Englishman.'

'I'm Canadian,' Malty insisted.

Pyotr looked at him with a blank expression that did not care if he was from Mars. 'You caught something this morning. An unlucky rat. Where is it?'

'We ate it.'

Pyotr shook his head and then looked at his new boots. 'Pity. I could have traded it for things you might need. You should not just eat food when you find it. If you can hold your damn stomachs then you might build up some trading capital. For capitalists, you are lousy businessmen.'

'I have an American near death and two of my own men are down to less than fifty kilos. They have about a week before they'll collapse and die. If this weather keeps up the way it's going, they won't even have that.'

The guards settled their dispute by establishing a rotation system whereby some of them would stand watch for fifteen minutes while the others worked with the prisoners, then the guards would be relieved by those working and so on.

Malty picked up the axe at his feet and set to work on a pine tree in front of him. He wore woollen mittens he had stolen from a dead man at the side of a road years before. That was when he was in Siberia and the temperature dropped to minus fifty. Then the guards just sent them out to work and waited for them to come back. Those who chose not to come back died, those who could not find their way back or were late back died. Those who did get back often begged to be let into the camp again. Sometimes the guards were too slow and those prisoners died, too.

The tree fell to his left and Malty had time to rub his hands and gather what strength he had for the day's work. You could not stand around for too long or you would start to seize up like an engine. He had seen many men begin to seize up, seen them try to move limbs that would not move, seen the horror in their eyes and heard the squawks that passed for screams.

Others just sat down and died. They would drop their tools, walk away, sit down and die. The guards never tried to stop them, no one did. It was the only dignity allowed and often guards would do it, too. Once or twice a guard would go mad and begin to shoot all the men in his charge, keeping the last bullet for himself. Once or twice a prisoner would overpower a guard and kill everyone with him and then himself. There were other variations too numerous to dwell on. Everyone kept their thoughts short and their energy for keeping warm.

'There's a guard looking for English lessons,' Ivan Pyotr whispered to Malty. 'I think he wants to go to London or America. He'll pay in rations. Hell, I offered but he wants a native speaker. Jumped-up bastard. Never have made it in the Okhrana.'

'He must be very desperate,' Malty said.

'Of course,' Pyotr agreed. 'I don't think the rations are his. But don't expect the classes to last too long. How many more cigarettes have you?'

'I want something worth while.'

'A woman!' Pyotr raised his frost-coated eyebrow.

'Who sold out Mikhail Kevenko to the gallows then?' Malty asked.

'We were partners,' Pyotr said.

'Then you were lucky,' Malty said.

One of the guards yelled at Malty then and he jumped back

into action, chopping at the tree he had felled with a sudden fury, more to keep warm than to work off the build-up of fear the guard's words had caused in him.

'Man gets his prick up in this sees it break off, Comrade,' he said to Pyotr.

'I'm an Okhrana colonel, Squadron Leader. And I have not been officially relieved. I believe the Tsar is indisposed.' Pyotr went back to his own work. Once he swung round to Malty and this time the thin Tartar looked like a snake ready to bite. 'I knew a man with cholera once, he tried to shit himself when the temperature was fifty below or worse. We found him frozen, impaled on his own shit.'

The work parties came back just before dark, when the wolves began to howl and the fires were the only light in the camp. Once the sun had finally given up the struggle with the day, the winds came from the north and shredded anything not inside the wooden walls of the huts.

Swell Johnson lay on a bottom bunk at the end of the shed. His legs were hanging over the edge of the bunk and his head was propped up on a piece of stuffed material. A small crust of bread lay on his chest, and Malty found himself eyeing the individual crumbs on Johnson's blanket.

'How are you, Swell?'

Johnson answered true to his name. His eyes rolled in their sockets until the lids slid over them. 'I think I gotta get outta here, Vic. I got short-time written all over me. Maybe it was somethin' I ate.'

'Remind me,' one of Malty's men said, 'just in case I got it wrong, just who were our pals during the recent war with Germany and Japan?'

'The freedom-loving Union of Soviet Socialist Republics,' Malty replied.

'Oh, great,' the man said. 'For a moment I thought I'd been standing at the gates of a German POW cage waiting for release only to find myself thrown into a worse cage, accused of spying by our allies.'

'No, that's a different Union of Soviet Socialist Republics,' Swell Johnson said. 'They helped the Germans carve up Poland, invaded Finland, Latvia, Lithuania and Estonia, and then took some of Romania. Our Union of Soviet Socialist Republics came to the aid of Poland, pre-empted a German invasion of the Baltic republics, took back those bits of Romania rightfully hers and forestalled an invasion by aggressive Finland.'

'See, you're not so bad, Swell,' Malty said.

'I feel very warm, you know,' Johnson said. 'They did some shit job on me in the meathouse.'

Malty nodded. He had long ceased to feel emotion for the sick and wounded, just resignation at the course their difficulties would take.

'What the hell were you doing here?' he asked.

'Nature!' Johnson said. 'I came to see the wolves. Swell, ain't it? I told 'em in Moscow. You think they believed me? Swell mess, swell story. I gotta get outta here, Vic. They get me again and they'll kill me.'

Malty did not reply but the look he gave said he wished Johnson an easy death. Swell was using up food and blankets unnecessarily.

'You think you might be able to get up tomorrow?' Malty asked Johnson then.

'You think they'll send me to the infirmary if I don't?'

The infirmary was a death sentence. No one who went there ever came back.

'I don't think there's any infirmary at all,' Malty said. 'Men are just taken a suitable distance from the camp and killed. But don't worry, Swell, you're important.'

'Swell.'

'I talked to Pyotr,' Malty said. 'He can get you some milk if we hand over more cigarettes.'

Swell shook his head very rigorously. 'No! Without them, we're screwed, Vic. These bastards'll eat us alive.'

'If we don't get out of here soon, we'll all end up eating ourselves,' Malty said. 'You think our governments know we're here?'

Swell Johnson tapped his side. 'Not much left on me to know about. There's bits of me all over this country. But, hey, they must know I'm here.' He went to speak more but held his tongue.

About fifty metres to the south of Camp Thirty-Six, a small lake fought the forests around it for space. Gradually, the lake was losing the battle and for a few weeks in high summer it would become no more than a piece of bog, cut off from its water supply and overgrown with foliage. Only the arrival of winter staved off its demise, but each year the lake lost a little more of its integrity to the trees and their allies.

From the other side of the lake, Anatoli Beshov could now envy those inside the camp, while an elk sought food beneath the snow and then pushed its nose into the ice at the edge of the lake. The frozen surface of the lake was scarred by long grasses and the remains of fallen trees and small plants. Occasionally, a beaver would pop its head above the ice and search the landscape, wondering if it was time to ride the spring again. But spring was struggling badly this year; winter still had strength to expend.

'See him?' Jack Summer blew into his hands and then picked up some powdered snow.

Beshov shook his head. 'It's lock-up. Anyone not inside is dead. Which we will be if we do not move now.' Something caught Beshov and shook what passed for a soul inside him and for a few seconds he was powerless to move. 'I take it you have never been a guest in one of Stalin's hotels?' he said to Summer.

'Spent some time in Germany,' Summer replied. 'Didn't like it much. Tried to escape.'

'We don't even know if he's still alive,' Beshov said. He was trying to influence Summer and the latter detected this and took the binoculars from Beshov.

'You know, you better hope he is,' Summer said. 'There's a gap between the watchtowers on this side. See it? If the man on the left looks away, there's a blind spot. The other man leans out that way, towards the open ground ahead of him.'

'That gap is planted thick with mines,' Beshov countered. 'They don't have to look there. All the way to the shores of this lake. If a man got through the mines then he had to swim the lake. Not possible in this cold. In summer they have a man over here. If we go in there, we won't come out.'

'Olga tells me you killed a family of eight little girls, all by your lonesome,' Summer said.

'You want to kill me, too?'

'Not especially,' Summer said. 'I just want to see your face when you think about it.'

Beshov became agitated and made an excuse to get some

distance between himself and Summer. He crept back through the snow to where Alexander Trepper waited with the horses.

'He's mad, you know,' Beshov said to his old comrade. 'They're both mad. Brytenn and him.'

'Keep away from me,' was all Trepper said.

'Why would I harm you, Alex, you're the only one of us who knows the way back. But look at that place. Do you think we can get in there?' Beshov tapped his head and watched Summer make his way towards them, through the snow.

They stayed where they were until it was fully dark, and then started back to Aktjabrj.

'Then we'll have to go in across the lake and through the mines,' Cooper Brytenn said the next day. He said it as if he were expecting Beshov to object, and when the Russian did object, Brytenn sighed.

'We could wait for them to come out,' Alexander Trepper said, 'on work details.'

Beshov smiled very slightly. 'Yes,' he said. 'Let's deal with this problem practically, instead of trying to be heroes, Brytenn.'

Brytenn went to argue but found the pain in his ankle had crept up on him and was now preventing him concentrating. 'Olga, my leg,' he said in an almost pleading tone.

She prepared a phial of morphine and everyone had to wait while she injected Brytenn. He used the time to prepare his case and reassert his authority. He did the latter by asking for small things from everyone round the table. Only Summer refused to co-operate. He was focused on Olga.

'Turning you into a nurse, is he?' Summer commented. 'How much of that stuff have you taken, Cooper?'

'It's just for the pain,' Olga said.

Summer stopped what he was going to say. 'I think Beshov has a point, Cooper,' he said instead.

'That right?' Brytenn said. 'Well, it's good that you don't have to make the decision, Jack.'

'And you don't have to go,' Summer said to Brytenn.

Something might have blown up if Beshov had not interrupted. 'We don't even know if he's there,' he shouted at Brytenn. 'Right?' he said to Trepper.

Trepper shrugged and nodded. But when Beshov looked to Summer for support, the American refused to give it.

Brytenn stopped everything and asked to be left alone in the small annex, with the maps, for a few minutes. He used the time to regain control of himself. Inside, a latent fear was resurfacing, the same fear he had felt weeks earlier on the Finnish border, a sharp sensation that caused his skin to change colour in places and all those pretensions he often used to cover his weaknesses suddenly to vanish. And even with the morphine, Cooper Brytenn began to have a headache.

'Here, drink a lot of this,' Sasha said to him. The big Ukrainian, who seemed to appear from nowhere, was holding two bottles. 'You are sick.'

Brytenn nodded and took a bottle. 'How are the troops?' he asked. He had worked with so many Sashas in his time, most of them dead now, men and women who gave everything and you just knew were going to get nothing more than a bullet in return.

'I think you are perhaps pushing yourself into quicksand,' Sasha said. He tapped his bulbous nose and then picked it. 'I know this because I was in the desert with Montgomery. Long Range Desert Group. Sometimes an officer would push us into quicksand, just because he could not think of another thing to do. But once you are in quicksand, there is little you can do to get out.'

'I have my orders,' Brytenn said.

'Sometimes that is not enough.' Sasha toasted him.

'Can you ask Olga to come in here, please,' Brytenn said. 'I think my ankle needs attention.'

Sasha downed another glass, raised his eyebrows. 'Alcohol is a better mistress,' he said. 'Than morphine,' he added. He left the annex, slapped one of his younger men on the shoulder and told him to fetch Olga.

Across a large room, full of equipment, Beshov and Summer, who had been staring at one another in the uncomfortable realisation that they had become allies of convenience, used the moment to approach Brytenn again.

'We have to take chances, gentlemen,' Brytenn said.

Summer might have said something to redress his earlier criticism if Olga had not appeared and knelt down at Brytenn's feet.

'I hope you're not thinking of tagging along, Cooper,' he said.

'Look,' Olga said to Summer. 'He shouldn't have come this far with an ankle that size. Try and say something positive, Jack, or just shut up.'

Summer obeyed. 'So we still go in by the lake and the mines?' he asked Brytenn.

Brytenn did not even think before he nodded his head. 'Me too,' he said.

Beshov swore.

15

Roulette

The frozen corpse of Yuri Podvoysky, locked in its ashen death agony on a small road between Belgium and Germany, caused Patrick Twilight to think of a child. Any menace the little Russian's ugly face had once had was now melting into the residual spring snows and the ditch water, being replaced by an almost stunned boyish grin, so inane that it might have been speaking to Twilight.

'Half our problem solved?' the Administrator asked. 'Or a bigger one added?'

'Do you know the legend of the Gravedigger?' Twilight asked.

'It's a mountain in the south Caucasus. Near where they train people like Podvoysky.' Reinhard Gehlen had a satisfaction in his voice which belied his suspicions. 'They say if the snow falls on the south side only . . . well, they're superstitious people, the Russians.'

'Georgians,' the Administrator said. 'The Gravedigger points the way for all. Beware the Gravedigger.' He rubbed his hands. 'Isn't that how the saying goes?'

'There's still snow on the south side,' Twilight said then. 'Nothing on the north side. First time since 1917.'

'So you think Podvoysky was sent to kill Girenko?' the
Administrator asked Twilight.

'That's certainly the way it looks,' Twilight replied.
'Except . . .'

'Gravediggers usually don't end up like this,' Gehlen said.
He flexed his slight body, rubbed his Savile Row suit and
pursed his slightly feminine lips. His academic calm lost itself
in his suspicion. 'And what was a Gravedigger doing chasing
an old Tsarist police officer? They're sleepers. They work their
way into positions of influence and then dig the graves of the
enemies of the revolution. Any half-baked assassin could have
taken care of Girenko.'

'Tell that to Podvoysky, General,' the Administrator said.
He looked around at the emptiness of the flatscape and the
small groups of police and soldiers around them. 'Why's the
body here?' he said. 'Patrick?'

'To point the way for us,' Twilight said.

'Or to point us away?' the Administrator asked. 'So what's
Reggie Spane up to? And for whom?'

'Who is Reggie Spane?' Gehlen asked.

'One of our difficulties, General. I'll fill the CIA in and
they'll fill you in. I do think this should all be done on a
professional basis. Patrick?'

'I think Girenko might be a Gravedigger, too.'

'So where does that leave us?' The Administrator was from
a generation for whom freedom and kindness were symbiotic
and expected. It was a paternalistic approach to liberation
where clearly defined classes relied on the support and
guidance of one another, where the end was wisdom, not
gain, where enlightenment made its last attempt to bridge the
gap between desire and attainment.

'Girenko told me he wanted to die.' Twilight touched Podvoysky. 'That was my lever.'

'He obviously changed his mind,' Gehlen said.

'Or never had any intention of dying,' the Administrator said. 'But if not that, then what?'

'It could still be Brytenn,' Twilight said. 'Girenko's succeeded in making sure just about everyone working for us in that part of Russia will be in contact with Brytenn. If they anticipated Brytenn, then they just have to follow him. Simple, really.'

'But how would they know we'd move on his information?' the Administrator said.

'And how do we explain this?' Gehlen added, pointing to Podvoysky.

Twilight shrugged and tipped his head back and watched an aircraft pass overhead.

Trudi Weiss watched another American aircraft skim the rooftops before touching down at Templehof airfield in Berlin. Later, she sniffed her way along a spindly street near the Kurfurstendamm, past two old women hauling firewood on trolleys, before turning right. It had been an empty night and she was debating whether to try her luck in the Tiergarten or go home. She chose the latter.

'Busy?' The man standing in the semi-darkness of her kitchen was smoking.

Trudi Weiss opened her long coat and untied the small scarf around her neck. She squinted at the darkness before opening her mouth. 'I take it you have a key,' she said.

'Yuri Podvoysky gave me one,' Misha Girenko replied.

She made a dash for the door. Girenko stopped her.

'He's dead, Trudi. You're alive. Stay that way.' He pulled a thousand dollars from his pocket and showed it to her. 'Yours,' he said.

She smiled, touched it, relaxed for a while, then took her shoes off, went over to a cupboard, pulled out a bottle and poured herself a drink. 'No matter how much you expect death you cannot escape the surprise,' she said. 'But money always helps.'

Girenko sat down at the table with her, took a drink and listened. There was something of the musical instrument about her voice and something of the opera about her reactions.

'What else do you want?' she asked. 'I serve in many ways.'

Girenko shifted, cold and nervous, jerking his head left and right at every sound from outside. 'I'm a priest,' he said.

'So what do you want?' she asked.

'I need to go east.'

'I take it you don't want to walk through the Brandenburg Gate. What happened to Yuri?'

'Yuri helped me,' Girenko said. 'I can't tell you any more. But I'm here because of him.'

'I almost believe you,' she said, dwelling on Podvoysky for a while. Then she became hard again and that instinct that had brought her from the mountains of Yugloslavia took over. 'You got more cash?' she asked. 'I can always use more cash. Coal. I need more coal.'

She stood up, came over to him, put her arms around him and mapped him with her body.

A large map covered the floor of Alexander Trepper's living room, and moved only with the slight breeze coming under the door and the few insects crawling from underneath the paper.

Cooper Brytenn sat watching Olga Sharankova examine his ankle with a fascination that had very little to do with his interest in his injury. Both of them listened to Beshov explain the layout of Camp Thirty-Six.

'The prisoners' accommodation is here to the east, in three distinct areas: ordinary criminals: you know, killers, rapists, thieves, that kind of thing; politicals: enemies of the state, counter-revolutionaries; and then the specials: these are any-one who cannot easily be fitted into the previous two categories but who might be of some use at a further time. They used to keep all former Tsarist police officers here, and the occasional party official caught embezzling. I was held there. And, if he is still alive, then that is where our friend Pyotr, Ivan the Terrible, will be. Though I doubt he's very terrible right now.' Beshov paused to shake his head in astonishment at what they were planning, then continued. 'Watchtowers are all designed to cover each other.' He pointed to the various areas of the perimeter fence and then gave a description of how they covered one another. 'At night, they shine their lights along each fence every two to three minutes. And of course there are dogs.' He looked to Jack Summer for confirmation.

'A tight space, Cooper,' Summer said.

'And we're going to need to build a raft,' Brytenn said, ignoring Summer's warning. 'In case the ice on this lake gives way. I don't want people in that lake with nothing but their balls to hang on to. Jack?'

Summer nodded. He was distracted by Olga's hands for some reason, probably the way they touched Brytenn's wound, but he regained himself quickly enough and no one noticed. 'One or two of us might well get very wet and very cold.'

Beshov came in again with a detailed description of what Summer and he had seen, and again stressed how difficult it would be. 'Mr Brytenn, our man, Ivan Pyotr, must have the keys to the kingdom.'

'Surely then we could wait for the work parties to come out? Get Pyotr then?' Alexander Trepper asked.

Brytenn figured Beshov had put him up to it. 'No,' Brytenn cut him off. 'It leaves us too exposed.'

'Too exposed!' Trepper threw his head back and looked for support around the table.

'Give him more money, Jack,' Olga said to Summer. 'The sooner we're in and out, the sooner we're gone, Alex. And you're free again.'

'Till the next time,' Trepper complained.

'Go find a nice boy,' Beshov said. Trepper had failed him and the SS man wanted his pound of flesh.

Trepper, if he had been a man with any spare courage, might have hit Beshov then. Instead, he cowered, only to find Beshov taking advantage of his retreat by being seen to agree with the same man he had insulted seconds before.

'There's a chance his idea might work,' Beshov said. 'Right, Jack?' Beshov's eyes narrowed to little dots. The friendly stare that followed slightly shook Summer.

'We go as planned, Herr Sturmbannführer,' Brytenn said.

'You are definitely a little mad, Brytenn,' Beshov said. 'Maybe that stuff she keeps putting into you is affecting your brain.'

Suddenly, as if they were back in the Swiss hotel bedroom again, Brytenn stood up, grabbed Beshov and pulled him across the table, which surprised no one more than the Russian turncoat. Brytenn's anger especially concerned him. 'You should concern yourself with what is required of you,' Brytenn said. Then he let Beshov go, steadied himself, then slumped into his chair, leaving Olga to check his ankle.

'Okay, okay,' Beshov said, raising his hands. 'Professional disagreement. Please give Mr Brytenn some morphine, Olga.'

'Does he have to be allowed to talk all the time?' Olga Sharankova asked Brytenn. 'You see this?' She pointed to a scar on her head, just visible between the stubble. 'He did that.' She broke Beshov's stare. 'And you don't even remember.'

'Sturmbannführer Beshov,' Brytenn said, 'is the key to our kingdom.' He tried to smile but instead cried out slightly when Olga pulled his bandage too tight. 'Tell me it's getting better,' he said.

'You need a doctor, and you need rest,' she replied. 'Not me. Or morphine.'

Brytenn became serious again. 'What I need is a volunteer,' he said. 'For the minefield.'

The silence that followed was broken by Jack Summer. 'Me,' he said. 'I'll do that.'

Brytenn agreed. And both men watched Olga prepare a morphine shot.

Later on, Brytenn and Summer sat alone, drinking tea in the small annex, discussing the plan. A rather frenzied Alexander Trepper, having failed to make any headway with one of Sasha's young helpers – something everyone noticed but no one commented on, not even Beshov – now played his accordion by a fire in the next room, while Olga and Sasha prepared the weapons on a long, woodwormed table. Beshov slept in a corner, with a bottle beside him. He had been defeated for the moment and was willing to acknowledge it.

'I have a horrible feeling that great art is essentially fascist,' Brytenn said to Jack Summer without any prompting. 'Know what I mean?'

But Jack Summer did not know what he meant. He managed to conceal his ignorance while still wrestling with the subject, his facial contortions resembling the same muscular movements the pain from Brytenn's ankle often brought on.

'I saw some fascists shot in Germany,' Summer said. 'Man, they were brave guys. Just spat at the firing squads.'

'Contempt for life,' Brytenn said. 'I'm not impressed.'

'You've killed before. You'll kill here.'

'Because I have to,' Brytenn said. 'The finest excuse.'

'Have you taken more morphine?'

'I am compos mentis, Jack,' Brytenn insisted.

'You're full of shit sometimes, Cooper,' Summer said. 'It's the system, you know, all the system.'

'What do you mean?'

'Will decide this.' Summer spread his hands. 'Either we're right or they're right and no amount of armies or us or anything else will make it different. If their system works and they're happy in the end, then they'll win, and if they don't, then we'll win.' He pronounced those last words so softly, Brytenn could barely hear them. But they registered.

'Do you miss the States?' Brytenn asked.

'I'm trying not to,' Summer replied. 'But then we Americans have a way of transporting our world with us that goes far beyond the superficial. Olga says we carry our nationality in our eyes the way no other people do, in our movements, in our heads. You only have to look at an American to tell he's homesick. It is our very belief in America that points us out. The States is a burden I cannot afford out here, you know, Cooper. You should remember that. And Olga is a girl who likes to have men who need her.'

'Invaded your patch?' Brytenn asked.

Summer walked over to a jug of cold water and poured some into a cup. 'You know we're losing here. Six months, a year, they'll have us all. We each have our tortures, we all play with reality to prevent the pain. You were decorated in Italy?'

Brytenn nodded.

'There's no glory here,' Summer said then. 'There's not much of anything. There's just the slow realisation that what you know only exists because you know it and whatever else there is does not matter until you find it out.'

'Well, maybe I have glory for you.'

Brytenn pulled out a small black notebook and handed it to Summer. Summer took it and put it to one side before reading it.

'Radio message from Munich,' Brytenn said. 'It seems there's a chance our Soviet hosts know where we are and why we're here.'

'When did you get this?' Summer asked.

'Trepper's basement transmitter has its uses,' was all Brytenn would say.

'And you're going ahead?' Summer said.

'Impossible not to. I know what I'm doing, Jack.'

'Jesus. You think he gives a shit? Stalin? My God, he's airbrushed out half the men who helped him get where he is now. They rewrite history here as a matter of course.'

'We all rewrite history.'

'Not by the hour. I suppose you want me to say, no, we don't all rewrite history. Is that it? Well, fuck you, Cooper.'

'I thought I'd tell you about our problem, Jack.' Brytenn had a sneaking feeling he had better not go further with the argument, so he began to examine his wound again. The last shot of morphine was beginning to wear off. 'Look, Washington is a little more than anxious not to go to war,' he said quietly, without looking up. He pulled off his bandage and touched the wounded ankle. Summer looked at it, too. 'Another general war would be unthinkable. Do you understand me, Jack? If it takes a hundred sordid little conflicts and the like to prevent another general war, then I'm for it. And if we're the price of it then it's a fair exchange.'

'Jesus, Cooper, what the hell goes on up there in that brain of yours?'

'Whatever the outcome, we are charged with this task and will complete it. You want millions dead again? You've been here too long, Jack. Time to get out.'

'Your war will never happen.'

'Damn sure it won't. If I can stop it.'

'I know the Russians. They lost twenty million or more in the last one. You should see the villages with no men. You think they want that again?'

Brytenn shook his head and continued dressing his wound. 'Did they tell you I was betrayed by communists in Italy?' he asked.

'No,' Summer said. 'No, they did not tell me that. That why you volunteered for the Agency? I came here because I was bored. So maybe you can call that a breakdown. I was so bored I took a motorcycle across the States and broke up a few towns on the way. There I was standing in front of my mother's

home, kitbag over my shoulder, sun shining over the hills —
I'm from Tennessee, you know — all the warmth of home there
before me and I just could not face it. The ordinariness of it all
made me throw up, you know. So I watched my mother in the
kitchen, then turned around and walked off.

'I bought a motorcycle and headed off across the country.
Wound up in a fight in Arizona.'

'So how'd you end up here?' Brytenn asked, slightly envious
of Summer's record.

'Lawyer was an old OSS hand, recruiting for the CIA. Got
me off. Got me hired. Sent me back to the field, where I
belonged. I came here because I spoke Russian. You?'

'I learned Russian two years ago.'

'Smart fellow.'

'I like to think so.' As soon as he had said these words,
Cooper Brytenn felt as foolish as he had sounded, and tried to
push it to one side with a smile. 'I think the swelling is going
down here.'

Summer ignored him and went to the map of the camp.
'She'll kill him if she gets the chance. Olga will kill
Beshov.'

'You make sure she doesn't,' Brytenn said. He felt easier
talking with confidence about someone else and defended
Beshov more than he might have in other circumstances.
'Look, I know what he is, Jack, no one knows more than me.
Do you find you rub your hands more nowadays?'

'Why, Cooper, you're almost Russian. So the slate's wiped
clean for that bastard. The old Anatoli Beshov died in Berlin,
this Anatoli Beshov was reborn a defender of Christianity
against godless atheism.'

Brytenn grinned like a churlish schoolboy who thinks he's

smarter than the rest of the class but has not the wit to realise he should not make such a point even if it is true.

Then Beshov appeared at the door like a shadow and hovered there, chewing on a piece of black bread. He licked some salt from the back of his thumb. 'Silencers on the weapons?' he asked.

Brytenn pulled himself from where he was sitting, grabbed a stick and hobbled across to the map. He stared at it for a while. 'Do we need noise?' he said to Summer.

'This minefield,' Summer replied. 'Once we've made a path through it, we can put a series of sweeteners for those who would follow. The thing will be to cut communications, so they cannot call on help.' Summer turned to Beshov. 'You'll have to get that radio shack.'

'You take care of what you have to and I'll do what I have to.' Beshov pulled a revolver from his belt, spun the chamber, put the gun to his head and pulled the trigger. The click that followed was lost in the shouts from Summer and Brytenn. Trepper and Olga came in.

'You can prove yourself in action,' Olga Sharankova said.

'There was nothing in it,' Trepper added.

Beshov opened the revolver and emptied three bullets from the chamber. 'Fifty fifty,' he said.

16

Arctic Willow

That night they set out. Just before first light they were fifteen kilometres from Camp Thirty-Six, in a driving snowstorm broken only by the pines and larches which buffered their approach. They travelled in file, horses nose to tail, each rider wrapped up from head to toe against the elements, alone with only their own thoughts and the possibilities of the forest.

Without the comfort of morphine, which he had refused this time, the possibilities of the forest exercised Cooper Brytenn every time his horse took an unexpected dip or jumped something he had not seen, or forced him to avoid something he had not anticipated. And a creeping migraine began to shut down one side of his face. As for thought, he would have preferred to talk.

First sun and faint moonlight showed steam from his animal's nose breaking up into strings in the wind and fresh powder snow covering its mane. There were times when Brytenn thought the animal would just freeze, with him on it, and years later the whole group would be found frozen in line, nose to tail, and people would wonder who they were and what they were doing there. But then he would feel the horse's warmth, and if the warmth of the horse's body began to undermine the numbness the cold had brought to Brytenn's ankle, he would often wish the animal would freeze. First light brought first talk, though.

'I bet that hurts now,' Jack Summer muttered through his scarf, 'I bet it hurts like hell.'

'A man creates his opportunities, Jack, but life provides him with his abilities,' Brytenn replied.

Summer did not hear all of it. 'Well you shouldn't have come with that ankle,' he said. 'I told you that.'

'I'll take that as concern,' Brytenn replied. His own concern was a simple desire.

Summer blew out. He leaned back in his saddle and shouted. 'Olga, you think he should have come?'

Olga shrugged. And except for a long look she gave Brytenn, she said nothing. Her actions angered Summer, though.

'Mr Brytenn is a man who wishes to move mountains,' Beshov said, without turning his head. 'Right, Mr Brytenn?'

'Just small ones,' Brytenn said.

Summer, who could not even begin to conceive of the things that drove Cooper Brytenn, which angered Brytenn, just swore and checked his compass, wiping small snowflakes off the face with the back of his gloved hand.

'Have you ever seen an arctic willow?' Summer asked Brytenn a few minutes later. 'They grow, lying down, slowly . . . but they still grow . . .'

'And they never get up,' Brytenn said.

'You should perhaps take the foot out of the stirrup,' Olga said to Brytenn. 'And let me give you something.'

Brytenn shook his head. 'Not yet,' he said. It took all his

will and a degree of concentration on the minutiae of his situation: the ragged oily-wet hair of his horse's mane; the smell of leather from the scarred reins and rotten saddle; the occasional sudden snorts from his animal's nose, followed by snap jerks of its head, which unbalanced Brytenn; the noise of its feet over different types of ground, which made him anxious, and of branches cracking on contact with his body, which irritated him. And, of course, the perpetual sound of his own moistened breath.

They climbed under the cover of hundreds of skeletal trees, to the distant sound of a lone wolf, between melting banks of hard snow reinforced by fresh falls, over soft ground hardened beneath by permafrost, through deep drifts, a slow plodding march, marked only by the routine stops for direction and water.

Only Trepper, out in front, seemed impervious to the whole event, never even turning his head left or right, eyes focused on each ridge at the end of each stretch of the forest ahead.

The next ridge left the heavy tree-cover behind and was a combination of blue and white that seemed to blend with the cloud so much that it became the sky. Brytenn could feel his heart move at the thought of breaking free of the forest, but he did not know if it was joy or fear. He thought he must have kicked his horse by accident because he felt a sharp pain and the animal began to move faster and upset his rhythm. Or perhaps the animal just felt what he did.

Then Trepper raised his hand.

'You see that,' he said, pointing at a blanket of snow along the edge of a fold in the landscape. 'We have to go round.'

'But we went through the last time,' Summer said.

'That was then. The horses will sink. Too deep. We must go round. The falling snow will cover our tracks.'

'Much further?' Brytenn asked with the same voice one asks a dentist about drilling.

'Up that way,' Trepper said. He pulled out a map. It was quickly covered in snow. 'There's a kind of pass – a small valley – along a river. But keep to the treeline. You can be seen and there may be work parties. These camps don't apply normal work practices. That right, Herr Sturmbannführer?'

If Trepper was attempting to get the upper hand with Beshov, he failed miserably.

'You might just get an Iron Cross for this, Trepper,' Beshov replied. 'Or perhaps the Mother's Cross.'

'Bastard!' Trepper replied.

'I think Trepper has us doing penance,' Beshov said to Olga. 'What's your crime, love?'

She did not so much ignore him as kill him with her eyes and walk over his body, an action that appeared to amuse Beshov rather than send him off in a cowed retreat.

'I ask you this,' she said to him, 'is it right that a man who has caused so much misery should be so happy?'

'You think I'm happy?'

'You should be, you're going home.'

Dawn hit Camp Thirty-Six in the western Urals like a bad joke. The sharp northern wind with its near-blinding snow stopped everything. No one got fed. No one moved.

Except Victor Malty. He and Ivan Pyotr met in hut number three of the special compound, to discuss the sale of various tradeable items, and swap what might be described as food by people who live around garbage tips and back alleys. Anything swapped was put aside. Hunger was not a good enough reason to eat. And while the two men sat on a bed at one end of the hut, the rest of the skeletoid prisoners lay beneath whatever coverings they had watching the transactions with concentrated disinterest, listening to the anger of the wind and the creaking pleading of the timbers of the camp. Pale, almost transparent creatures, with glass eyes and what Victor Malty called 'that other-world look', these zeks watched because they had nothing else to do.

The alarm was sounded almost as soon as the snow stopped and the rain began. Guards with a fiery terror in their eyes ran towards a hut at the end of the compound, then stopped and clustered on the hardened rutted ground around the hut, while the rain began to soften the soil under their feet and two men in fur and beards went inside to confirm their worst fears.

'What is it?' Malty asked. He was watching from the doorway of his hut, chewing on a small nut, which he refused to swallow until the last drop of flavour had been sucked from it.

'Plague,' Ivan Pyotr replied from where he stood in the compound. The old policeman shook his Tartarish head. 'I've seen it many times.'

Then the order came for everyone to evacuate. Reluctantly, the prisoners complied. And only when they were out in the compound did their desire for life return.

The condensed panic carried on the faces of everyone in the compound, prevented from overextension by the cold and the sleet now falling, huddled for cover in the intensity of the morning air while a lampshade sun showed red and orange through the ragged clouds and mountain haze.

The mountains were long and blunt and steel blue, and the

sky was heavy with the weight of its calling. And below them, each lump of flesh and wool shrank to the position of least exposure and watched the routine at the plagued hut.

'I've heard of them shooting a whole camp because of this,' Pyotr said to Malty.

'It's really plague?' Malty asked.

'Sure. You think because it's gone from your country, it's gone from everywhere. Out in Siberia, there are animals with it all the time. I've heard camps out there fall to the plague every few years. Once they came across a place they hadn't heard from for over eight months and they found the whole place dead from plague. They burned all of it. Two thousand stinking corpses. And no one could use the river for three years. But that was a long time ago. They say it comes from Mongolia, or China. Those Chinese are dirty.'

A guard in a mask went over to the infected hut and painted red crosses on it; then, individually, the guards backed off as one while a man with a flamethrower came forward.

'There are men inside!' a prisoner yelled.

He was told to shut up and a sergeant of the guard drew his pistol and fired into the air. 'Everyone, quiet, or I'll shoot you all.' He had the red face of a man who might do worse than he said, and the dark eyes of one who had.

The other guards pulled their weapons into position. The man with the flamethrower opened fire. For a few minutes, after the screams of the sick, while the flames took hold, everyone took advantage of the fierce heat being generated by the burning hut to warm themselves.

Then the guards began pushing the prisoners back, like a herd of cattle, towards the wire at the perimeter. But when the guards got too far away from the burning hut to avail themselves of its heat, they began firing into the air and then moving back towards the heat, still shouting at the prisoners to keep away from the burning hut.

There was now a gap of some ten metres between the prisoners and the guards, and the prisoners were angry at having been denied the heat of the flames. Some of them stepped forward, more desperate for heat than they were afraid of death.

'Down on your knees, all of you!' the sergeant in charge shouted at them. And he fired into the air again.

'They're going to shoot us,' one of the prisoners said.

He might have been right except that a flame moved from the burning hut to the one next to it, as if something had lifted and carried it.

Ivan Pyotr yelled a warning to the sergeant, who turned around and fired at the second burning hut in frustration. The other guards scattered and then came back at the sergeant's orders to deal with the second burning hut which, because of the strength of the wind, was now in danger of setting fire to a third. Snowflakes sizzled in the fires and the wind fanned the flames so much that the guards kept having to move to avoid being burned.

The sergeant shouted at one of the watchtowers to call for the commandant.

'Jesus, we'll either burn or be shot.' Swell Johnson was standing beside Pyotr, looking for all the world like he had plague, stooped between two men, holding him under the arms, a ragged remnant of the football quarterback that had come to Russia to snap a few photographs of Murmansk a few weeks earlier. And the grey blanket around him only made his face look more ghastly, like an apparition. He just about managed to support his words by pointing to the huts all around them.

The gate to the special compound was opened and a very young guard, with a very red face, ran along the dirt path to the small collection of log buildings sitting on a rise at the treeline. This was the commandant's office and home, and the guardhouse.

But the second the young guard entered the commandant's office, a third hut in the special compound caught fire. For a few seconds everyone's eyes were fixed on the flames, and no one noticed the gate was still open, moving silently back and forth in the wind.

Guards in fur hats and heavy coats rushed from the other compounds, boots struggling in the snow and ice, some dragging weapons along the ground, only to be told to go back to their posts. The guards in the special compound began to back away from the flames, this time unwilling to either take advantage of the heat or do anything to prevent what was about to happen. Their sergeant fired a warning shot in the air and threatened them with worse than death if they did not do their duty and help put the fire out. But none of them was listening. As the fire gathered strength, they began to break up and run for the gate.

It was Victor Malty who started the prisoners' revolt. He hit the guard nearest him in the face. The man, huge but half concentrating on what was going on behind him, was knocked off balance, and loosed off several rounds from his submachine-gun. The bullets killed two men to Malty's right. Malty slammed his foot into the guard's neck, took the submachine-gun and killed the sergeant in command of the guards.

For a second or two, everything was silent except for the sound of the fire and the wind.

Then Malty yelled an order at the other British and American prisoners. And they turned on their guards.

Eight of them seized weapons and rushed the half-open gate. But three of them were shot dead. Those behind them stopped. It looked like the guards would regain the initiative. Until an American prisoner elbowed a hairy Muscovite the guards used as a stool-pigeon and threw him at his masters. In panic, the guards shot him. And while they came to terms with what they had done and a few voices cheered, Victor Malty shot the two guards nearest the gate, and Swell Johnson, though he could barely stand, grabbed a rifle and shot a guard in one of the watchtowers. The recoil knocked him to the ground, while Victor Malty shot the only guard left at the gate, a decent if dull man they had all traded with at one time or another. The escaping prisoners went for the guards in their way, killed them and ran over their bodies.

While the remaining guards in the special compound were in disarray, reinforcements from the rest of the camp and the guardhouse hurried towards the escaping prisoners with less than full enthusiasm. Some just ran away. And then another hut caught fire, and any guards remaining inside the special compound fled, too. The rest of the prisoners rushed the gate.

Ivan Pyotr, like most of the rest of the prisoners, had done nothing much except stay alive up to this point, his institutional face merely following the action around him, as if the very act of doing nothing but watching would save him from any future retribution he was sure would come.

Now, however, as if struck by a sudden realisation that his thirty-year-old situation had changed in the space of a few minutes, the old man swelled with some of the strength that had once earned him the nickname 'the Terrible', picked up a pistol and shot a guard in the next compound. By this stage, most of the prisoners from the special compound were dead or through the gate and the camp guards were trying to deal with an uprising in the other compounds.

Almost reluctantly, Ivan Pyotr walked out of the camp across a path of exploded mines and body parts, bullets shooting by his head, virtually oblivious to what was happening, eyes only on the treeline and what might lie beyond.

Cooper Brytenn watched the sun give up the struggle for the day and the temperature shelter in the bowels of the earth only to be replaced again by the savage bandit elements of the Asiatic taiga pouring over the walls of the Urals. And Trepper and Sasha came galloping back through the trees and the falling snow.

'Something's wrong,' Sasha said. 'There's firing. Soldiers everywhere.'

'We have to get out of here,' Trepper added.

HOLES

17

Taiga

Vladimir Romanovili wandered among the remains of scores
of British and American prisoners, against a background of
glowing orange and sulphurous sky and a heavy Siberian wind.
Behind him, the bodies of thirty or more guards were laid out
on a stretch of icy corrugated ground. Blood stained the snow
around them.

'If I didn't know it, I'd say a couple of them were executed
by a Chekist,' Romanovili said to the lardish camp commander shivering beside him. 'See where the bullet entered his
head? That's where a Chekist would put it.' Romanovili
touched the back of the commandant's head. 'How many
of the foreign zeks got away?' he asked.

The camp commander had to blow his nose and wait for
what passed as thoughts to crisscross his brain, while he
prayed he would not be held responsible for what had
happened.

'We're not sure,' he stammered. 'No more than five,
possibly fewer.'

'Don't you keep numbers? What about the zek Pyotr?'

Romanovili's limited reaction to the breakout, often

apparent in those of his disposition, sent his colleague into a state of terror. 'The weather,' the commandant said, 'is making a search difficult. And the fire may have burned some of them.'

'Where are the living?' Romanovili demanded.

'I have them all in the remaining huts. Chained up. Am I to shoot them?' At that moment, this heavy, nasal, beaverish man would have shot the world to stay alive.

'What do you think?' Romanovili asked.

'I was a victim of circumstances.'

'I'll mention that to the politburo.'

The camp commander began to wipe his forehead. 'I am a victim of circumstances,' he kept repeating to himself while Romanovili marched off towards his waiting German helicopter.

Cooper Brytenn watched the single Interior soldier, struggling through the snow and the low branches of the taiga south of Camp Thirty-Six, with a degree of uneasiness he always felt when faced with raw faith. Brytenn looked around at the worn faces of his companions. His own pain had given him another headache, which dragged the left side of his face down towards the snow.

For two days they had been like this, scrambling from one forest dugout to another, hemmed in on all sides by a thousand Interior Ministry troops and their equipment, with only the weather and the night for allies. A game of ever decreasing circles as each sweep narrowed the room for manoeuvre and each manoeuvre set them up for a new sweep.

Occasionally, Brytenn found himself glancing over at Olga Sharankova and letting what emotions he could not control linger on her, something he was convinced made him gauche and disagreeable. But it was necessary. And his craving for relief from the pain in his ankle made it impossible to hide. He needed morphine, no matter what he said to the contrary, and perhaps that was another reason for his staring at Olga.

'Five more back that way,' Olga mouthed. 'I think they're lost. Should we move on them?'

Brytenn looked to Jack Summer. There were times when the responsibility just became too much.

Summer drew his finger across his neck, then slipped into position beside Brytenn, pulled a large Siberian machete from his high boots and pulled the hood of his long white winter jacket over his head.

'Let him come a little closer,' he whispered.

He signalled to Anatoli Beshov, who sighed and moved forward. Behind them, a horse snorted. Summer and Brytenn turned and scowled at Alexander Trepper, who was struggling to keep the animals concealed behind a low wall of scrub.

Beshov crawled into position about fifty metres ahead, behind a moss-covered rock, while a small animal moved in the thin trees. The sound of broken branches carried on the still air and the snowfall began to stop.

Then some of the Interior soldiers behind the young man in front called for him to slow down. He stopped and told them to catch up. A deep voice from behind him told him they would be in serious trouble for getting lost and suggested they should go back. Summer moved around on their left flank.

Beshov asked by sign whether he should kill the young Interior soldier ahead of them.

Brytenn watched the young man a little more, almost hoping he would lose courage and turn back towards his friends, who were virtually stopped now and calling to him.

But the young Interior Ministry soldier, whose acne was pronounced and whose tongue was resting on his lower lip, kept coming towards Beshov. Mist was descending rapidly from the tops of the trees.

'He has courage to burn,' Brytenn whispered to himself. Admiration and envy fought each other inside his head.

The mist came down like a stage curtain right as the young Interior soldier reached Beshov. Beshov drew his knife and looked back at Brytenn.

'Tell him to kill him!' Olga whispered to Brytenn.

But Brytenn just kept staring.

And that was when Victor Malty came out of the trees.

In an instant he drove a sharpened stake through the young Interior Ministry soldier's ribcage. The young man's acned face screwed up and blood and saliva poured from over his tongue and out of his twisted mouth. A second later, he was in the snow, Malty on top of him.

Brytenn was fixed by the sight of this death. It took Olga Sharankova to make a move.

She tapped Sasha and they both sprang up from where they were hiding. The two rushed forward, took positions behind trees and emptied their silenced weapons into the forest ahead of them. The click of the bolts sounded like breaking branches. Three of the following Interior troops were killed in the first volley. The other two dropped their weapons and ran.

Summer and Sasha went after the first. Sasha downed him with a single shot about thirty metres into the trees. Summer walked up to him and cut his throat.

The second man was faster, built tall like a long-jumper, with angled shoulders, and his fear made him run faster. Olga, who was a short woman, could not keep up. But Beshov, who was now charged with the excitement of combat again, kept pace and began to gain. Both men disappeared into the mist.

Behind them, Summer and Olga made Victor Malty put his hands on his head. Cooper Brytenn stuck his weapon into Malty's face. 'Who are you?' he asked the pilot.

'You're not with the Interiors?' Malty replied in very bad Russian.

Before Brytenn could answer, Anatoli Beshov reappeared from the trees, running. 'There's more Interiors coming; we have to move,' he said. He lifted his weapon and drove it into Victor Malty's skull.

The whole of Brytenn's party stood around Malty. He was bound and gagged and lying in a small pit. And they were all in a small cave north-east of Aktjabrj, a tiny warren of tunnels everyone called the Hole. A freezing coffin, Summer called it. He had been the last to suggest they go there and the last into the place when they did. And he sat near the entrance, where he could see the light.

'So what do we do with him, Brytenn?' Olga asked, staring at Malty. She turned around and walked over to Jack Summer before Brytenn could answer. Summer went to put his arms around her but she shrugged him off. And only then did she realise he was the one who needed comforting.

'Kill him!' Beshov said. 'Now!'

'Shut up, Beshov,' Brytenn said then. It was a peculiarity of his moments of indecision that he was often at his most decisive immediately after them. His headache had begun to ease but his ankle was still killing him.

'Okay, okay,' Beshov said. 'Look, Brytenn, let's just call in your aircraft and all fly back to Munich. The drinks are on me. How long do you think we have before half the Interior troops and Chekists in the country are descending on this area?'

This argument might have developed if Victor Malty had not begun to stir. He rolled over on to his face and began to choke and cough. Beshov went over and turned him over. 'Christ, I gave you a lump,' he said.

'Who are you?' Brytenn asked Malty for the second time.

Malty spoke a few words, then waited. Perhaps for another blow, perhaps because he could not quite remember everything that had happened to him. His explanation, when it came, was name, rank and serial number.

Beshov immediately began to laugh. 'Why should we believe him?' he asked. 'He comes to us out of the forest; he's probably a stoolie.' He went to hit Malty again but Brytenn held him back with a pistol.

'You're beginning to make me angry, Herr Sturmbann-führer,' he said. 'And you remember what happened the last time you made me angry.'

Beshov withdrew. 'Look, I was just trying to put some perspective on our situation,' he said.

Suddenly, Olga Sharankova lashed out at Beshov with her hand and caught him across the mouth, splitting his lower lip, then apologising to him before hitting him again. She let her confusion defuse itself in the words she uttered. 'Just leave him alone; can't you see what he is?'

Brytenn reached out and grabbed her. His strength surprised her. He held her for a moment and took away some of her anger. It hurt him more than he let on.

'Please . . .' he said as she backed off.

Beshov merely smiled and wiped his wounds, and that

angered her more than anything. Jack Summer, who had been holding back till now, still sitting on a rock in the corner, chewing a piece of bread, studying the walls of the cavern, playing mental patience with himself, stood up and came over to her now. He reached out for Olga's hand and she took his. And after that the situation calmed somewhat.

'You'll appreciate we have to be sure, Squadron Leader, or you're dead,' Brytenn said to Malty. 'What happened in the camp?'

Malty talked slowly and deliberately, never straying from the events, pausing for breath after a few sentences, stalling over words, correcting himself a few times, trying to get some bearings, explaining he was not sure of when it had all happened or what day it was now.

'It's Friday,' Cooper Brytenn said. 'You've been wandering in the trees since Wednesday. How did you stay alive? We've been avoiding patrols constantly. The whole area's crawling with Interior troops. Only the weather is with us. How did you stay alive?'

Malty smiled almost painfully and shook his head.

'Ivan Pyotr, do you know of him?' Brytenn said to Malty then. 'He was a prisoner in that camp.'

Malty looked at the eyes of each of the men and the single woman before deciding to answer. Twice he looked at Anatoli Beshov after that, in case the SS officer was planning to hit him again.

'Look, who the blazes are you?' Malty asked then.

Brytenn went over to a pot of soup and poured a bowl, broke a piece of bread and dipped it in the soup, then put the bread to Malty's mouth. 'We're your salvation, Squadron Leader. Now if you'd answer the question.'

'Pyotr?' Beshov said. 'Ivan Pyotr. They used to called him the Terrible.'

'I know him, I know him,' Malty said. 'I have men back there, Mr . . .'

'Brytenn. I'm sorry, Squadron Leader, but anyone you left back at Camp Thirty-Six is dead. Sasha?'

The Ukrainian seemed to be recalling some other incident while he spoke. His whole face trembled and the strongest of his features withered. 'They killed them yesterday.' He drew his hand across his neck. 'The camp is destroyed.'

'All of them?' Malty asked. 'There were fifteen hundred prisoners in that camp. Seventy-four of them were my men.'

'I'm sorry,' Brytenn said. 'Now, Ivan Pyotr. If you please, Squadron Leader . . .'

Malty nodded, not sure of what he would say next.

Ivan Pyotr, meanwhile, was huddled in a makeshift shelter, made of the remains of an old woodcutter's hut a few kilometres to the east, feeling the last of his body heat seeping away into the earth, trying to stop Swell Johnson from going into a shock from which he would not return, and sometimes wishing he would. Many of Pyotr's motives in this were selfish: he needed Johnson's body heat, what there was of it left, to supplement his own. And there was a certain bond developing between them. The company of strangers, they called it in the camp.

'Where the hell is he?' Swell Johnson asked again. 'You think they have him? If they have Malty, they'll have us. We should move. I think we should move.' He had been going on like this all day, ever since Malty had gone out to look for food.

'And where are you going to move to?' Ivan Pyotr asked him.

'You should leave me, then.' Johnson nodded as if agreeing with himself and then seemed to lapse into unconsciousness before speaking again.

Pyotr could not help watch an icicle melt on the branch of a tree in front of him. The tree was tall but had bent early on in its life and despite efforts to grow straight again could never quite manage it. Its branches covered half what remained of the old woodcutter's hut, the snow did the rest of the job, great banks of it they'd had to tunnel into that first day after their escape, cold, bewildered, hungry to the point of agony, led only by Malty's strength and his certainties.

'He'll be back,' Pyotr said when he was sure Johnson was conscious again. 'Look, I know men, and Malty'll be back. He's the sort who'd come back from the grave if he promised it, or willed it. How do you feel?'

'Swell.'

Pyotr smiled. 'You have a mother and father?'

Johnson nodded.

'I had a son once. He'd probably be about your age. Maybe a bit older. Nice wife, too. They killed her. The Bolsheviks. Just took her out one morning and shot her. I was a colonel in the secret police, but I suppose you know that.'

'So how come they didn't kill you?' Johnson asked.

Pyotr touched his head. 'I know things.' He bared what teeth he had left. 'Thirty years they've had me here, just waiting for me to . . . shit, there's movement out there . . .'

When Malty had finished his story, Brytenn turned to Trepper. 'Get back to the village and contact Munich. Request

173

the pick-up. And I want a landing strip cleared tonight. Get whoever you can to help.'

'In this weather?' Trepper said. 'No one will help. Especially with the Interiors patrolling. We'll be lucky if the villagers don't turn us all in.'

'The villagers have no choice now.' Brytenn's voice was quite cold and slightly disturbing for those who had never heard it like this before. 'They work for us and get a chance to get out or they stay here and wait for a bullet in the back of the head.'

He took Trepper outside the cave, slipped him some money and talked to him for about a minute before the older man prepared to leave.

'My God, you're learning,' Beshov said to Brytenn when he came back in.

'Why do you want Pyotr?' Malty asked.

'That is not your concern, Squadron Leader,' Brytenn said. 'Your concern is us at the moment. If I decide to trust you, then you will live; if I do not, then I will kill you myself.'

The strange thing about this was that Malty did not take Brytenn as seriously as the American did himself, but instead kept looking across at Beshov to see what he was thinking, as if that were the real barometer of his fate.

'I am who I say. If you have a radio, please confirm it.'

'Squadron Leader, if we did that, we would just confirm that there was a man named Malty, shot down over Germany, nothing more. A waste of transmission time and an unnecessary risk. They can track our transmissions, you know.'

As Brytenn led Trepper to one side, Malty closed his eyes.

He closed his eyes again when they reached the place where he had left Johnson and Pyotr the following evening. There were signs of life: small bones, crumbs of a black bread Beshov recognised, raw flesh in strips, like it had been torn from the bones, and human faeces neatly placed in one corner and frozen like a sculpture. And footprints. Scores of footprints.

'Well, I hope whoever was here wasn't on that when it froze,' Beshov remarked about the faeces.

'The footprints?' Brytenn asked Olga.

'Interiors.'

Malty looked at Brytenn. 'Why would I invent such a story?' he asked. 'To bring you here? For what?'

Brytenn called Summer over to him and the two men walked out a few metres. Summer's disposition had changed considerably since they had been in the Hole.

'What do you think?' Brytenn asked.

'I think it's over, Cooper,' Summer said. 'Let's go.'

Summer went over to Olga but she left him to answer a subtle summons from Cooper Brytenn. 'I think I need something now,' was all he said. And she reached into a saddle bag for some morphine.

Brytenn looked back at Victor Malty, looking for all the world like a prisoner awaiting execution. 'I believe you,' Brytenn said, without hesitation. 'For what it's worth, Squadron Leader. You say he was with an American . . .'

18

Beria

The same evening, above the wall between the Secrets Tower and the Annunciation Tower in the Kremlin, Lavrenti Beria, the poisonous bespectacled chief of the Soviet nuclear programme, met his master, Josef Stalin. A depressingly cold mist veiled the Moscow River in front of them, while yellow lights struggled to illuminate the pastel colours of the Soviet citadel.

'Tell me, are there still supplies stored in the passage running from the Secrets Tower to the river, Lavrenti?' Stalin asked.

It was the kind of question Stalin often asked Beria these days, to check his knowledge of secret police activities. Beria's replacement as secret police boss in 1946, his promotion to the politburo in compensation, and his appointment as head of the Soviet drive for an atomic bomb, should have negated such enquiries, but the former Georgian criminal had managed to insert his own men into key positions in the new security ministries and, with his new rank and position, he was virtually as powerful in those areas as he had ever been. And being one himself, Stalin knew his Georgians.

'I'll ask someone if you like,' Beria replied, swinging himself around to the area between the Annunciation and Archangel Cathedrals, watching a small cat seek shelter against a white wall. A single tree then caught his eye and drew it to the last of the Napoleonic cannons around the Arsenal. 'It's cold, Josef; couldn't we go inside?' A car rolled up the hill from the Borovitskaya Tower gate and swung round towards the great Tsar cannon.

'I was thinking of opening the Annunciation Tower as a prison again,' Stalin said. 'Like Ivan Grozny. For special prisoners. So we would not lose them.'

'Probably a good idea,' Beria replied, resentful of the games he was forced to play with his leader.

'You look troubled, Lavrenti,' Stalin said. 'The cold, or something else?'

While Stalin's face sometimes resembled a jackal's, Beria's was like that of an overweight bird of carrion. Relentlessly suspicious eyes dominated his sharp expressions, and a sense of impending demise lay behind every action he took.

'If I was back in full command of security then the kind of thing that happened at Camp Thirty-Six just would not happen,' he said.

'And who would make our bombs?' Stalin asked. 'You are the only one I trust with such a project, Lavrenti. The only one. You think an old illiterate like Khrushchev, or perhaps Molotov, should look after our bombs?'

'You have a way of making argument superfluous.'

'I think I'll give up smoking a pipe, Lavrenti,' Stalin said. 'It's bad for my health.' It was the kind of off the cuff, seemingly innocuous remark that members of Stalin's government feared most. Beria had seen men dragged away and shot for disagreeing with Stalin on the most mundane subject, for suggesting the most trivial change to something dear to the leader's heart. The kind of fear Stalin engendered was a relentless weight of apprehension, where a man was reluctant to comment on the weather for fear of being labelled a counter-revolutionary in Stalin's mind. And once that happened, the path was sure and straight and quick.

'The tobacco figures for last year were quite good,' Beria replied.

Now the ball was back with Stalin and he made expressions with his face that only Georgians understood among one another.

'And Podvoysky?' Stalin asked.

'He definitely met Khrushchev.'

'And so have we,' Stalin said.

'But we have not defected.'

'Do you recommend I have Nikita Khrushchev arrested and charged?'

'It would work as an instrument of encouragement, for the people, to have a senior figure in the politburo charged and found guilty of being in the pay of the Americans. If they march on Berlin, then we should have a traitor.'

'We don't know why they met.' Stalin shoved his hands in his pockets. 'And I have a sneaking regard for Khrushchev. Like Molotov. You know I did not replace Molotov because he was going soft on Berlin or because he let Tito get away from us. I replaced him because I was feeling sorry for him. That bloody wife of his . . . at least Khrushchev doesn't have that problem.'

'Have you considered Khrushchev and Molotov together?' Beria asked. 'As a force?'

'You're a very suspicious man, Lavrenti. Sometimes I wonder if you have suspicions about me. Oh, I realise you should not allow personal feelings to enter the realms of revolution but when you approach seventy, Lavrenti, sometimes you look back on your life and see where things might have been neater. I have done everything I have done for the greater good.'

Beria recognised another possible trap, so he skirted around it. 'If Podvoysky was acting under Khrushchev's orders, and Khrushchev was trying to broker a deal over Berlin, then the Americans must know we are trying to force their hand.'

Stalin allowed himself a long pause. 'Are we?' he said.

Beria drew a handkerchief from his pocket and wiped his mouth. 'The die is cast, Josef. We must press on.'

'Your first strike?'

'It would appear logical.'

'They are straining to supply Berlin as it is, Lavrenti. All we have to do is maintain the blockade. And if they are forced to smash their way through, then we will indeed be entitled to counter-attack their aggression.'

'Arrest Khrushchev.'

Stalin shook his head. 'No,' he said. 'We'll do nothing. When we move, Lavrenti, we will move like the arctic winds. It is something you never forget, if you have had the privilege of being imprisoned.'

For a long time the two men stood silently, Stalin performing small movements, Beria easing the strain on the muscles of his legs.

'There is another small matter I believe I should raise with you, Josef.'

'I hope you don't want more money, Lavrenti. We cannot afford any more money.'

'No, it's not that. Do you recall a man named Girenko, Josef? A Tsarist police officer from the Ukraine. He was imprisoned by us years ago, then escaped. I believe he interrogated you on several occasions.'

Stalin's face had completely changed and he lost his voice for a few seconds. He regained it only after an immense effort. 'What of him?'

'He's turned up in Paris, on a murder charge. It appears he killed a priest years ago and took his place in a monastery. The French have been asking questions through intermediaries.'

'Would they send him back?'

'To the firing squad?'

'That is where a man like that belongs.'

'So I thought.'

Later, Beria headed across the river to Gorki Park, something he was in the habit of doing after a particularly disagreeable meeting with his leader. There was a sense of being safe in having the river between them, and Beria felt secure enough to dismiss all but five of his bodyguards and get out of his car. Some children were sliding on the remains of an ice patch, and Beria went over to them and shared a joke and some toffees he always kept in his pocket for such occasions. There were times when the company of children was the only thing that made Beria feel real any more.

Vladimir Romanovili was watching a couple kissing across the park when Beria found him. Three of Beria's men took up positions with their backs to their boss, while Beria and

Romanovili walked up a small mound and into some cover. A few very thin trees and a large thorn bush covered them from all but the most prying eyes.

'What did he say?' Romanovili asked.

'What do you expect he said? Nothing. He said absolutely nothing. I want the Vasili file, Your Imperial Majesty.'

'I wish you would not call me that, Comrade,' Romanovili said. 'I have never been a royalist. And I have never understood the joke.'

Beria called two of his men over. They held Romanovili while Beria hit him in the stomach, twice. Then the two bodyguards left and Beria helped Romanovili up.

'Now, Comrade, you will gather what breath you have and think of me with respect. Otherwise I will have you in the basement of the Lubyanka with a battalion of penal soldiers dancing on your head and committing the most foul acts of brutality on your body. You must be aware of those units and their capacity for savagery.'

'What do you want me to do?'

Back in the Kremlin, when the darkness had taken over, Josef Stalin came out of the Annunciation Cathedral and walked down to the Borovitskaya Gate before turning back past the armoury to the Poteshny Palace. It had begun to snow again, very lightly. At this point in the day, Stalin began drinking. Very slowly, staring out of the window. Nikita Khrushchev found him virtually unconscious later on.

'Podvoysky is dead,' Khrushchev said.

Stalin did not seem to take it in. Instead, he started talking as if to someone else, quoting Lenin's speeches, and while he did this he looked like nothing more than a wretched old man fighting with his past.

'I should have been the priest,' Stalin insisted. 'Not that policeman.'

'And we don't know where Girenko is.'

19

Raw Meat

After pausing to buy a newspaper and check the clouds overhead, Patrick Twilight arrived at Broadway Buildings at about five thirty in the afternoon of 26 March, the same Saturday the horse Russian Hero won the Aintree Grand National.

It was a rusty evening and the Administrator's face bled into it, giving Twilight a sense that his superior was something more than finite and something less than tangible. Twilight sat huddled, feeling the electric sensations of the bile in his stomach surging up to his mouth while he shook. He needed another drink.

'Girenko's in Berlin,' the Administrator said. He passed Twilight a photograph. 'Name's Trudi Weiss. She arranged for Podvoysky to come to Wiesbaden by American transport from Templehof. It wasn't too difficult to sweat the man who took her money. She has Girenko in her flat. It seems Podvoysky had young Trudi book a return ticket. And while we were running up and down the various borders of the Iron Curtain, our priest just made use of this ticket and popped back into Berlin.'

'Why the hell would he do that?' Twilight said, very aware that his Huntergatherers had not been the ones to find Girenko.

'Because there is no Vasili file,' the Administrator said. 'All this was designed to close down our operations between Moscow and the Urals.' He passed a sheet of paper across the desk. 'Interior Ministry troops raided a group Brytenn used yesterday morning. Poor bastards. Friend Girenko definitely sold us raw meat, Patrick.'

'But what about Podvoysky?' Twilight asked.

'A lover's tiff or something,' the Administrator said.

'Girenko is definitely Spane,' Twilight insisted.

'Whoever he is, he's already caused us enough trouble for two lifetimes, and this time he could be about to sink a lot of valuable ships operating in hostile seas. We should have just called his bloody bluff and let the French cut his damn head off. Anyway, pack your bags, we're flying to Berlin in an hour.'

Misha Girenko raised his head and surveyed the neatness of the kitchen around him. The asthma attack he had had for two days now was beginning to ease and as he said a few prayers to himself he sipped a small glass of schnapps to warm his chest.

'Are you a priest?' Trudi Weiss asked him.

Very deliberately, he reached into his pocket and pulled out a stole. 'You wish to be forgiven for something?'

'Many things,' she said. She let small tears out and soon her face was covered in them. Girenko gave her a small towel lying across the table and she dried her face. 'But not now.'

Girenko spoke Latin, placed his hands on Trudi's head and said some more prayers.

'I almost believe in you,' she said. The electricity in her eyes shorted, producing a dull lazing effect on the rest of her body. 'I'm not afraid of you any more.'

'Perhaps you should come with me.'

She pulled the lapels of her dressing gown across her breast, not from modesty, but because the excitement of having him there was making her shiver. She sat down beside him.

'Yuri said that to me. Look, I don't want to know why you're here. Just keep paying me . . . Father.'

'You're quite a woman, Trudi . . .'

'There are people destined to live their lives in a moment,' she said.

'Like butterflies.' He put his hand out and took hers and held it to his greying face.

'I intend to live that much longer,' she said.

'I'm sure you will, Trudi.' He grinned. 'You haven't asked me about Yuri?'

She smiled. 'I want to go out and buy things,' she said. 'Coal, cigarettes, anything that I can trade. You know what they call the western sectors of Berlin now? The German gulags. We are Stalin's prisoners as much as anyone in one of his camps. What did you come here for?' Then she thought for a while. 'No, don't tell me. Just give me some more money.'

'You should leave this city,' Girenko said.

'And go where? And with what? It may be a prison, but it's my prison. Look, don't go getting soft with me. I play the game well, Father, so listen to what I say, do what I tell you and pay me well. And don't try anything.'

He raised his hands in a mock surrender.

'Will you shop in the eastern sector?' he asked.

'With you here?' She laughed. But more from fear than anything else.

When she came back from her shopping trip two hours later, Girenko was waking from a sleep. He had a Bible, some Catholic vestments and a novel beside him.

'Been reading Proust?' she asked. 'Trying to recapture something?'

'Impossible,' he replied.

'We are going to the opera – I bought two tickets. There's a full moon and the stars are out. There's light everywhere.'

Girenko smiled for the first time since they had met, almost relieved that she no longer felt threatened by him. He took her hand and kissed it. Then he held her face as if it contained all the things he had ever been looking for. 'I want to tell you things,' he said. And for a moment they shared the experiences only people in their profession knew about.

'Tell me,' she said. 'Tell me about yourself. Tell me about Yuri. Tell me things that will make you smile. Tell me things that husbands tell their wives or fathers tell their daughters, if you like. Tell me anything.'

He withdrew his hands, went to the window and pulled the curtains back. 'Just checking on the stars,' he said.

Patrick Twilight sat in the shadows of an all-night cafe near the boundary between the eastern and western sectors of Berlin, watching a cat in a small pool of moonlight, listening to three teenagers argue, telling the Administrator a story he had been told, of a Gravedigger agent sent into a group of White emigres in 1927.

'He killed them all between 1927 and 1945 and won the Knights Cross with oak leaves from Hitler while doing it,' Twilight said then.

'Well, if friend Girenko is expecting a Victoria Cross,' the

Administrator replied, 'he can forget it.' He looked more like a bush than a tree now, huddled over his coffee. 'What are you getting at, Patrick?'

'What would make him go back to Russia along a shadow line?' Twilight said.

'How do you mean?' the Administrator asked him.

'I mean that this Girenko kills a man sent to get him, and is now heading back to his homeland like an infiltrator. If he was legitimate, then all he had to do was walk into the nearest Soviet embassy and they would have had him home in the diplomatic bag the same day. He could have walked right through the Brandenburg Gate at any time since he got here. Or any one of our sector crossing points. But instead he shacks up with a woman whose boyfriend he's just killed.'

'So you're saying he's not in favour at home.'

'Not with everyone,' Twilight said.

'You are a depressing bastard, Patrick. They say a man who has lost his beliefs becomes harder to see. You have to strain when you're looking at him to make out his outlines. It's like he's beginning to lose faith in his own existence.'

'I want you to let Girenko go,' Twilight said then.

The Administrator's reaction forced a look of contempt from Twilight. Then he looked into the Administrator's eyes with a degree of envy he reserved only for those who were truly stupid.

'Haven't you ever eaten raw meat?' Twilight asked.

Girenko and Trudi Weiss started before first light, during a particularly cold false dawn, when the moon decided to show its muscle for one last time and the sun was halted by a strong bank of cloud and a haze from the canal. Only the drone of the continuous flight of aircraft kept the whole city from sleeping, a constant warning of a coming conflict.

It was a lonely cold feeling for Girenko, walking through these cobbled streets, through a mist that seemed a curtain on time. He had never really loved a woman in his life, but now he felt a stinging need to protect Trudi Weiss, a simple necessity spurred on only by the short time they had spent together, so he held on to her arm very tightly and kept his eyes peeled for what he expected would be scores of military and plainclothes policemen.

'Walk me to the spot,' he said to her. 'Then go. With my blessing.'

Eventually, they reached a disused factory on the sector line, a no-man's land of exchange between the eastern and western sectors of the city, a safety valve of unpoliced interconnection, where black marketeers and others with something to hide – sometimes just people having affairs in another sector – moved between the sectors unfettered by the normal rules of control.

'Each side knows the others use it, each side allows it to happen, sometimes just to get their people in and out without notice. A bit like Switzerland during the last war: everyone knew the others were using it, but each of them needed it open more than they needed to capture it, so Switzerland remained untouched.'

She led him to a series of derelict buildings along the demarcation line between the zones, where the morning would arrive last and the sun would have difficulty lighting once it rose.

'I cannot thank you enough,' Girenko said. If he meant it or not did not seem to matter.

Trudi Weiss kissed him and they held each other for a while, until she called him Yuri.

A single shout interrupted Girenko's response.

Two British military policemen were approaching from the south end of the street, guns raised, five more from the north. And there were plainclothes men behind them. One of the military policemen went down on one knee and took aim. Trudi Weiss shoved Girenko through a hole in the wall of one of the derelict buildings just as the first shot rang out.

'Help me!' she cried.

But Girenko had left his feelings with her, and disappeared into the maze of passages between the sectors, with only the sound of his feet on the wet stone giving away the direction of his movements. The men following him stopped. Patrick Twilight looked at Trudi Weiss, lying on the cobbles.

'She looks nothing like her photograph,' he said.

'Well, she's been through so much,' the Administrator said. 'Come on, I'm freezing.'

Two of the military policemen lifted the body and placed it in the back of their jeep.

20

Ruins

The first traces of Aktjabrj's fate were in the melting snow, running by the horses' hooves. Small dark flecks and tiny pieces of charred wood; then the odour found a gentle spring breeze and, after competing with early apple blossom and the pine resin, won the day. The sky was a bright blinding blue and the sun was so warm Brytenn was in shirt sleeves and Sasha bent down from his saddle to scoop up some snow for his face. But the smell began to dominate everything, so much so that the whole party began to wish for the cold again.

The plateau took a sharp dip and the forest broke up into what appeared to be a series of smoking bonfires. Tall trees threw their arms up in the face of the flames while the sky bled slowly across the brown and white landscape. And burning Aktjabrj seemed to be shivering.

Alexander Trepper was hanging from an apple tree in his garden. Several fresh blossoms had settled on his lips. He had been castrated.

Three smouldering skeletons down, the old woman who had given Brytenn bread and salt and the man who had played music and toasted the Tsar were lying face down, as if asleep, a single gunshot to the back of each head. Olga and Summer slid down from their horses and Brytenn directed Beshov to move on ahead, down the tiny street, while Olga flanked left of the hamlet and Summer went right, down the backs of the burning houses.

Each home had a single dead body in it, alternately shot and hanged. Nothing was left standing except the hanging trees. Felled trees lay like withered corpses across picket fences and burning homes.

'Nothing.' Olga Sharankova dipped her head.

'Where are the rest?' Brytenn asked.

Sasha, who was about to cut down a man who had been his friend, growled, 'Where do you think? In there somewhere.' He gestured towards the forest. 'In a nice pit, where fresh trees will grow strong for next year.'

'Don't cut him down!' Beshov barked.

Sasha almost threw his knife at the SS man.

'You'll give us away. Leave him. Leave them all, we can do nothing for them now.'

Brytenn watched as the eyes looked to him, and for all the world he wanted someone else to make the decision. 'Do what he says,' he said finally. 'So what have we left?' he asked Victor Malty.

That night they stayed in the village's cadaver, and listened to the sounds of death. It was a clear night and Brytenn forbade a fire. The cold enhanced the stars and the stars seemed like frozen tears. Brytenn paced up and down for an hour until his ankle could take it no more. The morphine in him was having less effect now. So Brytenn just sat down where he was and began to drink.

'If Trepper hadn't taken that transmitter out, maybe this wouldn't have happened,' he said.

'It's not your fault.' Jack Summer took the bottle without asking and began downing it in large amounts. 'Believe me, I wish it were because I wanna blame someone.' He sat down beside Brytenn. 'When I came home from the war, I stayed with my sister. I loved my sister. I stayed with her because I was scared to go back home. Anyway, one morning she comes into my room and tickles my nose, the way she had when we were kids. Her husband had to pull me off. I was going to strangle her. And I don't think I was even awake.'

'That's what I used to say,' Beshov said. 'I'm the victim, you know.' He grinned at Olga Sharankova and threw her some salted meat. She ate the meat before swearing at him.

'Well, Squadron Leader, it seems you are no better off now than you were in that camp,' Brytenn said then. 'Just a bigger prison. And probably less food. I could advise you to give yourself up but I won't.'

'So what do we do next?' Beshov demanded of Brytenn.

Brytenn shrugged. The confidence in his voice contradicted the words that came from his mouth. 'Hope,' he said. 'Maybe Trepper got through to Munich before they castrated him.' Brytenn looked at his watch. 'We were this close, Jack, this close to Pyotr. I wish you had not left him, Squadron Leader.'

'What's so special about Pyotr?' Malty asked.

Beshov put his finger to his lips. 'That's Mr Brytenn's secret, isn't it, Mr Brytenn? You have a lot of secrets, all tucked away in that self-righteous little brain of yours.' He stood up. 'So now, here we are, stuck in this shithole village, no way out. No fucking way out!' He kicked Brytenn in the leg, just above the ankle. 'You fucking bastard, Brytenn, you've killed us.' The second kick never made it. Sasha swung his leg in under Beshov's and upended the SS man. Beshov was on the floor looking up at the stars and Olga Sharankova's knife.

'Go on, sweetheart,' Beshov shouted. 'Do it.'

'Don't,' Brytenn said. He could barely speak with the pain, but he managed to lift himself. He put his hand to Olga's. 'Please!'

'You're too soft,' Olga said.

'Do what he says, Olga.' Summer had her other hand. The two men pulled her back slowly. 'You don't want this bastard to die quickly, do you?' Summer asked her. 'Maybe the Chekists will get him, and maybe they'll work on him with piano wire and a kitchen knife.'

Brytenn put his hand out to Beshov, and for a moment the Russian thought about laughing. Then he took the hand.

'You're right,' Brytenn said. He had lost his confident veneer and was relying on something inside he was not in control of. He might have called it training, but it was more. 'Sasha, set up our radio . . . just in case.'

'How long can we afford to stay here?' Summer asked.

'Not long,' Brytenn said.

Each of them slept away from the others, one always on guard. Summer came over to Olga but some time later she stood up and walked outside the house they were in and did not come back. Summer did not follow her. Olga found Brytenn sitting in what had been a shed, drunk, and in so much pain he could not unclench his fists. The pain was not all his ankle.

'You'd better let me look at that,' she said anyway. 'Give you something.'

She knelt down beside him and shivered. Then she began to

undo his bandage and feel the wound. 'I think it's probably broken now,' she said. 'Here, eat this.' She pulled a potato from her pocket and gave it to him. 'It needs better strapping, or you'll never make it.'

'To where?' he asked. 'You might be right about me.'

'Hey, come on now,' she said, nervous and smiling at the same time. It was the first time he had seen her smile and in the starlight it had an extra quality above that of just a girl smiling at him. 'I intend to grow my hair long again one day,' she said. She took his hand and held it tightly, then she bound his ankle even tighter. 'Sorry,' she said when it hurt him. She kissed his lips and sat down beside him. He put his arms around her.

'I'm beginning to doubt myself,' he said.

'I won't let you.'

'And Summer?'

'Doubt is not his problem. Just fatigue. He doesn't care any more. He does this to pass the time. It's like a game of football. His heart is not there, the way yours is. He is a talent looking for a cause.'

'And I am a cause looking for talent.'

'I did not say that.'

The crackle of the small, short-distance radio no one had even bothered to lie beside stopped anything else being said. Sasha was already at it. He pulled its headset from under a large canvas bag. The surprise on his face was mirrored in all those around him.

'It's the Skymaster . . . the aircraft.'

After the initial contact with the Skymaster, Brytenn gestured to Summer, who took out a radio code book and began to set down instructions for Sasha to send. For a moment, when the sound of the owls and the wind had died, all there was was the punctuated strains of the radio as Sasha began to make continuous contact with the aircraft and each of them exchanged positions.

That was when Beshov approached Brytenn with the same caution he would a minefield. 'Look, eh, Mr Brytenn, this isn't very easy for an SS man, but I'm sorry for what happened back there. I guess I lost it.' He put out his hand.

Brytenn shook it but said nothing. Beshov thought he might reply, just out of decency and good manners.

'One hour,' Sasha said then, distracting Brytenn's attention. 'They'll be here in an hour.'

'What about a runway?' Olga said. 'I take it Trepper never got around to clearing one.'

'Shit!' Beshov said. In their excitement, no one had thought about a landing strip.

Brytenn left Beshov. 'Is there anywhere they can land at short notice?' he asked Summer.

Everyone focused on Summer while he thought.

'About five kilometres that way,' he said, 'there's a strip we've used before. But it's very short, and not ideal for a four-engined aircraft. However, if the cold keeps up and there's not too much water, yes, I believe they can land there.' He took a map and went over to Sasha.

'Just pray they got in under the radar,' Olga Sharankova said. 'Or your escape is going to be a beacon for the Interiors to find us. Draw them like moths to a light bulb.'

'You're not coming?' Brytenn asked her.

'This is my home now.' She smiled something like resignation.

Brytenn took that and managed to show affection to Olga Sharankova, which she did not now return.

'I'll admit it is difficult to let Beshov go,' she said to him. It was an explanation that she did not need to give, and Brytenn was welcoming of it. Suddenly, in the middle of their small intimacies, the radio moved from mostly intermittent communication to continuous codes and call signs again.

Brytenn went over to Malty, who was buried in his own thoughts. 'Ready to go, Squadron Leader?' Brytenn asked. 'You'll be quite a sight when we get you home.'

Beshov slapped Malty on the back. 'He's fine. Nothing a few meals won't take care of. You married, Squadron Leader?'

Malty returned nothing but contempt. Beshov took his hand away and went back to Brytenn. 'So we failed,' he said to Brytenn. 'It was a damn foolish exercise anyway. Don't worry, Malty, you're not to blame because the Interiors got to Pyotr before us. Is he, Mr Brytenn?'

Malty's displeasure was now palpable and he backed away from Beshov and Brytenn, as if he were having too many thoughts for his mind to cope with.

'You were lucky,' Brytenn said to him, 'they were unlucky. That's about it. The powers that be are going to have a time explaining you when we get back.'

'Come on, time to go,' Summer said.

The landing zone was a long clearing in the trees, about as wide as the wings of a Skymaster, but only just, with small pyramids of sticks, covered with snow, on either side at intervals of twenty metres.

'Use anything to get them lit,' Brytenn said to Summer. The pain in his leg kept him on his horse while Sasha dismounted first, walked the length of the strip and then came back to Brytenn.

'Clear,' he said.

'With any luck the Interiors are miles away, around warm fires, toasting their work,' Summer said. He dismounted and set the portable radio up under one of the smaller trees. It crackled into life again.

'The fires, Sasha,' Olga said. 'You and me.'

Sasha winked at her and one by one they began clearing the snow from the beacon pyres and throwing petrol on to the heaps of sticks. Then Olga began to light the pyres with a flare gun.

'Well, we can't send a flare into the air,' she said to Brytenn.

As soon as the last heap was lit, Brytenn could hear the sound of engines, a distinctive low hum, pulling him towards the south. Summer was guiding the machine towards them, using Sasha at the other end of the field, with three lighted sticks as a definite fix on the site for the pilot. Brytenn looked up at the sky and saw nothing but stars.

'How's your ankle, Mr Brytenn?' Malty asked him, more as a means of calming his nerves than anything else.

'A mess,' Brytenn said for similar reasons. 'Like all of this.'

'I don't think so.'

Brytenn thanked him.

'Okay, here she comes . . .' Summer took his headphones off and grabbed his kit from the horse. He handed it to Brytenn.

'You're not coming either?' Brytenn was not surprised.

'There's some stuff in there for my family. See they get it.'

'You'll be caught.'

Summer just looked at Olga.

The aircraft came round the landing strip twice in wide circles, then throttled back and turned into the wind. From being the dominant sound the aircraft now competed with the wind and the night creatures and the radio. It touched down right where it should as if the pilot had been so used to the area that he could pick any spot and place his machine there.

Brytenn dismounted. Olga gave him her shoulder.

'You should both come,' he said to her. 'It's over here.'

This time she chose not to speak.

The aircraft did not stop engines when it touched down. Instead, it taxied down the hard wet surface of the landing strip and turned back with the wind.

'He's heading down to face the wind,' Summer said. 'Come on, we'll pick him up there.'

Beshov ran towards the aircraft first. Olga Sharankova told Summer to provide cover while she and Malty helped Brytenn towards the opening cargo door. A small man in a flying suit appeared at the back of the aircraft and beckoned them.

The night had now become dull, and a thin mist which had been hanging on the trees at the very end of the landing strip was beginning to permeate through the whole landscape, causing the small torchlights to diffuse. Beshov reached the aircraft, shook hands with the loadmaster and then turned to Sasha, who was now the forward cover for Brytenn and Malty.

The big Ukrainian put himself next to the aircraft, and put his hands together to lift Beshov through the opening. Small flecks of icy rain now began to pass along the fuselage and mix with the smoke from the engines and the gathering mist. Beshov hauled himself up on to Sasha's hands and the two men traded threats and insults.

Sasha shouted at the loadmaster for help and then shoved

the SS major into the aircraft, Beshov grabbing the cold steel of the fuselage to help himself in. As he did so, he said something to Sasha.

'You . . .'

Sasha's facial expression changed from anger to agony in the space of a second. A bullet hit the aircraft above Beshov's head and forced him and the loadmaster off balance. The loadmaster toppled forwards out of the plane and on top of the Ukrainian, and the two men fell into a wet boggy hole. Then an engine exploded. Sasha stood up, covered in flame, screaming.

Summer ran towards the aircraft as the loadmaster stood up, fell back and died. Cooper Brytenn pulled Olga Sharankova to the ground and both of them rolled and fired in the direction of the trees behind them. The aircraft began to move forward.

It moved some distance down the track, bouncing on the bumpy ground, splashing up water, digging up pieces of muck, bullets tearing into the fuselage, smashing glass, the remains of moonlight and starlight bouncing on the fuselage as the pilot struggled with the machine and a burning engine.

Brytenn found Malty at the edge of the field. Three Russians Interior soldiers were running at them from behind the aircraft, and behind the soldiers a jeep with a machinegun mounted on the back and a small searchlight had stopped and was engaging the escaping aircraft. The tracer bullets seemed to dance on the aircraft, like small fireflies, until a second engine caught fire, and the aircraft turned off the straight line it had adopted. Malty tore Brytenn from the trance, and Jack Summer, to the right, killed the three Interiors running at them.

The final explosion, when it happened, lit up the whole area for an instant. The aircraft hit the trees just as it was managing to lift itself off the ground. The aircraft burned for a time before the whole thing went up, straight up towards the sky in a gigantic towering flash which caught several of the Interior soldiers. Small figures running about on the fringes of the trees like torches were all that Brytenn could see as he retreated into cover.

THE GRAVEDIGGER

21

Circles

Driving along the frontier between the western and eastern zones of Germany in late March 1949, a London newspaper reporter wrote that he had last seen a military build-up like this in the months before D-Day. His report was spiked under the British D-Notice system, whereby newspaper editors will not run anything deemed to jeopardise British national security. The offending article was replaced by one that commented on the preparedness of the British army of the Rhine for all eventualities and how well they were getting on with the locals. Patrick Twilight, who had a copy of the original and had contributed to its replacement, underlined a comment on the number of times the word tea was mentioned in the piece.

'Germans don't come running out with cups of tea,' he said to the Administrator.

'We know that and anyone who has served here knows that, but it might be true and that's all the public at home have to believe,' the Administrator replied. 'What would you rather hear? That we're on the brink of another war or that tea supplies in the Hamburg area are good? I like tea.'

Twilight counted the number of tanks lining the roads, and noted the unit identification on the soldiers sitting under netting. They were making tea. 'Do we know how many of our people Brytenn had with him?' he said to the Administrator.

The latter shook his head. 'We're going to face a hell of a stink if any of these boys turn up in London and contact one of the newspapers. A lot more problems than the current state of tea in western Germany.'

'Did we know any of this before?' Twilight asked. 'That these fellows of ours were held in Soviet camps?'

'We know what we know,' the Administrator replied. 'Anyway, they're probably all dead now.'

'How many people might they have over there?'

The Administrator shrugged. 'Maybe some of our lads in the frenzy after liberation got a touch of the red in them and headed east voluntarily. Some, perhaps, less voluntarily. Look how many of them voted for a Labour government. I hope that bloody aircraft's as untraceable as the CIA say. They've set a date in Washington, you know. A sort of line in the sand.' He pulled his gloves off. His hands gradually lost the redness the gloves had given them, and the slight chill from the east was turning them white. 'It looks like Girenko has succeeded in drawing out most of our little resistance in the western Urals and its surroundings, with his Camp Thirty-Six tale. And now they'll be torn apart by Stalin's dogs. If the mountain won't come to Mohammed, then bring Mohammed to the mountain, as they say. We should have picked him up.'

'I stand chastised,' Twilight said.

'You need a change, Patrick. Girenko'll be made a hero and they'll be rid of another headache in their rear. Only a few isolated refuges and Ukraine left on our side, and we've nothing to play with. There was no Vasili file, I'd say.'

Twilight shook his head. 'As you say.'

The Administrator put his hand on Twilight's forearm. 'We can't afford to leave anyone who knows anything behind, Patrick.' For a moment the two men's eyes met and held a stare.

'Can we ever?'

For two days Brytenn's team had cut between the sweeping Interior troops and headed north along the line of the Urals. Then, on the third night, holed up in a shallow pit, almost covered over by a fresh fall of snow, a sweating and obviously frightened Summer held fast by Olga, they had started south again, while the Interiors moved north. Before they moved, Olga had to talk to Summer for fifteen minutes.

'He was in a tunnel in Germany, in a prison camp, when it collapsed,' she explained to Brytenn.

Brytenn already knew.

They passed so close to an Interior camp the next night that the dogs began to bark and only the snow prevented their masters from acting on the animal's excitement. When the night was over and the sun came up and began to undo the cold's work, Brytenn just stopped and sat down on a rock. He could go no further. He gave the order to halt and they fell asleep for an hour in a ravine, among fir saplings. And when they woke, no one stirred.

'We should move,' Jack Summer said to Brytenn after a while.

'Where to?' Brytenn asked. For the first time in many years the fact that he did not know what to do was showing on his face. He began to undo his boot and examine his ankle. 'I don't think it's so bad,' he said to no one in particular. Then he lost himself in the details of his wound.

'We must put distance between them and us,' Summer insisted. A kind of automatic survival instinct was running Summer now and he seemed to be about to take over the team. 'Cooper!'

It took time for Brytenn to look up and nod his head. And as he did so, Olga appeared from a depression in the trees holding a small bottle. 'Where had you in mind?' Brytenn asked Summer. But his eyes were on Olga.

'Jack's right, we should keep moving,' she said, passing Brytenn the bottle.

'Weather's good for moving,' Victor Malty commented. He was brushing snow from his clothes, and shivering. The pilot looked utterly miserable.

'And for hunting,' Brytenn said. He watched the small dot of an aircraft pass overhead, slipping in and out of the heavy grey clots of cloud which stained the sky here and there, while the freezing wind broke the landscape into sizeable chunks, thinking about himself and the way in which he had changed since he had come to Russia.

'We can't hunt, Cooper,' Jack Summer said.

Brytenn smiled. 'I'm forty today, you know,' he said.

'Congratulations,' Olga said. 'But . . .'

An elk came out of the trees and caught the whole party unaware. They all swung their weapons into position. No one fired.

'Let's have something to eat,' Brytenn said. 'To celebrate my birthday.' He pulled a small handgun from his pocket, probably not enough to do the job on an elk. Summer placed his hand on the weapon.

'You want to bring every soldier in the area down on us? There's Interiors everywhere, Cooper. The sound will carry.'

'So what?' Brytenn asked. 'Out here, there are no directions, just space.'

Summer shoved the weapon down again.

'I command here,' Brytenn said.

'If we still had silencers, I'd say yes, kill it,' Summer said.

'Well, we don't. We don't have anything. And soon we'll start to eat each other. You ever eaten . . . ?'

'I remember a story my mother used to tell me, of an emperor and his clothes. Do you know it, Cooper?'

Brytenn started to quote from various novels, for no real reason. 'Scared I'll put you in another hole?' he said to Summer then.

Summer lifted his rifle and shot the elk.

For a moment Brytenn stared into the distance. And then he began to laugh. It was an uncontrollable shaking laughter that brought tears to his eyes and mucus from his nose. He was back in a boat, alone with his dying friends, talking to them, their eyes fixed on him for six days.

'I threw them in the water,' he said to Olga Sharankova. 'I threw them in the water.'

'What are you talking about?' Olga asked Brytenn.

He nodded towards the distance, where the sun was. 'See the tall wisps?' he said. 'It's Aktjabrj. We've come full circle.' He moved his arm round and round. 'Can't you see? We were only five miles from land and I threw them out, my friends, I threw them out because I couldn't stand to look at them any more. I didn't know if they were dead. I didn't care . . .'

Summer began to laugh now, for no other reason than Brytenn was, and his fatigue began to make his mouth lose shape. 'In the Pacific, we wanted to know about an island, so we sent out a patrol. Seven men. One week went by, they didn't come back. Two weeks . . . three . . . four . . . eleven weeks and nothing. So we assumed they were dead. We assumed there were plenty of Japs on the island. When we hit it, there were no Japs and we found our patrol. All out of their minds. First time they tried to find the beach they went round in a circle. Found the remains of their own camp. Didn't recognise it. After that, they just wound up going round in circles. Ended up running from themselves.'

The two Americans were convulsed with laughter. Olga hit both of them. It had no effect.

'Do you know what date it is?' Brytenn asked Summer.

Summer shook his head and began to convulse with laughter again. 'Leader of that patrol was my best friend.' He stopped everything immediately and just froze there looking into the trees.

'It's April the first, Jack. April Fool . . .'

When Brytenn picked himself up and began walking towards the village, Olga went to follow. Victor Malty stopped her. 'Let him be. We used to have things like this in the camp. It's best to let it work its way through. How about some food?'

'Squadron Leader, are you inviting me to dinner?'

'I warn you I'm married.'

'So is she,' Summer said, in a clumsy attempt to reinforce his claim on her.

'You should go with him,' Malty said to Summer.

Summer refused.

Brytenn walked on ahead, down a winding snow path, over pleated ground, to the first house in Aktjabrj. Trepper's body was gone but a disembowelled pig lay on the doorstep, fat running from its body and frying in the embers of what had been the house. Brytenn knelt down and picked something up before moving on to the next house.

He had an old man's face now, as he hobbled on a stick, sprouting short hairs, its colour changing with the rising sun, its shape taking on a form that resembled the many movements of personality he had passed through during the years of his work but dominated by his own private terrors.

'If you want to breathe again, then stop.'

The pistol to the back of Brytenn's neck freed him from the troubles of his mind and he was almost grateful.

The men ate the flesh of the animal Summer had killed with a degree of appetite that defied their sense of repulsion for what they were doing. Only Olga Sharankova ate the raw meat unself-consciously. 'I lived in Poland during the Nazi times,' she explained.

'I've spent years in places like that, back there,' Malty said, nodding in the direction of Camp Thirty-Six, 'but I never got used to it.'

'We should start a fire,' Summer said.

'And draw the Interiors?' Olga asked him.

'They're probably cooking. You don't hear their commanders telling them not to start fires because we'll see the smoke. You gonna just follow him blindly, Olga?' Summer gestured towards the village. 'We've had fires before, and we've had Interior units chasing us. And we've seen them off. You know what it's like trying to find something in this country. And we know it a hell of a lot better than those boys do. So we lead them a merry dance and then pick them off in small groups when they overextend.'

The food had sparked Summer's confidence and supplemented his basic instincts. He was talking now without much thought for anything.

'Yeah, lie low, wait for the trouble to pass, then begin again. Just you and me, Olga, and whoever we can recruit. We can do damage here. We can make things happen. Have old Uncle Joe wondering if one day we'll come visit him, take him away. Think of the resources we can tie down.'

'You must be very frightened of returning home, Mr Summer,' Malty said.

'Ain't you?'

'I have not had your advantage of having seen it. I am relying on memory. Memory is a faithless comrade and an unreliable adviser. But I must go, I suppose. Just like you must stay here.'

'See!' Summer said to Olga. 'The Squadron Leader, here, thinks I should stay. You want to have a look at my lice?'

'Stop it, Jack, just stop it. He's been gone twenty minutes, you know. Brytenn.'

She threw her meat down and was about to walk away, when Brytenn appeared out of the trees to her right. He appeared so quietly she was startled and sat back down immediately.

Ivan Pyotr was standing behind him with a gun.

LIMERICK COUNTY LIBRARY

22

Swell

Swell Johnson lay on a straw mattress in the basement of one of the burned-out houses in Aktjabrj, his eyes shut, his skin the colour of rancid milk, a thin film of sweat on his brow and his lips so dry them seemed like they would just crumble into dust and fly away on the wind.

'How are you, Swell?' Malty asked Johnson.

Something like the expected answer came back, but it might have been just a sigh. Whatever it was, only Cooper Brytenn did not hear it. He was standing at the door of the cellar, looking at the faces of men he had sat in a boat with for ten days years earlier.

'We hid here after the Interiors came,' Ivan Pyotr explained. 'Even they don't come back to torch a place twice. I thought I heard voices before – you maybe?'

'These were our people,' Jack Summer explained. He was genuinely shaken by the sight of Johnson and held Olga's hand for a moment, for no reason. She did not stop him.

'He'd be better off dead,' she said of Johnson.

'No!' Brytenn said, then stepped outside.

'So you came all this way for me?' Pyotr laughed. 'Did you

hear that, Swell, these people came to rescue me? If you ask me, they're the ones who need rescuing. I always said you people from the West were soft.' The police colonel's laughter was as genuine as a two-dollar bill and about as welcome.

Olga took out what she had left of her medical kit, a few rags, some ointments and a small bottle of iodine, and went to work on Johnson's face. 'At least he'll feel a little better,' she said.

Behind her, Brytenn gestured to Malty from the door.

Outside, in the remains of a wooden house, Brytenn hobbled over to a charred window frame and examined the carved reliefs on the outside wall. 'What are we going to do with him?' he asked the pilot.

'What do you mean?' Malty asked.

'Yeah, Cooper, what do you mean?' Jack Summer was lighting a cigarette, something which seemed out of place given their circumstances.

'We can't take him with us, look at him.'

'You want to put a bullet in him, bossman?' Summer asked.

'No . . . no . . . but I think we should leave him where he can receive proper medical attention.'

Olga Sharankova had appeared at the door and took a drag of Summer's cigarette.

'You know what Chekist medical attention will be,' she said. 'They'll put him with the rest. In a bed for life.'

'Look at our position,' Brytenn said. He began to wave his hands as if he did not believe what he was saying himself. 'We have hundreds of kilometres of open ground to cover before we get near Finland, and no horses left. Even assuming we do get fresh mounts, until we clear the railway line at Syktyvkar, we'll be evading Interior troops by the regiment. No, my job is to get Pyotr out. At all costs.'

'We could call in another plane,' Summer said.

'With what? Our radio's range is too short,' Brytenn countered. 'And even if we could . . .'

The conversation died in Brytenn's logic and, for a few moments, only the wind spoke.

'Well, I've got news for you, Mr Brytenn.' Ivan Pyotr was now standing behind Olga, holding the pistol he had stuck in Brytenn's back. 'You're not going north.'

'It's the best way out,' Brytenn insisted. 'Longer, granted, but wilder and easier to evade detection.'

Pyotr nodded and took a cigarette from Summer. 'I haven't had one of these in so long I had quite forgotten what to do with them.' He lit the cigarette. 'If you want to find Vasili you'll have to go south.'

'Who's Vasili?' Malty asked.

'You didn't think we did all this for an old policeman?' Summer said.

'It's here, in Russia?' Brytenn said. 'The file?'

'Well, where the hell else did you think it was?' Pyotr said.

The following morning struggled to be born. Vladimir Romanovili stood near the remains of Brytenn's aircraft, now covered in a fresh snowfall, while two of three patrols radioed back their positions in the forest and reported they could not find any trace of those who had escaped.

Romanovili was swearing to himself while he examined documents found at the crash site. He had a strong pain in his left side and wondered if his heart was beginning to let him down now. For a few seconds, he wished it would. But only for a few.

'We're right behind them,' he said. 'I can smell it. They're on foot, perhaps wounded. How far can they get?'

Lavrenti Beria sucked in air and threw back his shoulders as if to impress his junior. 'Tread carefully, Your Imperial Majesty. We don't want your sense of smell knocked completely out of joint, do we.' He took a map from his coat pocket and traced his fingers across it. The tremble of a man perpetually in fear of being the next victim of his own rage kept Romanovili transfixed, while Beria examined a swathe of territory around them.

'So what would you do if you were lost in the taiga?' Beria said. 'North to Finland. Longer route, but harder to find you. Or south. Pyotr worked for the reactionaries in the south during the war against counter-revolution.'

Beria had been late to the cause and like many late to a cause felt it his duty to catch up by outdoing all those who had been there before him. He had the most insulted mouth Romanovili had ever seen, which looked perpetually offended or on the verge of being offended. Romanovili pulled a bottle from his own pocket and offered it to Beria.

'I'd head north,' Romanovili said to Beria. 'But if they head that way they could just slip out of the country and . . .'

'Then I think you'd better find them. I'll see you again in Kazan.'

Beria allowed his eyes to follow a young girl across the line of a small hill about fifty metres away.

'Who's she?' he asked.

'She works for me,' Romanovili said.

Romanovili knew it was his superior's habit to have his henchmen kidnap young girls for his own delectation. He was one of the few cronies of Stalin to have personally murdered people, something he shared with Stalin, and of course they were both Georgians.

'Bring her to me,' Beria said. 'When you're finished with her, of course.'

At this point, Romanovili began to think to himself, and wondered if Beria had noticed it. Thoughts had become the only refuge in the perpetual winter of the Stalinist ice age. Things were frozen, awaiting the thaw.

As soon as I find what they're after, he thought, Beria will kill me. I am a dead man waiting for rest.

Cooper Brytenn had similar sentiments. But nothing happened that night or the next day, except that the further south they moved, the worse the weather grew, and the temperature dropped again. April appeared to revert to January. Malty and Summer carried Swell Johnson on an improvised stretcher, while Ivan Pyotr brought up the rear, deep in thought, like a card player with his last hand in front of him. And the combination of Swell Johnson and the police colonel deep in thought forced Brytenn into himself.

He remembered small things from a childhood that resembled a frozen river in his mind, a simple surface, white against the clear blue sky, birds and humans sliding on the same surface, and the fear of the centre for all, for the surface was unsure.

Keep to the edges, his mother would yell.

'How is your ankle, Brytenn?' Olga Sharankova asked suddenly because she was feeling left out. It brought Brytenn back to reality. He raised his stick to show he could walk without it. But the pain on his face when he did it showed he could not.

'Just keep me pointed in the right direction,' he said. Then he glanced over at Swell Johnson and was glad his old friend was still unconscious.

'Otherwise we might have to leave both of you,' Summer said.

'I'd save you the trouble, Jack,' Cooper Brytenn said.

'You know you're quite a man, Mr Brytenn,' Ivan Pyotr said, perhaps with a little sarcasm in his voice. Brytenn did not detect it.

'Coming from you, I'll take that as a compliment, Colonel,' he said to Pyotr, just to get away from thinking about what he had said before.

'Me?' Pyotr said. 'I'm a simple police colonel who through force of circumstance found himself the centre of an ugly little power game.'

'Would you prefer to be anonymous?'

'Sometimes I would prefer if I had not been born. You know I don't think I like being free.' Pyotr's strong Tartar looks seemed to wither at that moment. All Brytenn could do was stare at Swell Johnson again.

'Tell me when you want morphine,' Olga said to him.

He did not reply to her this time.

'Mr Brytenn,' Malty said then, 'what do you have in mind exactly? If you wouldn't mind explaining. Just to keep me filled with hope.' He exhaled a freezing cloud and coughed while he lifted the stretcher from his shoulder for a moment before replacing it.

'I have in mind to find us some horses, Squadron Leader, and after that I will tell you as you need to know. We're heading for the Volga, I can tell you that, Squadron Leader. Right, Colonel Pyotr?'

'Everything leads to the Volga in this part of the world,' Pyotr said.

'So what is this Vasili file that has us marching through the last snows with most of the Interior Ministry's best on our tails?' Olga Sharankova asked.

'Can't tell you that, Olga,' Brytenn said.

His smugness irritated her. 'Then it must be a load of bullshit,' she said. 'I usually find that when people refuse to tell me something, it turns out to be a load of bullshit. Your friend won't last, Colonel.'

'He'll last, right, Squadron Leader Malty?'

'If I last, Swell will last,' Malty said. He said it in a prison tone, and it carried a prison value.

'And you're all right, Squadron Leader?' Brytenn asked. 'I could try lifting him, if you want.'

'No way, Cooper,' Jack Summer said.

'Just keep moving,' Malty replied.

Brytenn could not conceal his disappointment.

That night, when they stopped, Brytenn went over to Swell Johnson, while the others slept. It was a mild night by the standards of the taiga, and Johnson opened his left eye and said something. Brytenn closed the eye.

'Can you hear me, Swell?' he whispered. He dampened a cloth and put the cloth to Johnson's dry lips. Johnson sucked on the cloth and then relapsed into unconsciousness. Brytenn used the cloth to wipe Johnson's face.

'I'd swear you knew him.'

Olga Sharankova was sitting up behind him, scratching herself and pulling on another piece of clothing.

'You want to take a look at my ankle?' Brytenn asked her.

'You want to tell me anything?'

'I have nothing to say. You know, you could walk out of here and vanish. This need not have anything to do with you.' He touched her arm and they held a stare which embarrassed both of them.

'Are you trying to tell me something, Brytenn?'

'I'm trying to show you things. I have what I want, and you helped me to get him. Now you can go. Take Jack Summer with you. Get out of here yourselves.'

'What does that policeman know that makes him so important?'

Brytenn moved his hand to her face and gently drew his finger across her chin. 'We'll have to split up, you know. As soon as we have the horses. If we offer them two targets, then there's a good chance they'll miss one, and an even chance it'll be the one we want them to miss.'

'And the others?' she asked.

In the morning, Brytenn announced his decision to split up to the others. 'As soon as we find horses, Colonel Pyotr, Squadron Leader Malty and I will travel separately.' He stared at Summer. 'You and Olga will go together, Jack.'

'And him?' Malty asked, looking at Johnson. 'What about Swell?'

For a moment Cooper Brytenn's fear got the better of him and he felt he was displaying all the confusions inside him on his face. 'We'll take care of him,' he said.

'How?' Olga asked.

Brytenn ignored her. 'I'll give you a rendezvous, Jack.' He began searching for a small one-time code pad and scribbled details on a square of paper, muttering things from a novel Malty remembered reading a decade or so earlier.

'I'll look after Swell,' Malty said to Olga then. 'That right, Mr Brytenn?' But Brytenn was not listening any more. He seemed to be a man revelling in his own loneliness at that moment, something Malty almost envied.

Then Olga stood up and shook her head. Some of the early morning sunlight caught the tiny small blonde spikes and created a showering effect around her head.

'I'll go with you,' she said to Brytenn. 'You'll never make it without me, you don't know anything about the system here. They'd spot you a mile off. How is it that you Americans always think that because you study a culture and learn a language you can just walk through it. There are other languages, Brytenn, and you just cannot speak them.'

Even Summer could not argue with her logic.

23

Divisions

But they could not split up. At first, they could not find horses, then the Soviet military and the Russian weather drove them into hiding. Hours in cold pits and tunnels smaller than coffins, staring into darkness, just listening. Hours of silence. Sometimes, when it just got too much, Jack Summer would simply break free and scramble out into the open air. And then they would begin walking again. No one ever said anything to Summer about his problem.

On the fourth day, they did manage to acquire horses at a collective farm where the winter had been bad and their money was welcome. But Swell Johnson got worse. They threw him across a horse for a day and Olga collected mosses from the forest and mixed them with drugs she had and fed them to him. But the cold was stronger. Finally, Swell fell from the horse he was lying across.

'You should shoot him,' Olga said very calmly to Brytenn.

'No,' he insisted. He looked at Malty and Pyotr, both of whose faces now betrayed their lack of faith in Johnson's future. The two men just stared past him.

'Look, maybe we should leave him,' Summer said.

'He'll die out here,' Brytenn said. 'And we're not going near any more farms. I asked you to leave him when he still had a chance.' With each word he spoke, Brytenn wondered if Johnson could hear him. 'We could have saved him by leaving him,' he added, almost as an afterthought.

'We needed hope then,' Pyotr explained. 'Do you understand?'

'Mr Brytenn has never been in prison,' Malty said.

'We all have our prisons, Squadron Leader,' Brytenn said, wishing he had not. He limped over to some small trees, feeling the pain in his ankle more than he had for some time. 'Get me something for this, Olga. Please.' He began hacking at a tree with a machete.

Jack Summer joined him. 'What is it with you, Cooper?' he said.

'Maybe Beshov was right,' Olga said. 'Maybe he is crazy.' She handed Brytenn a phial of morphine. 'That's all I'm giving you,' she said. 'Do it yourself.'

He snatched it from her without a word.

While Brytenn injected the morphine, Olga began to help Summer with the tree. Brytenn joined them as soon as the drug began to take effect. And the three of them began to construct a litter for Swell Johnson.

'I don't know, all this work reminds me of prison,' Ivan Pyotr said to Victor Malty.

Malty went to check on Swell Johnson. 'He's still alive,' he said with some disappointment in his voice.

When Brytenn and Summer had fixed the litter behind Brytenn's horse, they placed Swell Johnson on the litter.

'I won't leave you, Swell,' Brytenn whispered into Johnson's ear. Then he looked around to see if anyone had noticed. But all of them were busy with their own survival, except perhaps Olga, who had taught herself to concentrate, even in moments of great stress, on several things at the same time. She seemed to be watching Brytenn in much the same way she had watched Beshov. Some part of Brytenn even considered the possibility that she had shot Beshov during the gun battle at the landing strip. But that led on to other possibilities he was not willing to contemplate.

'You know sometimes you make me feel sorry for Beshov, Olga,' he said to her before they set off again.

'I feel no sorrow for him,' she replied. 'He is where he belongs. You are under the influence of morphine.' She shook her head.

They made one hundred and fifty kilometres over the next three days and crossed the main railway line to Perm and Sverdlovsk on a Sunday afternoon in the rain.

And in the vastness of the taiga, Cooper Brytenn felt he was losing his authority again. Especially when he took morphine for his ankle.

Though together, the group broke into a series of loosely connected units strung out and barely held together. Only Olga talked to Brytenn, and then not very often and usually to argue over his ankle and the morphine he demanded. Malty talked with Pyotr, as if they were back in prison, something Brytenn was not comfortable with. And Summer did not talk to anyone, except once to Swell Johnson, when Johnson woke for a few hours and the others were asleep.

It was about that time that Olga began riding next to Brytenn. There was nothing conscious in it, and she sometimes dropped back or went ahead as requested, but if it came to a choice of post, she chose to be beside Brytenn, instead of

Summer. What made her do this even she was not sure of, but the bond of affection between them, subtle as it was, was very noticeable to everyone else.

'What attracts us to people?' she said to Jack Summer much later. 'Perhaps need more than anything.'

As he rode through the forests, Summer's eyes fixed permanently on Olga Sharankova, as if the stare itself were enough to keep her with him. It can take but a lack of one emotion to convince you of another's triumph. Summer had been dropped into Russia two years earlier, an empty vessel seeking to be filled, with the sense of adventure only real in people who know little and care less, and the desire to do what he did best. Now, he was losing it. As sure as the snow was melting.

The land appeared to have no end. They would cross a forest the size of a small state and then a prairie the size of another, only to find another forest.

'I was talking to Swell,' Summer said to Brytenn at the end of a day in which they had made more ground than Brytenn had hoped. It was a sudden remark, while Olga was examining Brytenn's ankle. It might have been to attract Olga's attention. If it was, it did not work. She continued looking at the ankle.

'What did he say?' Brytenn asked Summer.

'This and that,' Summer replied. 'Says we should leave him.'

'He doesn't know what he's saying,' Brytenn said. There was no emotion in his voice. Just determination and resignation.

'Okay, okay, you wanna know what he said?' Summer said then. 'He said nothing that made any kinda sense. Zip.' Summer threw down what he was holding and pulled out a cigarette. 'I hate just watching him. Just there.'

'He's bad luck,' Ivan Pyotr said.

Malty went over to Johnson and touched his head. 'He might as well be dead. I've touched dead men warmer than him. I'm sorry, Swell. You know you make promises and you mean them . . .'

'He knows your name, Cooper,' Summer interrupted. 'Only damn word I could understand. Knows the bossman.'

'You have to kill him,' Olga said very quietly while bandaging Brytenn's ankle again. She did not even bother looking up.

Again Cooper Brytenn replied in the negative.

'Privilege of command, Cooper,' Summer said. 'You'd be doing him a favour.'

Brytenn exploded. 'If we had left him in Aktjabrj, when he still had a chance,' he said. 'When he could have been saved. Should have been saved.'

'He might as well be dead,' Pyotr said.

'We don't have any choice, Mr Brytenn,' Malty added.

There was an ugliness in these two men's accents that Cooper Brytenn had only ever detected in Anatoli Beshov's before this. He thought of the SS officer and felt the sudden need to wash. Just to scrub himself for an hour and feel clean.

'I used to wonder how close any of us were to what Beshov was,' he said to Olga. 'If he was not dead, then maybe we could ask him where the line is and how you know you've passed it. Because there's no going back once you have.'

'What the hell are you doing here?' she said.

Brytenn stood up, hobbled over to his horse, untied the strap of his saddle bag and pulled out a pistol. He checked the magazine and then cocked it. 'You do it,' he said to Summer.

Summer refused the weapon. Brytenn went round each of them and each of them refused the weapon in turn.

Then Brytenn walked away, stood for a moment, and came back. 'I wanted him saved. You know?' He knelt down beside Johnson, and asked him how he was. Nothing came back. Then he looked around at each of the others again.

'It's up to you, Cooper,' Jack Summer said.

Brytenn looked around him one more time, almost pleading with them to help him, and then put the pistol to Johnson's head. He closed his eyes and began to squeeze the trigger. It seemed like an eternity before he was stopped, and when he was he could not believe it. He kept the barrel at Johnson's head.

'There's no need.' Victor Malty put his hand on Brytenn's and pushed it to one side. 'I knew he was too cold. There's no pulse.'

When they had buried Johnson, Brytenn turned to Olga. 'I was right to leave him, he could have been saved.'

But she did not understand him.

They moved on in silence. Two days later, when the moon was a broken silver disc, they saw what might have been a large lake, but when the darkness came, the water went with it and by the middle of the night, the snow was falling again, in a kind of crushed ice form, and they had reached the edge of a forest.

There, they stopped and slept very badly in holes, Summer at one stage refusing to stay in his, preferring to bed down with the horses. No one, not even Olga, argued with him, but when they all awoke, without a hint from anyone or anything, Brytenn took full command again.

'Kill the horses,' he said to Summer.

Summer's mouth opened so wide you could have stuck an

apple into it. But Brytenn had his map case out and a piece of Summer was almost glad of the order.

'Over there,' Brytenn said. 'That's the Kamu river. It runs into the Volga. That way, about five or ten kilometres, that's the railway line to Kazan. We're deep in Tartar country, Colonel Pyotr. Right?'

'It's been a long time,' Pyotr replied.

'Yes, well, no more horses. From here on, we get respectable. Morphine, Olga. Please.'

'So, where do we go?' Olga asked, taking out a phial and jamming it into his leg. It had become so routine for one or other of them to do this that it did not interrupt the conversation. It did slow Brytenn down enough for Ivan Pyotr to intervene.

'Stalingrad,' Pyotr said. 'Right, Mr Brytenn?'

Brytenn took out a map of the area around the city named for Stalin and was making calculations and writing in a small coded script. 'That's just it,' he said. 'Just as Colonel Pyotr said.'

Summer was going to issue a litany of reasons why going to Stalingrad was just about the worst thing they could do when his eyes were diverted by movement in the trees.

The outline came out of the early morning mist and the strings of slow-falling snowflakes, left of one of the small shafts of light provided by the weakest of dawns, the remains of the moon's light and what stars there were left in the sky. Brytenn picked up a rifle. 'Come out,' he said.

A middle-aged man of about medium height, with a heavy white beard, walked slowly from the trees, smiling. He was wrapped in winter clothing and armed with a shotgun.

'You might have guarded yourself a little better, Mr

Brytenn,' he said. 'I almost gave up on you. And a man my age can catch cold out here every night.'

His smile widened and the smile took Summer's mind off Brytenn while the bearded man continued to approach. He walked silently over ground that usually broke under small animals.

'Not so fast!'

Olga stepped out from behind a tree and placed a pistol to the bearded man's head. He raised his hands.

'Schenck . . . I thought you knew me better than that.' Brytenn, who, though still in some pain, seemed to have regained every bit of his self-assurance, held out his hand.

'You have created quite a stir, Brytenn,' Schenck said. 'There have been arrests everywhere. Interior sweeps all over.'

'I suppose I should ask who he is?' Summer said.

'Who he is and how he got here and why he's here,' Olga added. 'And why I shouldn't kill him now.'

Brytenn beamed with arrogance, some of it morphine-induced. 'Schenck's a little card I placed up my sleeve when I sat down to this game, Jack.'

'Ace!' Schenck said.

'I had Trepper put him on warning,' Brytenn said. 'Among others. Just in case. To be honest, I didn't know if Trepper got through, or if the Interiors had picked you up, Schenck.'

'Every Tuesday, for six weeks,' Schenck said. 'I was to come here. Tedious, yet effective.'

'Blind snatch, we call it, Colonel Pyotr,' Brytenn said.

'How many other blind snatches do you have working around Russia?' Summer asked Brytenn.

'You're not the only Agency game in this part of the world,

Jack. You're an important one but not the only one. Schenck has been with us for years, one way and another. Right, Schenck? Olga, you can take your gun away. He's friendly. He's going to take Jack and the Squadron Leader to where I want them. Now you've decided to come with me.'

'And you three?' Summer asked Brytenn. 'How will you go?'

'Not your concern, Jack,' Brytenn said. 'Your concern is to follow Schenck's directions and turn up where expected, when expected.'

'We're the decoy,' Malty said. 'Right, Mr Brytenn? Best not know the intentions of those for whom we're decoying. And I thought I'd escaped.'

'If you do as you're told you will,' Brytenn snapped.

Olga Sharankova wanted to shout something at Brytenn but held her tongue. 'He's right,' she said to Summer.

Brytenn pulled out another map from his pack and began scanning it. 'Colonel Pyotr, could you join me, please . . . alone,' he said, as if he were asking the old prisoner to step into his office. He paused once to look up at Summer. 'We have help, Jack.'

For about five minutes, Brytenn and Pyotr discussed the map. Summer was tempted to interfere but the very training that defined him made him back off. He sat in silence with Olga and Malty, while Schenck ate some cold meat he was carrying. He offered a flask to the two men beside him and some of the meat to Olga. Only Malty accepted. And he took some meat.

'You look well for people who have outrun half the Interior troops in the Urals,' Schenck said to Brytenn afterwards. 'They're all gone north. Though we've had patrols here, too.

This is a damn hard country to police, east of the Volga anyway.'

'You see, I have things under control,' Brytenn said to Summer.

'Of course you do,' Summer said. 'Just who is he?'

'He's a man left behind by time and circumstances,' Brytenn said. 'Right, Schenck?'

'You might say that. Can we move? I have a safe house you can use for a night. Warm, with food.'

'You see, Olga, all the comforts,' Brytenn said.

She did not answer him.

Brytenn thought for a while and did not let her antipathy upset his confidence for one moment. Perhaps he was at his most convincing when he was least confident, he thought, and he looked at Olga to see if she had noticed that, too. It did not matter if anyone else in the party noticed, but if she did then Brytenn would not have been able to make it last. He sighed.

'How will you move?' Schenck asked him.

'By train. Right, Olga? Husband, wife and grandfather. You don't mind being a grandfather, Colonel Pyotr?'

Pyotr just shook his head. 'I don't feel young enough,' he said.

'You had it all worked out.' Olga Sharankova shrugged the way Slavs do when they are sure but expecting the worst.

'You don't have to come with us, Olga,' Brytenn snapped. 'You can stay with Schenck. He'll look after you.'

'And who would look after you?' she said.

Summer nodded and plucked a piece of bread from a dark loaf he was holding. 'And I thought I had you figured, Cooper.'

That remark made Brytenn take a decision he had not

intended to. 'Could I speak with you, Jack?' he asked. And when Summer followed him away from the others, Brytenn was pulling out a map.

They split up the next day.

24

Strangers

Perhaps if Vladimir Romanovili had been paying more attention to what he was doing and less to what might befall him he might have noticed the hidden pattern in the small details of the many tracks leading from the same forest the following morning.

Cooper Brytenn had done his best to camouflage his real intentions by feeding poison to his horses and then scattering the animals, but if his pursuers had been more attentive to their work than the spring rains, they might have figured out that at least some of his people had headed for a small railway station about twenty kilometres back to the north.

And sitting in a very small room, in that same railway station, hours after his old companions had gone, smoking a cigarette for want of anything else to do, parts of his face still slightly burned and bruised, Anatoli Beshov might have told his captors why Brytenn had chosen to kill his horses and take the train.

Beshov's face had a slight twitch in the cheek muscles and his hands were quick and fidgety, and he had smoked three cigarettes halfway down before taking the one he had now.

'Sturmbannführer, you look distinctly unwell.' Lavrenti Beria sat across the table from Beshov, scribbling in a small notebook, occasionally taking his pince-nez from his nose and cleaning them with a small dust cloth he held in his pocket.

'The doctors say he is well.' Near Beria, Vladimir Romanovili stood back against the wall, tapping his foot, sometimes catching the eye of Beshov, sometimes ignoring him. Beshov made a point of watching Romanovili even when he was speaking to Beria.

'Health is so much a matter of perspective, isn't it, Beshov?' Beria said. 'Perhaps your friends have come south for theirs.' He smiled. 'Though I doubt it, don't you?'

'Brytenn is a man with things to prove,' Beshov answered.

'I think what Comrade Beria was suggesting,' Romanovili said, 'was, might there be a chance they have Pyotr?'

'Well, you don't have him.'

'You should understand, Beshov,' Beria said, 'that your life is dependent on your usefulness to us. If they have come south instead of heading north, which would be the easier route out, then they have come south for a reason. And that reason can only be Colonel Pyotr.'

'You have used a hammer to crack a nut, you know,' Beshov replied. 'Scattered the pieces far and wide. And now you want me to gather them up. On the vague promise of my life. The Americans pay, you know. Reinhard Gehlen pays.'

'They would not have thought twice about sending you to your death, Beshov,' Romanovili said. 'The Americans. They would have killed you long ago if you were not so useful to them.'

'I'm always aware of my predicaments.' He started to smoke again. 'But you need me.'

'We need Ivan Pyotr,' Beria said. He slammed his fist on the table.

While Romanovili and Beria were talking with Beshov, Cooper Brytenn and Ivan Pyotr sat either side of Olga Sharankova on a train bound for Moscow, and by the time Romanovili and Beria had come to terms with this as a possibility, Brytenn and his companions had changed trains at Kazan and swung south to Ulyanovsk where they picked up an early Volga riverboat facilitated by the mild winter as far as Saratov.

They stayed in a small hotel between the river port at naberezhnaya Kosmonavtov and ploshchad Muzeynaya. The hotel was run by a Volga German who had evaded deportation to Siberia in 1941 by marrying a local communist official. She was a squat woman with a deeply unGermanic face which resembled a piece of dried fruit.

That night, as Romanovili's men searched up and down the Perm to Moscow train line, Brytenn and Olga walked prospekt Kirova in the moonlight, while Ivan Pyotr slept.

'You don't fear he will run away?' Olga asked Brytenn.

'Where to?' he replied. 'He has run away. His decision has been made. He is bound to me now. He knows it. I know it.'

'And when you finally release him?'

Brytenn sighed. 'You are not always good for me, Olga.'

'What makes him important?' she asked then. And Brytenn wanted to tell her, if only to enhance his own importance.

'I'm not sure we should get the train tomorrow,' was all he said. 'I think we should switch tack.'

Olga accepted it. 'Another boat?'

He shook his head. 'If they've guessed our direction, which

they must have by now, then it's just a matter of checking the various transport systems. No, we should find ourselves a truck. Something with an offensive smell in the back.'

'I'll bet you already have one in mind,' she said.

'There'll be time to wash when we get where we're going.'

'I think that's your problem, Brytenn. Remember, I'm Polish.'

Brytenn started to laugh but Olga did not join in.

'How is your ankle?' she asked instead.

'Do you miss Jack?' he countered, and not just because he wanted more morphine.

Jack Summer and Victor Malty made another two hundred kilometres in the back of Schenck's truck that night, covered in hemp. The tail end of winter followed them in the shape of a large angry mass of a mountain storm, lying across the tops of trees, spitting sleet ahead of it, a sheet of rain moving slowly towards the horizon.

The road was buckling in the contest between late winter and early spring, brown bog and bolt axle breaking on the sudden dips from hard permafrost to molten quagmire, ruts reducing the journey to a slide from side to side, small birds nestling in the cover of the truck's load, one or two peasants in small carts forcing the vehicle to leave the road for a harder surface, then fight its way back to the main route in time to meet more ruts and disintegrating surfaces.

'April is a schizophrenic month,' Schenck said when they stopped that night. He pulled the jute covering from the back of his truck. 'How are you?'

Summer indicated he was all right but shook his head when looking at Malty. 'I think he's running a temperature but he's freezing.'

'I'm all right,' Malty said. 'Just a little flu.'

'Where next?' Summer asked Schenck.

'You look at me with too much suspicion for comfort,' Schenck said. 'You think I'd drop you off at an Interior camp? Perhaps at the Lubyanka?'

'Your accent,' Summer said. 'Where are you from?'

'You should be worried where you are going. There's still a long way and you won't have me from here on.'

They walked along a track through a forest of birch, thin trees with silver barks, bending in the strong winds from the Urals, covered on one side by large flakes of snow which were now falling with the temperature, the hardened ground rutted in uniform folds, studded with round stones, a soft sheen of ice forming on the crust, the crust breaking now and then under the feet of the three men making their way towards the small house at the very end of the track.

The house was brown and bent a little to the left, as if many years facing the wind had slowly begun to push it over. It was dark inside except for a weak fire and two candles that barely lit the area around them, and the small torch the truck driver was carrying.

'You two stay here,' he said, 'I'll be back in the morning.' While Malty lay down, Summer grabbed Schenck, but he did not have the strength to hold the driver, who pushed him off. 'Do you not think that if I wanted to betray you I would have brought you straight to the police? I said I will be back. I will be back. There is bread and salt and vodka on the table. Eat and sleep.'

'Why do you do this?' Summer asked Schenck while he was leaving. On one level Summer already knew the answer because he had seen scores of people like Schenck, but on another he needed to hear it from the mouth of this man Brytenn had produced from a hat. There was an element of control in all of it. What else did Brytenn have up his sleeve?

Schenck first thought before answering, then scratched his beard. 'I first came here in 1914, as a prisoner of war,' he said. 'I was locked up for twenty years. When they let me out, I could not go home. I did not want to go home. Somewhere near Klagenfurt, there is a woman with children, probably with grandchildren. My wife, and . . .' He stopped there and left.

'Hey,' Malty said to Summer then. 'Leave him alone. He's a good guy.'

'And I suppose you can tell at a glance?'

'I'm a prisoner,' Malty said.

Malty and Summer were playing cards for small twigs when Schenck returned. And Malty looked to be making progress against the illness that had reduced him to a shivering wreck earlier. In fact, if anything, Summer now looked less healthy than his colleague.

Half a bottle of vodka sat at Jack Summer's elbow, while the remains of a loaf of black bread lay on a plate in the middle of the table. But only Malty seemed to have eaten any of the bread. The two men paused to watch Schenck enter.

'You've been a while,' Summer said. 'Did you go to meet Brytenn?'

A flurry of snowflakes had followed Schenck in and he paused to sweep them to one side, grinning while he did. Two of his teeth were missing and his tongue was a deep red hue that reminded Summer of inflammation. Which brought him to Brytenn again. And there he left it.

'It is arranged,' Schenck said then.

'If that storm keeps up we won't be going anywhere,' Summer said. More to re-establish some of his own status than any real comment on their situation.

'Oh, don't mind that,' Schenck said. 'Spring is here. The snow only comes at night now. The sun will take care of it in the morning. We only have to watch the rain. That's the real problem at this time of year. The roads are so bad.'

Schenck went over to a cupboard, pulled it back and took out a box hidden in the wall behind. 'I must make a few telephone calls,' he joked, checking his radio transmitter. 'To make sure your route is safe. Don't worry, everything is well-oiled. Brytenn is a clever chap. Yeah?'

Summer nodded, reluctantly.

'So where exactly are we going?' Malty said then. He presented his hand to Summer as if to emphasise his point. 'Three aces.'

'I swear this guy cheats,' Summer said.

'Or your mind is not on the game,' Schenck commented.

'You may be right there.'

'I think he's in love,' Malty said to Schenck. And he made the appropriate gestures with his hands. He began to collect his winnings. 'So where are we going?' he asked again. 'Look, if anything should happen . . . I've spent long enough in prison. I wanna go home, Jack.'

Schenck looked at Summer and shook his head. Summer drank from his bottle and that and everything on his mind that evening helped contribute to his decision in equal amounts. 'Get me a map,' he said to Schenck.

In the morning, the snow had stopped. Jack Summer woke with a slight hangover. Victor Malty was sitting at the table, drinking tea and studying Schenck's maps. He looked so well Summer began to wonder if the pilot had ever been ill. However, his own state of health was his main concern.

'Jesus, I went hard at that stuff last night,' Summer said.

'That, you did.'

'Where's the Kraut?'

'Austrian. There's a difference.'

Summer rubbed his head and searched for some water. 'Yeah, yeah, where is he?'

'Over there.'

Summer went to go over to Schenck but hesitated. A small trickle of dark blood had caught his eye and the sunlight at about the same time. When Summer swung back to Malty, the pilot was pointing a silenced nine-millimetre pistol at him.

'It's his,' Malty said. 'Mauser parabellum.'

'Why didn't you just wait till we got where we're going?' Summer asked. He placed the jug of water he was holding on top of a pine cupboard and lowered his hands to his sides.

'I have my own deadlines,' Malty said. 'Which I have neither the time nor the inclination to explain to you. Outside, please.'

'Why don't you just do it here?'

'Take him.' Malty looked at Schenck.

They walked about two hundred metres from the house, to a small mound, surrounded by birches, full of singing birds now the wind had died and the sun was beginning to melt the snows of the previous night. Summer carried Schenck on his shoulder.

'Look, who the hell are you working for?' Summer said once. ''Cause I can tell you, you won't live.'

But Malty ignored him until they reached a spot he had

obviously prepared while Summer had been sleeping. Summer's anger was mostly directed at himself. And at Brytenn. But for different reasons.

'Right, dig.'

Malty pointed to a spade and then stepped back. At first, Summer was inclined to refuse. What more could happen than was going to happen anyway? But his desire for life was strong and he found himself reaching for the spade despite his best efforts at dignity. Malty stood well back, so that Summer had no chance to get him with the spade.

'You'd gladly split my head,' he said.

There was no talk while Summer dug. He understood something of the nature of the people he had seen on newsreels digging their own graves in front of SS death squads. Then Malty told him to stop.

'Put him in there.'

Summer lifted Schenck and dropped him into the hole.

'Now, you, kneel down, hands behind your head.'

Right at that moment Summer wanted to say something. He went to say something, but a sudden wheeze and a thump to the the back of his head brought only blackness.

Malty threw the last piece of dirt on the grave and scattered loose branches over the site before tossing the spade into the trees. He was sweating heavily, an oily secretion that left a slightly putrid odour under his arms and a savage thirst in his mouth, something that might have been exertion or the remains of what had been on him for days now.

When he had cleared out Schenck's house, he pulled himself into the Austrian's truck cab, started the engine and drove off. As he was leaving, he glanced once in the direction of the grave.

A metre below the surface Jack Summer awoke into a nightmare. Face down on Schenck's face, without light or air, the dead weight of wet clay pressing him into the body beneath him, the moist slithering of worms around his ears, the painful cold of the earth devouring him.

'Olga!'

He wrestled the earth around him in a sudden burst of blind panic, a twisting, writhing frenzy; pushing, scratching, scraping, spitting, choking, feeling the first signs of give in the loosening soil, praying it would give way, then pushing whatever he had with all the strength he could bring.

It took five attempts, five ghastly failures, five pleading, panicking efforts to break the earth's hold, and almost at the same moment he had screamed defeat at the silence, one of his hands broke free, then an arm, and, very slowly, a cold spitting rain welcomed him to the fresh air.

Outside, he rolled around in the rain, spitting and swearing, shaking until he soiled himself, then falling forward on to the ground, while the rain began to clean him. And now he was crying, screaming hoarse screams that no one heard and crying Olga Sharankova's name.

25

Tsaritsyn

Many hundreds of kilometres to the south, Olga Sharankova returned to a safe house near the Volga River, north of Stalingrad, through puddles left behind by rain, brilliant sunshine dancing along behind her.

She made her way down a soft hillside through ground scored with bluffs, past what must have been a battle-ground. Old rusting German tanks littered the area, like grotesque sculptures, and the remains of uniforms pushed out of the softening earth in small gaseous bumps, causing Olga to stop and contemplate the possibility of an entire German infantry company rising from their graves at that moment.

Six years after the battle, Stalingrad still bore the immediate scars of war but was slowly being wiped clean of the holocaust of 1942 and 1943. Olga had been there in 1945, when the place still resembled an ant hill kicked to pieces by some angry giant, and the people were gaunt and pallid and stooped like overripe corn someone had forgotten to harvest. Now they were beginning to straighten up, still carrying fatalism like a birthmark but more robust. They had had their catastrophe.

And survived. She was about to make comparisons with herself but decided not to.

She could remember the war only as a series of small visitations. First the Germans, then the Red Army, then the Germans again. Then each of them visited within hours. Then people left their houses and took to the forests. But the visitations continued.

Olga Sharankova listened to the wind in the rusting shells of the tanks and the flapping of small pieces of uniform and backed off up a steeper slope than she needed, through thorns and high grass before she reached the ridge of a bluff and she could see her destination.

The house was supposed to be derelict, a lonely protrusion on the flatscape, a coagulation interrupting the free flow of the land, buried in the jaws of a small fold and surrounded by a few tall trees at distances that made their presence a mystery. They provided no cover. Distance and the land did that. Far beyond the house, on what was probably a road, Olga could see a cart.

Then Cooper Brytenn came out of the house and went over to a well. He pulled a bucket from the well and filled what looked like a trough and splashed water on his face before beginning to shave. She watched him shave for a while and then cocked her pistol and checked the ammunition in it before coming down the slope in the cover of small trees and lengthening grasses swaying in the gathering wind.

'Any joy?' Cooper Brytenn cleaned his face before coming to meet her. He seemed to have developed a second layer of skin, so that his face gave you very different speech from his mouth.

'Nothing,' she replied. 'If they are caught, then this place could be full of security police and troops . . . now.'

'Then we have to assume they are not caught,' Brytenn said. 'Otherwise, you and I would have serious problems.' His smile did not convince her. 'We don't have these places growing on trees, Olga,' he added. 'And this one is reaching the end of its usefulness. I saw two lovers walking about a kilometre that way. They found a place to do what they had to. But sooner or later someone, maybe kids, will come here.'

'Did you try Schenck again?' she asked him.

'No reply. We must wait to be contacted.'

'We should be in town,' she said. 'So many new people have moved here, no one would notice.'

'One more day here,' he said.

She came closer and Brytenn cleaned his face again. Ivan Pyotr watched them from the window. Olga noticed.

'How much do you trust him?' Olga asked Brytenn.

'About as much as I do you,' he replied. 'Look, I know you're worried about Jack. I am too. I kinda like the bastard. He's like a younger brother I once had.' This was a lie and Brytenn stopped immediately.

'Let me look at your ankle,' Olga said.

He leaned against the trough and raised his foot. And when she bent down to it, he touched her hair.

'You've taken more morphine?' she asked.

'Tell me what you think?' he asked.

'I think you should not take any more morphine. I cannot see any infection. Maybe it is healing.'

'I don't think so.'

That night Ivan Pyotr cooked a rabbit stew and the three of them ate in silence. Pyotr ate very slowly, sometimes stopping while his stomach attempted to cope with food it had not touched in three decades. Occasionally, the old police colonel belched or broke wind, and apologised to Olga, who could only smile for a short time because she was watching Brytenn.

'It is a terrible thing to be pulled in different directions,' Pyotr said to her when the two of them were cleaning the wooden plates in a stone sink afterwards. Brytenn was sitting at the window with a rifle in his hand and a map on his knee, in a degree of discomfort he wanted to conceal. Pyotr moved his shoulder in the American's direction.

'You should keep your thoughts to yourself, old man,' Olga said. 'I can look after myself.'

'I'm sure you can, my dear. Look, I was just trying to make conversation. Prisoners only have conversation. Nothing else. And I am an old prisoner, old and frightened. I used to inspire fear, you know. Now I am the frightened one. That is a bad state of affairs, believe me.'

'They will not thank you for what you are doing,' she said. 'Brytenn's people.'

'What else can I do? I served the Tsar with everything in my power. I gave my soul to him.'

'He's dead. And I don't believe in souls.'

'What did they do to you?' Pyotr asked. He put his hand on hers and she filled up and then pulled away, her hard face full of latent tenderness but held together by fear and hatred.

'She's a little upset, no?' Pyotr said to Brytenn later.

'She's worried, Colonel.'

'I don't blame her,' Pyotr said. He began to smoke a pipe. He handed the pipe to Brytenn, who felt he should take a smoke. 'We're so damned exposed here,' Pyotr added.

'You're not afraid someone will recognise you when we move?' Brytenn asked. 'An old enemy? Someone who was in prison with you?'

'I suppose it's possible. But I'm more concerned with people nosing in on us. Russians are annoyingly curious. How do you think the Okhrana did so well against the subversives for so long? Russians are born spies. Born informers. Spite, jealousy, all the great virtues of poverty, we played on them like little instruments. Stalin – Vasili – he was a prime example. We had him by the balls, but he could have said, fuck you, kill me, you know, take his medicine. No, he started slowly, but by the time he was in full flight, he was executing his own people for us, and enjoying it. There is a power in secrecy that only the poor know.'

'Do you wonder about the file?' Brytenn asked him.

'So near,' Pyotr smiled.

'You have no doubts?'

'I cannot afford to. And what better place for such a document than a church?'

'Stalin hates churches.'

'Only the big ones. Old priests, Brytenn. The communists have not moved against the small village ones. They are just closed, waiting for better times. I know my Russians. Village people may be collectivised but they still hang on to the faith. I picked my spot well, Mr Brytenn. The left bank of the Volga has been safe, through all these years of trouble. I even met men in Camp Thirty-Six who had seen the village where I buried the Vasili file. They were able to tell me about it. Political prisoners of one sort or another. Good men.'

Brytenn's mind had shifted back to Olga. Pyotr noticed.

'Never, in all my years, did I give up hope of getting out and retrieving my files.' Pyotr nodded furiously. 'A man must live for something.'

'I cannot guarantee you any more than the Vasili file,'

Brytenn said. 'The rest, wherever you have them, will have to wait.'

'And how much longer must we wait here?'

'Not long. There are footnotes being written, shall we say.'

Brytenn was staring at Olga.

Olga sat beside Brytenn at three in the morning, while a small rain shower cleared the air. She wore a blanket over her shoulders. 'I don't want to sleep,' she said.

'And I can't,' he said.

There was so much more in what they said that each of them was forced to pause and draw breath. She examined his eyes. He examined her body. She touched his forehead. She touched his ear.

'Don't ask me about morphine,' he said then.

She rubbed his leg without asking him anything about it. 'You should hear him snoring in there. Pyotr. I think he's happy. It's a long time since I have seen someone happy.'

'He's not happy,' Brytenn said.

Olga ran her hand up to his groin. 'Are you?' she asked.

'You're so confident?' Brytenn said.

She lifted her hand. He put it back and placed his in the same position on her body. She closed her eyes and said something in Polish.

What happened next was clumsy at first, and Brytenn had to roll off her when she could not receive his erection. Then Olga lay on him and he stroked her. It took time for her to become wet and they kissed while they waited.

'Try again,' she said when she felt ready.

'You want to dominate me?' he asked.

She rolled off. They lay, looking out of the window, laughing softly for a time, counting the stars, drinking from a bottle of vodka until she reached out for him. This time he entered her easily. It did not last very long.

'I lied to you,' she said later, when he was dressing. 'I'm exhausted. I just cannot sleep. I'm too worried.'

Brytenn sighed. 'Keep your worries to yourself,' he said.

As he did, Jack Summer's train entered one of those oceanic vistas of rolling hills punctuated by distant clumps of trees that resembled huge liners or merchantmen, while the land appeared to roll in the dawn sunshine and the gentle breeze beginning to push up from the south was slowly gaining the upper hand against the weakening Siberians, causing a ripple effect on the grasses and a striped colouring to the fields.

Every moment of his journey so far he had expected arrest. But twice the security police had stopped just before completing the search of his carriage, and once they had accepted his documentation without questioning him or looking at him properly. If they had they might have seen the coagulated blood on his hair, from the wound which made him sleep incessantly. He only managed to keep himself awake now by thinking about Olga, something he had struggled with for so many hours now he wondered, ridiculously he thought, if he would recognise her again.

So, very methodically, between the sharp pains in his head, he began to piece together a picture of her from the recesses of his memory, small mosaics of reassurance that told him he was on the right road. And he could rest.

Except that Malty was out there, with all he knew. Any rest

Summer had won for himself was lost when he thought about Malty. And then he passed out again.

When Summer regained consciousness he was on a bed. He staggered through a room he did not recall entering and into a bathroom he did not recognise. His head wound was bleeding again, and the headache made him want to shut his eyes. But as soon as he shut his eyes he remembered the grave. So he opened them again and found there was another face in the mirror. A girl's face. It was long and expectant, with tiny hairs above the lip and small lower teeth. And the eyes were brown and warm.

'I brought you tea and something to eat,' she said.

'Who are you?' he asked.

'I found you in my doorway. People said you were drunk. They called the police. I said you were my friend. Have some tea. Eat.' She put the tray she was holding down on a table and went to touch his head. He stopped her. 'You need a doctor,' she said.

'Have you called one?'

'What happened?'

'I was attacked.'

'Then I will get a doctor.'

She touched his wound. He did not stop her this time. She took a small cloth from behind her, soaked it in water and began wiping the blood.

'I don't need a doctor.'

'I think you have a fracture. I'm a nurse.'

'What's your name, nurse?'

'Anastasia. They call me the Grand Duchess round here, for a joke. Some joke. You?'

'Josef,' he lied. 'I was on a train. I came to Stalingrad. Then I don't remember.' He smelled his hands. 'Alcohol,' he said.

'Yeah, you reeked of it. I figured you for a drunk, too. Till I found this.' She held up a wad of money. 'Whoever attacked you wasn't looking for riches.'

'Where is this place?'

'This is the village of Vasili. Though we are told to say town now. Some town. But we're almost a suburb of Stalingrad, if on the wrong side of the river, so I suppose you could say we're a town. We all work in Stalingrad.'

Summer went to the window and looked out on the street. In the distance, over some rooftops, he could see flickers of light bouncing on the Volga, and beyond that he did not bother with.

'You live alone?' he asked.

'My mother is on her way back from Moscow. Please lie down. Eat, drink, rest. I have to go to work now but I'll be back later. Don't go out. There's no need. Mind if I use some of this to get things? I know prices are coming down but . . .'

Summer nodded. 'What street is this?' he asked then.

'There is only one street in Vasili,' she replied.

'Yes,' he said.

He ate a kind of sausage meat and cheese dish and washed it down with tea from a small samovar and a spirit that resembled perfume. The spirit made him drowsy and he slept again. When he woke, his wound was dressed and there was a note beside the bed. Anastasia had come back for an hour. There was a piece of fruit on the note. Then Summer remembered coming across the river, with some soldiers on leave, getting drunk with them to avoid the security police, telling stories.

Outside, in blasts of afternoon sunshine, he approached the address he had come for. At the very end of the street, like a giant monument, or a warning before the countryside, a three-storey house stood where the church should have been, a red-brick and wooden construction that seemed to have plagiarised several architectural eras and been rejected as a residence by all but those who manage to let years go by without really noticing what is going on outside.

The men sitting on the porch were young men who had missed the war, long thin men with gaunt faces and the timid arrogance of knowing they were the inheritors of a victory they had not contributed to.

They were laughing, drinking vodka and playing cards when Summer got to the picket fence across the street, and the barking dogs caused them little more than the odd glance out into the cold daylight.

'Jesus,' Summer muttered to himself.

Had he believed in a saviour, Anatoli Beshov probably would have spoken His name with the same solemnity as Jack Summer. But Beshov was too busy trying to save his own life to even consider the possibility of there ever being a supreme being 'stupid enough to take on human form', as he once put it himself.

'She led me on,' he shouted to Romanovili. 'Tell him. Tell Beria.'

Romanovili just looked at the ground, now flecked with small rusty puddles from a recent shower, and then over at the young girl in Lavrenti Beria's arms. Romanovili smoked another cigarette while Beria told his men to put the SS major down on his knees.

'I told you he was a useless investment,' he said to Romanovili. 'You witnessed what his kind did to our Motherland during the Great Patriotic War. For all we know, they left him behind deliberately, to put us off their scent.'

'No!' Beshov shouted. He tried to break free.

The two guards holding him, young Tartarish men from Kazan, who were far too strong for Beshov, shoved the turncoat down on the sandy ground, pulled his arms back and pushed his head forward.

'I was only having fun with her,' Beshov squealed. 'Shit, I'm only a man. The fucking bitch came on to me. I swear it.'

Which was the truth. Beria had told her to. For what reason, Vladimir Romanovili could only guess. Perhaps the old hatchetman just wanted someone to kill. Probably there was a deeper motive. Romanovili found he did not care. Better you than me, he thought. And in doing so he almost gave away his own feelings. Which Beria noticed.

'I blame you,' Beria said to him. Then he kicked Beshov in the spine and waited for his men to pull the SS major back into position.

Then Beria pulled out a pistol and cocked it. He placed it to the back of Beshov's head. 'You little SS shit.'

'I know. I know.' Beshov kept nodding. 'Please, you need me.'

'You're a disease,' Beria said. 'And I don't want to risk any more infection.'

The pause that followed was almost unbearable for Romanovili. He found himself trembling. Beshov kept speaking, jumbled phrases, pieces of useless information, details of Cooper Brytenn's team. And then suddenly, with a very calm voice, he said: 'I know where they might be. There's a safe house in Stalingrad. If they are headed down there, then that's where they'll be.'

Beria lifted his pistol. 'That's better,' he said. 'I knew you'd be more co-operative if we were able to impress upon you the consequences of holding back information.'

Anatoli Beshov collapsed on the wet ground, moaning, cursing Cooper Brytenn.

26

Reunions

Victor Malty emerged from a house just west of the river in Stalingrad with a new suit and the beginnings of a beard, the sense of a wounded animal all over his body, holding himself in the manner of one expecting to be arrested at any moment. The remains of the fever he had had were still with him but the sheer force of an iron will forged in Camp Thirty-Six meant that Malty could feel it breaking.

He walked straight up prospekt Lenina and then down a street of low houses with broken picket fences and a chorus of dogs.

The street was broken and speckled with mounds of gravel and lines of hardened tar. Each of the homes had a vegetable patch with the remains of the previous crop lying about, having thawed out, now preparing to decay in the gathering heat of the spring.

Each day the temperature rose a little more, and while some of the roads were still quagmires, the sun was gradually sucking the moisture from the earth and the beginnings of the summer dust were taking shape.

Soon the whole country would be dust and the hardest thing would be to prevent yourself from blowing away.

The cafe where Malty stopped overlooked a small pond with black swans and geese in it, moving with the seasons. There were people in shirt sleeves, too, drinking spirits and laughing.

'Victor!'

Malty smiled at the hand raised up from behind a newspaper and walked over to the man who had hailed him. The man's face was still buried in his newspaper. 'I'm glad to see you, too, Reggie,' Malty said.

Misha Girenko, looking younger now his hair was coloured, smiled, folded his paper and moved his seat over to allow Malty to sit next to him.

'No second thoughts?' Girenko said. His colourless lips and broken nose made him somehow less menacing than Malty remembered. But the pilot was still coming to terms with what he had done to Jack Summer. Everything Misha Girenko had been born to, Victor Malty had had to be taught.

'About a country that left me to stew?' Malty said. 'No, no second thoughts.'

Girenko looked around him, wheezed and coughed. 'Just so I haven't left you with any troubles.'

Malty looked around and then smiled. 'No.' He put his hand on Girenko's. 'I've always known what I was doing, Reggie.'

'Not here,' Girenko said. 'Let's go somewhere peaceful where we can play arias and drink vodka. And you can tell me everything in private.'

Malty looked around again, pained by what he had to say now. 'They're not there, Reggie,' he said. 'They're not where I was told they'd be. They must have switched safe houses.'

'Why would they do that?'

'I left no traces, Reggie,' Malty insisted.

'Maybe you were lied to,' Girenko said. He thought for a while. 'Well, they're here, somewhere. Come on, let's go.'

'You look well, Reggie,' Malty said as they were getting up.

'A little spell in prison. You know how it is. Mary's well. I've kept an eye on her one way and another.'

'I missed your letters the most, you know,' Malty said.

'Yes,' Girenko said, somewhat tired of their conversation already. Then he grinned. 'I wonder what your friends are up to. Let's go settle the matter, if we can.'

Then they left.

A few hours later, on the same side of the Volga, Cooper Brytenn watched the everyday pace of fatalism trundle through the high bluffs above the Volga while he made his way through the rebuilding process of Stalingrad. Twice, he was stopped by security police, twice, numbed by too many pain killers and pale from the strain on him, he was let go, the forged identity papers he had eliciting no more than a cursory glance that spring morning. The newspapers talked of imperialism and aggression in Germany, the people in the streets of prices and the dead. Always the dead.

Brytenn stopped at a cemetery that happened to be near a bus stop and the remains of a factory which had been the subject of vicious fighting during the battle with the Germans. Beshov had once said men who went to evacuate themselves were found impaled on their own frozen movements, and that one Russian ski unit found a German temporary latrine full of men whose urine had frozen them to the walls. But then Beshov lied like most people drew breath, Brytenn almost told himself.

'So where is he, this police colonel?'

Patrick Twilight stood next to the grave of a young officer of a Guards regiment, holding a newspaper.

'Good to see you, too, Patrick.'

Twilight thought Brytenn looked for all the world like an American pretending to be a Russian, and was almost inclined to run. But, aside from the obvious strain on his face, which was a bonus in Stalingrad, Brytenn's own self-confidence, the very thing that surely marked him out in a society like the Soviet Union, was enough to hold Twilight there.

'We shouldn't stand here,' Twilight said by way of compromise, 'it draws attention. And we haven't time for niceties. You've shifted safe houses?'

'Of course,' Brytenn said. 'Look, maybe Malty doesn't know about Girenko and his old lady. Maybe there's nothing to worry about.'

'I take it he and his companion still haven't turned up?' Twilight said. 'I think there's cause for concern, Cooper.'

'Keep it to yourself when we get to where we're going. And don't look so damned uncomfortable. You in trouble, Patrick?'

'Let's say I'm having difficulty treading water.'

'Jesus, I have to drop in by parachute, but you, Patrick, you just walk right in. I bet you even bought gifts. I'll tell you, you British have style.'

Twilight took it almost as a compliment. 'We've pulled out everything for you, Cooper. My way in is your way out. So far we're using every sympathiser we have on either side of the Volga. What's happened to your leg?'

'Nothing a good sawbones can't fix. You bring morphine?' Brytenn felt he was giving something away. 'Anyway,' he said then, 'it's good to see you, Patrick. Brings home that bit closer. I know you haven't been behind the lines for some time.'

'You wonder whether you still have it,' Twilight commented. 'I have to say there were times when I was quite terrified coming in. So many security checks. You people must have created some storm up there. I'm awfully sorry about the casualties. Still, all in a good cause, as they say.'

'You don't fool me with all that polite reserve nonsense, Patrick. It's the Reds I feel sorry for. What's the situation in Berlin?'

'Hairline. Some chaps in Washington want to just pulverise Uncle Joe. Some want to back off and leave Berlin. So you'll understand why we're pulling out all the stops here. We need an edge and this could be it.'

They walked down a lonely road to the north of the city, then took a walk by the river. 'So tell me everything, from the start,' Twilight said.

Ivan Pyotr was sitting at a window, writing a letter, when Twilight and Brytenn arrived back from the city. The old colonel was calm and his eyes had narrowed to small points on which anyone who wished to talk to him could focus themselves. Or hang themselves, maybe, Twilight thought.

'Delighted, Colonel.' Twilight employed that diplomatic sophistication some Englishmen, no matter what their class, receive as a birthright, and Pyotr found himself forced to shake hands. When he touched his letter again, his hands were wet and he smudged his writing. Twilight began reading the letter.

'It's for a friend,' Pyotr explained. 'Who may or may not be alive.'

Twilight backed off and apologised. 'There are some

aspects of this work I despise,' he said. 'You'll appreciate what I mean, Colonel. Give me the letter when you're finished and I'll see it's posted.'

'So you've come for Vasili, too,' Pyotr said. 'He's a very popular man. I am a very popular man.' All of a sudden, Pyotr swelled up with pride and Twilight could see residues of that strength that had once made the police colonel feared and hated. 'Flavour of the month, I believe the expression is. You have heard of it?'

Twilight indicated he had and sat down. He asked Olga Sharankova for a drink and she almost refused him. But Twilight stared at her sharply, and, unlike most other men, did not immediately fall for her, which gave him an advantage he recognised on her face. And she obeyed his request.

She sat away from them after that, cleaning weapons. Twilight kept his eyes on her while talking to Brytenn.

'So, what do you want to do?' Brytenn asked Twilight.

'Make our play,' Twilight said.

'Jack Summer knows the target,' Brytenn said. And now his own concerns were rising to the top. 'And I can't switch that.' He looked over at Olga for support.

'They might be waiting for us,' Olga said. 'If Jack and Malty are caught.'

'I appreciate that,' Twilight said, almost wanting to tell her about Malty but not quite sure of the significance of the pilot himself. 'But if that's the case, then we're redundant anyway. Colonel Pyotr?'

'Redundancy is something men like us dread all our lives, Mr Twilight. Yes? I'm not sure freedom is such a good swap for it.'

'I think I understand you. Perhaps that's what brings me here. Cooper?'

'Jack Summer will not talk unless . . .'

'He's trustworthy,' Olga interrupted. 'Completely trust-worthy.'

Twilight thought her aspect full of hate, but did not dwell on it for too long and did not question her about it. The hatred was not for him and in his opinion women usually reacted by playing the victim when accused of something of which they were guilty. He had seen it so many times it had become detectable simply by its effect on other things.

'You and Jack Summer were close, I take it?'

Twilight sat down beside Olga and offered her a cigarette. Olga refused. She watched him prepare his questions, and noticed that the emotions on parts of his face remained separate. He could smile without showing concern, he could be friendly without warmth in his eyes. He leaned in close to her.

'They have not found us,' she said.

'You were ambushed before.'

She looked around at Brytenn. 'They were waiting for us then. Maybe your SS pig brought them with his smell.'

'Do you know how close we are to war again?' Twilight asked her.

'What's in this damn file?' she demanded.

'Patrick . . . ?' Brytenn interrupted.

The two men walked out to the porch, a high wooden construction that creaked with each step they took.

'Are you up to this?' Twilight asked Brytenn. 'With that ankle?' He was actually looking Brytenn over in more detail than the American would have liked. Probing for the weak-nesses both men knew were there.

Brytenn, who had had to take two shots of morphine where

one used to suffice, ran his hand along some of the carved reliefs on the wall. 'I've come this far.'

'That wasn't what I asked. How worried is she about Summer?'

'Enough,' Brytenn said. Everything about him seemed close to tearing apart at that moment, just as Twilight had intended.

'Oh, I see,' Twilight said.

'Do you, Patrick?' Brytenn asked. 'I hope you do. Because there are times – and I mean a lot of times – when I can't see a damn thing. Not a damn thing.'

27

Reactions

Patrick Twilight took one more look at the map and then tapped his fingers on the table. 'Tonight, no matter what,' he said. 'We should go for the file tonight, Cooper. If they have Summer, then it's just a matter of time before they get it out of him. And that's our only advantage. Time. So we go now.'

Cooper Brytenn scratched his head. He might have been suffering with lice. Olga was convinced he was and had insisted on searching for them earlier. Now, Brytenn was trying to reach a decision and coming very close to failing. 'And if Jack's talked?'

'Then, we're finished,' Twilight said.

Cooper Brytenn became cold and his colour changed. He looked to Olga for support.

She put her arm on his. 'Jack won't talk,' she said.

'Everyone talks,' Ivan Pyotr commented. And in those words he revealed more about himself than if he had spoken for an hour.

'At least Malty knows nothing,' Olga commented. 'That's something.' Her eyes displayed a concern that confused Patrick Twilight. She seemed to grip Brytenn tighter as she spoke.

Cooper Brytenn turned suddenly to her, then threw a pencil across the map. 'Look, Malty might not be completely with us,' he said.

'Oh, Christ!' Pyotr exclaimed. Now his facial expression said everything.

'How long have you known this?' Olga asked Brytenn.

'Not long enough,' Brytenn said.

'That's not the point,' Twilight insisted. 'The point is, if the file is there, then we go for it, Cooper. That's what you're here for. That's what I'm here for. As for the rest, Olga . . . well, you know the current price of one of us.'

'I think they call this a peculiar kind of creek, Olga,' Cooper Brytenn said. 'I'm sorry.'

'I'm authorised to assume . . .' Patrick Twilight knew that he did not have to finish his sentence.

'No!' Brytenn said. 'This is mine.' He stared at Olga. 'It's just I can't leave him. Summer. Not just like that.'

Olga rubbed his arm and he backed away from her and went to the door. He opened it and drew breaths of fresh air which soon became clogged with dust.

'He's probably dead, Cooper,' Olga said. She followed him to the door. He went outside and down a small path to one of the trees. Twilight sat back in a seat and poured himself a drink.

'That man should not be here,' Ivan Pyotr said.

'Tell me one of us who should,' Twilight replied.

Brytenn was sitting under the tree, splitting grasses when Olga arrived. She came to him hesitantly and in small movements, picking things up and studying them, watching the horizon, as if expecting to see something she had not already seen.

'I was never in Italy, you know,' he said. 'Well, not during the war. I missed the war, actually. Oh, I wanted to go, and I volunteered the way you're supposed to, but something always turned up. I got to Italy about a month after VE Day. It was part of my job to send people back to Russia and Yugoslavia.'

He dug at the earth with his fingers. Olga sat down beside him and put her arm around him. 'How's your ankle?'

'I could do with more morphine.'

She touched his head. 'You're sweating.'

'The heat.' It wasn't hot. 'You got some more?'

'Twilight has it,' she said.

'But you're the medic.' He looked back at the house. Twilight was standing in the window, staring at them. 'He's trying to . . . Tell him I need more.'

'He won't give it.'

'Just get it,' he said to her. But when she went to leave him, he pulled her back. 'I'm sorry,' he said. 'Look, my ankle's good. Probably isn't that painful once you get used to it. I was probably hitting on that stuff too much anyway. I want to tell you things, Olga.'

'Don't,' she said. 'I'm not interested.'

'I have to,' Brytenn said. 'Otherwise . . .'

'You won't be able to move?'

He nodded.

'You know, sometimes when I think of my father, I cannot move,' she said. 'He was a barge man on a big river when I was a kid. So proud of him, we were. He was killed when a tow-line snapped and sent half of him into the river. I recall that day often. They buried the rest the way you bury a man but my mother never rested easy knowing half of her husband was fish food in the Baltic Sea.' She laughed. 'Every time a large fish was landed, she expected to find her husband inside. This kind of thing sticks in your memory and to this day I will not eat fish. And you think you have problems.'

Brytenn wiped her face, slightly ashamed of himself. 'We should eat something,' he said. 'I need to eat. Head's aching.'

He pulled himself up with great effort, went back into the house and brought Olga a cup of soup and a stick of sausage. 'Eat it quickly, we're moving tonight,' he said.

'You better think twice about that.'

They both looked up to see Jack Summer standing over them, a long shadow stretching into the trees.

'That goddam church of yours is a police station.'

'Where's Malty?' Brytenn asked.

'Who the hell do you think did this?'

Summer toppled over.

28

Vasili

That evening, not too far away, in a squalid little room near the Volga, during the beginnings of a thunderstorm, Vladimir Romanovili touched Victor Malty's mouth and felt revolted by the rigid skin. Then he looked up at Anatoli Beshov.

'So they are here. Your friends are in Stalingrad.'

'No friends of mine,' Beshov insisted. 'Though I did like the squadron leader. He had certain qualities I admire. But perhaps just a little too much personal loyalty for his own health.'

Romanovili threw his hand out and caught Beshov across the face. 'I will tolerate about this much more from you,' he said, demonstrating with his fingers. 'I have too many dead men, and now this. I'll tell you what we're looking for may well cause the deaths of many more people before it is over. We should have been quicker. Smarter. You know, Beria wanted to kill you when that safe house turned out to be empty. I saved you, Beshov.'

Beshov had a habit many men of his persuasion learn, of trying to mirror the feelings of those in positions of power over him, yet at the same time searching out a weakness. He allowed himself to be dominated but began eating away at Romanovili's defences. 'Then I am in your debt,' he said, chewing on a piece of food left uneaten.

That was when Romanovili snapped past him and picked up a piece of bread. 'Teeth,' he said. 'Whoever did this, he's left a bite mark.'

It completely upended Beshov, who scrambled around for a supporting platform, and found it in the body of Victor Malty.

'He was killed from behind,' he said. 'That's a spade wound.'

Romanovili, who was telling one of his men to take the bread for dental analysis, looked over at Beshov. 'What does that have to do with it? And what's a spade wound?'

'Do you know what a Gravedigger is?'

Romanovili nodded. 'Sure. GRU specialists. But so what?'

'Forget the teeth. This man was killed by a Gravedigger.'

Misha Girenko replaced the telephone when he heard the noise on the staircase; the old woman took some time to make it to the top and by the time she did, Girenko was sitting there, holding a book.

The woman dropped the small kitten she was holding. It ran across the floor and took refuge under Girenko's chair. Only a slender shaft of light illuminated its paws. The rest fell across Misha Girenko. 'You do recognise me, Mother?' he asked. 'It's Misha!'

The old woman took her time studying his face, the thin nose on her dried fruit face sniffing the atmosphere for any evidence her weak eyes could no longer provide. She shuffled closer to Girenko, who then stood up, forcing the kitten to seek shelter somewhere else. 'Misha!' The old woman raised her hands slowly to her son's face and began feeling for his features and with each one she exclaimed his name again and again.

'I need to stay with you, Mother,' Girenko said later. 'Not for long.'

For a time she just talked without really acknowledging him, and he wondered if she really knew he was there. She went about her tasks with a measured delicacy, dropping names to him and mentioning old fragments of gossip as if they were current. Girenko allowed himself to wallow in the softness of her voice and the smooth flow of her words, drinking tea while the sun began to fill the room.

The room was a small affair even by the small affairs of the time, and everything appeared to be everything else when you looked at it from a certain angle. The smoky atmosphere was accentuated by the factory fumes pouring in from the street and the small fires on the waste ground about a hundred metres away.

'You'll want food,' Mrs Girenko said then, unprompted, and began to lay the table.

'Have I changed?' Girenko asked her, as if he needed her to confirm he was who he thought he was.

'Yes,' she replied. She appeared to consider adding to the answer but went about cutting bread and wrapping meat in a salted cabbage leaf and placing it in a baking tray.

'So many years, Mother,' Girenko said. He was beginning to realise why he had left in the first place and intended mentioning his father. Then something prevented him and instead of sitting there drinking he stood up, went over to his mother and took the baking tray from her.

'You do remember me?' he asked her.

She stood still and began to cry and shake at the same time, so that it looked like the crying was a result of the shaking and the shaking a reaction to the tears. Then she began to shake her head and mutter little pleadings. Misha Girenko reached out and took his mother in his arms.

'I can't stay long, Mother.'

The spiteful invective coming at him forced Vladimir Romanovili back on his heels while Lavrenti Beria threw his arms around like a wild beast tearing at the flesh of some unseen prey, his big bulk slamming itself down on the floorboards with such force that occasionally one of them would spring up at the skirting board across the room.

'Would you have me for a fool? A fool?' he demanded. 'A Gravedigger! A Gravedigger! Bring me this Gravedigger's fucking head on a plate. Or yours!'

Then, as suddenly as the tantrum had begun, it stopped. Beria relaxed his heavy shoulders and lowered his arms to his side before pulling off his pince-nez and rubbing them with his handkerchief.

'Vladimir, do you understand what is happening here?'

Romanovili did not so much respond as try to repeat what he thought was on Beria's mind. 'The battle for the future of socialism.'

Beria's smile became laughter very slowly, like an engine turning over, and the Georgian began shaking his head and heaving his great chest. Romanovili felt forced to laugh too but his laughter never got the better of his fear.

'My God, you understand well,' Beria said. 'If what I believe is happening indeed is, then there are games closer to home being played out right now and our time is limited.'

Every question Romanovili was afraid to ask was evident on his face.

'Find Pyotr,' Beria said. 'With the messenger will come the message.'

Beria went behind his desk and pulled out a small pistol. He checked it and then pointed it at Romanovili. 'You see this? You see what I will do if you appear in front of me with nothing to show again? I will shoot you dead. With this. It's a twenty-two. A piss of a weapon. But I will use it on you.'

When Beria had gone, Romanovili came out into the Stalingrad evening for air and rubbed his brow. Anatoli Beshov was standing with his back to a wall, watching some men pass a bottle of vodka around. Further away, three children were playing in an upstairs room.

'Christ, that man will be the death of me,' Romanovili said.

'Or you will be the death of him,' Beshov said.

'Don't be smart,' Romanovili replied. 'You just remember you're alive only because I say so.'

'If there are Gravediggers involved then perhaps all your efforts will be in vain,' Beshov said. 'Who else would want what you're looking for?'

'It's obvious,' Romanovili said. 'Gravediggers are GRU, military intelligence. The Red Army.'

'So who in the army?' Beshov said 'What about Zhukov, conquerer of the Nazis, the greatest general we've had this century, now stuck down in the Crimea? How do you think he feels? He might end his career running a power station or accused of treason.'

'He would have to have political support.'

'Molotov,' Beshov said. 'Fired from the job he loved. Wife under a cloud.'

'Are you trying to scare me?' Romanovili asked.

'Perhaps Beria is the wrong player in this game. If I knew what was in the file Pyotr has.'

'You don't want to know.'

'If I am to help you.'

'You think that kind of talk justifies your existence?' Romanovili asked.

'I have to justify my existence?' Beshov asked. 'Why would the British or Americans seek this file? What use is it to them?'

'Forget it,' Romanovili said. 'And we must all justify ourselves, Herr Sturmbannführer. You led a team here in early 1943, yes? When the Germans were cut off. You brought some men out of the pocket. You brought some Americans out of the pocket, is that right?'

'I was a prisoner of war in Germany. Caught fighting for the Red Army. Anything spoken against me is pro-paganda designed to undermine the great victory of the Red Army.'

'They were an embarrassment to the Americans, these men you led out. Washington did not want them captured, so they paid us to let them through the lines.'

'I recall a village where the trees were in autumn flame and the partisans came one day and asked for a particular man. I do not recall his name, but he was not there and no one had heard from him in months. So the partisans began hanging villagers, the old men first, by age, the old women next, then the middle-agers, men and women, and so on. It went on all day. They left

276

one little girl when they left, the youngest person in the village. The Germans found her and looked after her for a few weeks. Then they shot her.'

'Are you trying to say there was an equality?' Romanovili asked.

'Oh, no. The Germans were far more merciful. She could not live with what the Reds had left her. She was too lonely. There are things worse than death, as they say.'

'You will not be so blasé when they are peeling your skin off in the cellars of the Lubyanka.'

'Then we had better succeed.'

'So where are they? Your American friend, Brytenn, and his followers?'

'They will show themselves,' Beshov said. 'You just be ready to strike.'

'I'm relying on you to point them out,' Romanovili said.

When Olga Sharankova curled into a ball in the corner of the safe house and began to cry, it happened so subtly that most of the men in the room did not even notice. Ivan Pyotr was the first to see her but he did nothing. What had been left to him in emotions he needed for himself now, because, as they drew nearer to their goal, his whole reason for being had begun to fade away.

When Brytenn looked at her, Olga just gestured to Jack Summer, sitting in a heavy chair, one eye closed, looking for all the world like a corpse.

'You think he can go like that?' she asked Brytenn. 'I think his skull is cracked under that bandage.'

'We need him,' Brytenn said.

'Look at him!' Olga shouted. This time she directed her

anger at Twilight, but he said nothing and stayed out of much of what followed until it had worn itself out.

Summer opened his closed eye, stood up, and staggered like a drunk, as he struggled to keep his feet. 'I'm fine, Olga,' he insisted. 'Fine.'

'No, you're not!' she exclaimed. And she dipped her head into her legs as if that fact had undermined everything that had ever held her together.

While Summer searched the other faces for support, outside the wind blew across the steppe and the rain drummed on the windows in large drops.

Brytenn came over to Olga. He took her hands. 'We need him, Olga,' he said. 'And you.'

'He's the last one,' she replied. 'Can't you see? All the others are dead. So even if they didn't plan all this just to get to us and kill us all, that's what's happened. And now Malty's out there, telling them where we are.'

'No,' Brytenn said.

'I sent him somewhere else,' Summer added. At the same time, he came across the room and stood over her. He was carrying a small knapsack. 'Take this,' he said to her. She pushed it away.

'Take it yourself. Look at him,' she said to Brytenn. 'He's not even thirty and he's an old man. You could set up house in his cheeks and sell the colour in his eyes to the devil.'

'I agree, we're not much of a crew,' Brytenn said.

'We're no crew,' she said. 'You, of all people, would make him go?'

'I'm going, Olga,' Summer said.

'Then you don't know what's good for you. You never have.'

'Are you coming?' Brytenn asked.

'If she doesn't want to come, then we should not force her,' Summer said.

'We're not,' Brytenn said.

Summer knew this was a point of authority and stood his ground in the face of Brytenn's arguments.

'She's not Swell Johnson, Cooper,' Summer said.

'What's that supposed to mean?'

'It means what it means.' Summer seemed unable to continue. It seemed that the two men might throw punches at each other but not over that. Then Twilight intervened and broke what remained of the argument into pieces.

'We'll travel in two sections,' he said. 'You, me and the colonel in the first, Cooper; Jack and the girl in the second.'

'I think Olga should come with me,' Brytenn protested. 'She's part of my team. My responsibility.'

'Precisely why she should not go with you, Cooper.'

'I might remind you I have tactical command here. Your own people in Washington and Munich have given it to me. Jack knows the situation. Right, Jack?'

'I think they should go together, Cooper,' Twilight said to Brytenn.

There was a moment when Brytenn looked like a little boy having his favourite toy taken away, but he managed to regain some of his dignity. He dropped Olga's hands.

Olga shook her head. 'You go,' she said to Brytenn. She reached out and touched his hand. 'Leave me.'

'Come on, sweetheart,' Summer pleaded with her.

Brytenn told him to leave her alone.

Again the two men faced up to one another.

This time Twilight went over to Olga and pulled her up.

'Sorry to be rough, but I need everyone onside right now.' He pulled a gun from his belt, cocked it and put it to her head. 'We have to be in Rostov by tomorrow night,' he said. 'This gets done now or not at all. Please get your equipment into place and secure all hides. Mr Summer, if you could assemble everything here before we move out. Sorry, Cooper, but Vasili awaits.'

Brytenn stepped out on to the porch and began to smoke.

29

Prize

Spring flowers perfumed Vasili's main street, while the last of the day's sun began to bake the ruts in the road and the wind threw dust into the sky in small shaky pillars. A chorus of pigeons in a copse of trees behind a line of broken houses drowned most of the music from a distant violin, and Cooper Brytenn paused to listen to Vivaldi from a nearby window. The sun died with the music and, as it did, Vasili itself seemed to be vanishing, too.

The shape of the old Orthodox church, which had stood on the same spot for two hundred years, was still visible in the police station that had replaced it; the red bricks bore the scars of war and reconstruction in equal amounts, while on top a slate roof had replaced the onion dome, portions of which were still embedded in the wall above the front door. Iron railings girded the front of the building, leaving a small driveway with two equal patches of grass and an old armoured car for decoration. Two police vehicles were parked in the driveway and a hose lay curled at one wall.

Cooper Brytenn, now using a stick, as much for effect as support, limped past the place once, then stopped at the end of the street, circled round and came back. Two or three people sat in the small square in front of the station, at least one of them drunk. Probably all. Vasili, like many similar places, was left to drink after dark.

Across the tree-lined square, to Brytenn's left, next to a wall full of posters, some dating back years, Patrick Twilight looked at his watch and gave a single nod to Brytenn, which Brytenn barely saw. Brytenn took one more look beyond the square, down the main street, through a gap in some flowering trees, to where Olga and Summer were sitting on a bench holding hands. Summer was busy looking around him, for a face he could just about recall. Olga was keeping an eye on Summer but only with a detached professionalism.

'You don't have to do this,' she said to him.

'I want to.'

If he expected an argument, he did not get one. Olga was too busy. The rest of her attention was concentrated on Cooper Brytenn and the police station. And Ivan Pyotr.

Ivan Pyotr stood across the street, holding a bag and looking like he might just bolt to prevent his own redundancy. Except Olga was too aware of his every movement, and despite their tentative friendship, the colonel was well aware she would kill him if told to.

They all held their positions and thoughts until there was enough darkness. Then Brytenn moved.

The single policeman on the concrete porch of the police station, backed by the remains of painted-over mosaics and Communist Party posters, lounged in an easy chair, a leather belt with a holster containing a small pistol hanging over the railings in front of him, while he cleaned a submachine-gun. The smell of gun oil mixed with the scent of the flowers while the moon appeared lazily from behind growing strips of cloud forming in the east. The falling temperature had the policeman considering the relative warmth of his station.

Brytenn walked on, greeted an old man coming from a lane which led down to a small stream and a collective farm that bred horses. The American watched the line of the steppe begin to vanish under the approach of night. Above him, the few stars showing through the strips of cloud that were forming in the sky seemed to point the way for him back to the police station. As he entered the grounds of the station, Brytenn found himself quoting passages from harsh novels he did not like.

'Yes?' The young policeman moved faster than Brytenn had anticipated and dropped his legs to the ground. The moonlight caught a squint in one of his eyes and he placed his submachine-gun to one side before standing up.

'I wish to report a crime,' Brytenn said.

'We're closed. Come back tomorrow.'

The young policeman dropped his eyes to the weapon he was cleaning and just had enough time to see Brytenn looking at the firing pin he had removed. Brytenn came up very quickly and shot him with a silenced pistol. The policeman fell back in his seat as if sleeping.

Jack Summer, barely holding himself together, periodically dizzy to the point of distraction, slipped uneasily over a market-garden fence to the left of the police station and made his way along the grooves of a series of allotments, towards one of the station's side windows. Olga covered him from a position in a small clump of trees which had recently sprouted leaves, urging on his every move, while Twilight and Pyotr waited inside the gates of the police station, just behind Brytenn.

Summer, now using every ounce of mental and physical strength he had left, having checked inside the station, made his way round to the front of the station and took up position on one side of the porch, pausing now and again to draw breath and control the dizziness and nausea that now accompanied all his exertions. Brytenn took the other side. While Summer gave Brytenn hand signals on what he had seen through the side window, in the soft light from the station Brytenn could see large drops of sweat running down Summer's face. And when the moonlight touched him, Jack Summer looked dead. He moved towards the front door.

Inside the police station a wireless set played faint ballet music, a kind of ponderous melody which never quite fully made it to the front door. Summer shoved his head through the door and looked inside.

As he had seen through the side window, three policemen were sitting around a table passing photographs to one another and smiling. One of them shouted into the night for his young friend on the porch to bring a letter in. Summer counted the remaining moments of their lives out with his fingers, then slumped down on the porch. Brytenn burst in to the station building and opened fire.

The three policemen fell over their card table with a silence that seemed almost respectful to the stillness of the night. In the distance, the violin became louder for a moment and then died off, too. Brytenn turned up the ballet music.

The night closed in on the scene as Twilight and Olga made their way through to the back of the building. Down small corridors, checking open doors. Four men in a far room were grabbing for their weapons with that sense of terror of men who realise they will probably die in the next few minutes.

They moved to cover one another with a reluctance that belied their situation and desire to escape. Twilight fired single shots and the policemen had their expectations fulfilled.

Olga checked the bodies and moved down the doors of the adjoining rooms. A fifth policeman was in a small kitchen, making coffee, his back to her. She shot him twice in the head.

'Clear!' she whispered.

Brytenn went to the door and told Ivan Pyotr, who was sitting beside Jack Summer; for some reason he felt the need to check with Summer before going into the station. Perhaps he was hoping Summer would prevent him from having to do it. Perhaps he was concerned for Summer.

'Go on!' Summer said.

Very reluctantly, Pyotr obeyed. He followed Brytenn inside.

Meanwhile, Jack Summer lit a cigarette. His hands shook the whole time. When two people walked past and spoke greetings through the darkness, Summer answered them. And then he threw up.

Back inside, Ivan Pyotr, somewhat shaken, in the same way he had been the day he broke out of Camp Thirty-Six, looked at the bodies of each of the dead policemen with a mixture of relief and sadness. Then his Tartarish looks regained their strength as he readjusted himself to a building he had last been inside thirty years earlier.

'So where is it?' Olga demanded.

Pyotr, already making calculations, began walking towards a back room and Cooper Brytenn hobbled behind him, as if guided by an internal map. Pyotr stopped several times, checked dimensions, entered two rooms and came out of them, then finally stopped in front of a fireplace at the back of the building.

'There,' he said, pointing. But he was afraid to go near the spot himself. 'It must be there. That was where the altar was. It has to be there. Dig there.'

Cooper Brytenn began to pick up the heavy grating at the fireplace and clear away the coals and ashes. It took him some time and Patrick Twilight found himself fascinated, holding his silenced pistol across his chest, occasionally glancing out of the window for signs of interest from the world outside.

'Soviet citizens are obedient,' Pyotr remarked to Twilight. 'A prisoner understands this. Take your time, Brytenn.' But he did not attempt to help him.

'You're that confident, Colonel?' Twilight said. It struck him that there should have been more interest in what they were doing, that the prize they were after was worth more than the bodies of a few provincial policemen.

'Get me the pickaxe,' Brytenn said to Pyotr.

The policeman pulled out the small pick he had in his bag and handed it to Brytenn, but was still reluctant to become involved in what they were doing. And all the time Brytenn dug into the concrete, the police colonel kept his eyes closed.

The box Brytenn pulled from beneath an inch of concrete was as innocuous as the whole suburban scene, the dust still on the brown lid, a small rusting lock keeping the whole thing in its place. It might have been a child's playset.

Patrick Twilight breathed out only once.

'I could open it but I think you should, Colonel,' Brytenn said. He handed the box to Pyotr.

'No.' Pyotr raised his hands.

'Please!' Twilight said.

So the colonel opened the small lock with a pocket knife

and lifted the lid. When he looked inside, his mouth opened wide and he rushed for the door.

Brytenn caught him.

'In the time it takes for an eye to see, a life is lost,' Ivan Pyotr said. 'You have opened me to the world, and I will be seen. Thirty years. Thirty years and the world catches up with you. We used to say when you dug up a grave you were digging your own. Do you not understand, you foolish man, we will all die now. I did not want this.' He shook his head. 'Out!' he said then. 'Out of here!'

On the porch, Jack Summer was answering a woman's voice from the darkness. 'We're closed,' he said.

'But I have something to report. My mother was robbed this evening . . .' As Pyotr came out on to the porch, to announce the Vasili file was not in the box, the nurse, Anastasia, stood in front of Summer, her mouth frozen. He shot her as soon as she backed off.

THE MOUNTAIN

30

Escapes

As if the bloody mess found in Vasili police station were not enough to have him shot, Anatoli Beshov's disappearance out of a second-storey window of their Stalingrad hotel the following night made Vladimir Romanovili slam his first into the mouth of the man nearest to him, knocking him across Beshov's room and breaking a side table.

Romanovili had a paraphrase of Oscar Wilde's words on his mind: losing one prisoner might have been considered a misfortune; losing two would certainly be viewed as carelessness.

'Find him!' he shouted. 'Find them!'

Then he went to a small desk in his own room, pulled out a bottle and began to drink from it.

'Beria will have my balls,' he said to himself.

Further down the Volga, as a long river barge pulled in alongside the grid-patterned streets of Rostov-on-Don, a long-limbed sun was beginning to crouch behind the horizon across the Sea of Azov as a line of chimney stacks pumped grey smoke in tall jets towards the rainbow clouds overhead. A thin strip of sulphurous yellow marked the join between the land and the sky.

Cooper Brytenn and Patrick Twilight slipped off the barge and, walking either side of a broken Ivan Pyotr, called at a small apartment run by two Armenians near the city's river-boat station.

At the same time, Jack Summer and Olga Sharankova stepped down from a train which had just arrived from Kharkov. Summer, who could barely stand by himself now, told Olga to leave him, but she refused. They marched past the apartment where Brytenn and Twilight were staying right at the moment the sun disappeared over the horizon and, arm in arm, headed up a main prospekt for the northern end of town.

'There it is,' Olga said. 'Do you see it, Jack?'

It was an old bank that had been converted into a hotel for factory workers. It was a plain solid cube of concrete that looked more like a pillbox than a hotel. Summer could hardly raise his head to view the place.

'Now, remember,' she continued, 'let me talk. You were hurt in a factory accident. Saved by your friends.'

He did not respond. He had said little since Stalingrad, and his very torpor was enough to convince security police and others who might have an interest that he was exactly who she said he was. A handsome man with glasses and a small birthmark checked them in and took their papers.

'I'll drop them up when I'm finished,' he said.

Olga was almost glad to agree to his suggestion. He made things seem normal.

In their room, Olga stared out of the window and checked the street for things she knew were not there. There were routines she now followed without thinking and they gave a feeling of security where there was none.

'I think no one believes what they see any more,' she said to Summer. 'People have become so expert at reading between the lines, and sifting for news as if on a rubbish tip. Please talk to me, Jack.' She came over to him and kissed him.

'You should not have done that,' he insisted.

Summer stood up and began to walk about like a man who suspects everything, including himself, picking things up and putting them down without examining them, speaking in short undirected bursts, hurling half truths and petty accusations, starting things without finishing even the start. Olga told him to have a drink.

'You had to shoot her,' Olga said.

'You know this, Olga?' Summer said. 'Did Brytenn tell you that? Did he tell you he had to shoot Swell Johnson?'

'He didn't shoot him.'

'No, he left him.'

'He was dead.'

'Is that what they call it?'

'Keep your voice down, Jack. And speak Russian.'

'Yes, of course, Russian. I dream in Russian, you know. Bad dreams.'

'Jack, you're bleeding again,' Olga said.

Summer touched his head. 'So I am,' he said, and then began to laugh. He could not stop laughing, and once he cried out Cooper Brytenn's name as if he expected Brytenn to share a joke. He collapsed soon after.

When he woke, he was talking to himself. Olga bathed his head with warm water. 'I was being eaten,' Summer said.

'I know,' she replied.

*   *   *

Patrick Twilight lay on a creaking bed, watching Cooper Brytenn watch the street. Neither man talked. The room was so small the bed touched the wall and the wallpaper was peeling and touching Brytenn's shoulder. Brytenn held the remains of a phial of morphine in his hand. And as the drug took effect, he began to relax with his own thoughts.

'So what do we do, gentlemen?' Ivan Pyotr asked finally. He was sitting at the door, pressing a warped floorboard. It made a creaking noise, marginally louder than the bed, and Pyotr looked like he was on the verge of tears.

Twilight turned with an irritated look on his face. 'We get out of here,' he said.

'Without what I want,' Brytenn added, his confidence now boosted by the relief of his pain.

Twilight looked at his watch. 'Where did you have in mind to look for it?' he asked. 'We have at best a day or two to contact the boat. Before our papers are thoroughly checked and found to be forgeries. If we're really lucky, we might have three days. Assuming it turns up. Turkey's a long way away.'

'All those years for nothing,' Pyotr muttered. He had muttered it before and the two men in the room with him ignored it now. Though Twilight did keep the occasional eye on Pyotr just in case the police colonel decided to make a run for it, or some other foolishness. Frankly, the old man was a liability now, but Twilight was not really in the mood for complete frankness. He needed options, and more than that, Brytenn needed hope.

Brytenn was making calculations of the safe houses they had in the Caucasus, people arranged for him who might turn out to be double agents or just turn around and kill them and bury them in the mountains. 'I don't like to lose,' he said.

'That's a foolish position for any man in our line of work to take, Cooper,' Twilight said. 'We usually end up losing, one way or another. Our only real victory is staying in the game.'

'Just who are you?' Pyotr asked Twilight.

'I'm a stupid man who took a job when he had nothing better to do, Colonel. You know the story because it's yours, too. A job that required a degree of lying until lying became the sole basis for what I do.' Twilight sighed, as if everything he had ever relied on had evaporated in the evening sunlight.

'Patrick's British,' Cooper Brytenn said.

'Isn't that all it is, Cooper?' Twilight asked. 'Sets of competing lies. Each side needs the other to be the sole receptacle for its fears. And we must fear to survive, because without it we would sit back and let the maggots take us early. And nature will not permit that. So we invent fears.'

'Imperial malaise,' Brytenn remarked. 'You'd compare communism with our system?'

'You don't have the same conviction as Mr Brytenn, here,' Pyotr said.

'If you were able to walk around this town, you would find that at least half the population probably helped the Whites during the Civil War; well, maybe not that many now because so many of them died at the hands of the Germans. So many of them do not even remember the Civil War. But those who supported the Whites turned round and supported the Bolsheviks when they came and would support Attila the Hun if he turned up tomorrow. People just want to live.'

'Well, maybe you should stay and live here,' Pyotr said.

'I don't want to. I'm happy with my hypocrisy because it is a fairly benign one. But do not make the mistake of thinking that I believe in it as an article of faith.'

'And if these men who are unwilling agents of Stalin decide to press on to London, will you sit and wait and change your faith?' Brytenn asked.

'No. I'll run to your country, Cooper, and hope they don't come there.'

'It's time to go,' Brytenn insisted.

Twilight stood on the corner of the street, looking at his watch, while Cooper Brytenn, still slightly high on the morphine he had taken, crossed between two cars, went over to a small kiosk and bought some cigarettes. Far down the street, almost at the limit of his clear vision, Olga Sharankova watched from a bus stop. Brytenn, happy at seeing her again, paused to look at her, then recrossed the road to Twilight.

'Tonight, eleven o'clock,' he said, lifting his stick and touching the pointed end.

'You go on,' Twilight said, nodding at Olga Sharankova.

Brytenn smiled and walked along the prospekt with a limp that seemed more pronounced now he had a stick, so much so that Twilight wondered if the American was not now faking it a little. Twilight followed Brytenn at a safe distance.

Brytenn caught up with Olga at the bottom of some steps near the river, beside a statue of Maxim Gorky. The statue had graffiti on it and two policemen were checking papers to their left.

'I'd swear you brought me down here to hurt my ankle again,' Brytenn said to her. If he hoped for some intimacy, then he was disappointed. Olga had too many things on her mind, though some of her facial expressions convinced him she was glad to see him.

'Jack is getting worse,' she said.

'How much worse?'

She remembered her conversation with Summer and the arguments over Swell Johnson and did not answer. Then it was their turn to show their papers. They smiled and the policemen, who did not appear too concerned with what they were supposed to be doing, glanced at what they were given and then at Olga, before deciding she wasn't worth it. She pulled her headscarf down over her forehead.

Brytenn whispered the time they would go in a kiss. And Olga held the kiss longer than was necessary to receive the message.

'Stay with me,' Brytenn whispered, not sure why he had.

'I have to go,' she replied. 'He needs me.' She touched Brytenn's hand.

'Will he be all right?' Brytenn asked.

She did not answer. Just walked off. Brytenn was still following her when Twilight intervened.

'I don't mean to pry . . .'

'Well, then, don't,' Brytenn snapped. 'Come on, we have things to do.'

When Olga reached her hotel again, Jack Summer was lying on the floor, in a pool of vomit. Several pieces of furniture were upended around him and a bowl of food and a cup lay in a corner. She got him to the bed and brought him back to consciousness, then cleaned him as quickly as she could.

'What happened?' she asked.

'The manager was up again. Asking questions,' Summer replied. 'Then the power went. No light. Oh, God, Olga, don't let them eat me.'

'We leave tonight,' she whispered.

He nodded. 'We'll go together,' he said. He gripped her hand and would not let go of it. 'We're a good team, yeah?'

'A good team, Jack.'

'The best.'

But he knew she was thinking of Brytenn.

Twilight and Brytenn moved around Rostov for the rest of the day, dealing in the small change of their situation. It was a long, boring dance between buildings and public parks, an attempt not to attract attention that may well have done the opposite. Ivan Pyotr had refused to come and as he was no longer useful to them, neither Brytenn nor Twilight was inclined to argue with him. Both of them might even have considered leaving the old colonel to his fate, except that Brytenn needed to feel good about himself. He took some more morphine in a toilet without telling Twilight. Twilight knew anyway.

'So who has it?' Brytenn asked Twilight over tea. More to distract the Englishman than anything else. 'The Vasili file?'

'Who knows?' Twilight replied. 'No one who needed to break into that police station. That concrete was down for years. Maybe the old colonel told someone years ago and just forgot.'

'Do you believe that?' Brytenn asked. 'Have we all been chasing nothing?'

'I don't know everything, Cooper. I just feel the movement of strings, somewhere nearby. Let's go pick up our charge and vacate this country.'

They walked back to their apartment by a circuitous route, taking time out to meet their Armenian hosts at another block where they were staying with their daughter and her family.

When they left, Brytenn was in need of more morphine, except that when he reached for another phial, there were none left in his pocket.

'We better move,' he said to Twilight.

It was Twilight who noticed the light in their room was off.

'He knows to keep it on?' he asked Brytenn.

'He knows.'

The two men began walking faster towards their house, Brytenn carrying his stick and not limping as much as before, each of them pulling small silenced weapons from their pockets, panting in the frosty dampness of the spring weather, knocking over a crate before entering the large turn-of-the-century block, then moving upstairs when Brytenn gave the signal.

They entered the apartment in cover formation, Brytenn ahead, his desire for morphine pushing him ahead of his desire to stay alive, Twilight concentrating on the business in hand, and wondering if his own readings were beginning to play themselves out. He saw the shadow first and called for its owner to halt. But something distracted his attention.

On the floor, Ivan Pyotr lay dead.

Misha Girenko came into view at almost the same time. He put a gun to Twilight's head. 'What more had he left?' he said, taking Brytenn's pistol and chewing on a piece of vegetable at the same time. 'His whole reason for existence is gone.' He took Twilight's pistol away. 'I did him a favour. Just like you. You know, gentlemen, I could have reported you to the security police the minute you stepped off that barge.'

31

Springtime

The whole of the next day drifted, and with it Cooper Brytenn who, without morphine, sank into a nervous lethargy that only displayed itself in sweat and pain. He leaned more than ever on his stick and limped like his leg would fall off. But no one had any time for Brytenn now, not even Olga. It was as if his defeat was now their defeat. Only Twilight looked like he had anything left in him to fight with.

From the moment they left Girenko's old beaten-up truck, in a rainstorm, through a long climb into the Caucasus, with each of them taking turns to help a semi-conscious and bleeding Jack Summer, over an early spring carpet that unleashed its glory in small flowers between the tall pines and the steep faces of the mountain, they all remained silent. Until, suddenly, on the other side of the mountain, between a small forest of pines and a precipice with a river below, they were in deep snow.

'Are you going to throw us all off, Misha?' Twilight asked Girenko. 'Kill us all here?'

'There are a hundred thousand troops and police searching for you,' Misha Girenko said. 'From Stalingrad to Tbilisi. If

I'd wanted to do you harm, do you not think I would have handed you over to them, instead of smuggling you all through their lines. My apologies for the discomfort of the ride but it was necessary.' He looked around him. 'This is a safe place, Twilight.' He grinned and told them to stop. 'Sit down,' he said. 'Hands on heads, where I can see them. I'll be back in a few seconds, so don't go away. I'm still a very good shot. And I'll be watching all the time.'

Curiosity more than anything kept Twilight from trying anything. The others obeyed without question. Brytenn might have said something but he had to help Olga keep Summer steady.

Misha Girenko walked ankle-deep through the remains of a snowdrift, while six small furry animals crept across a lengthy treeline in front of him, through the broken branches of downed boughs, under a gloomy leaden sky, barely able to keep itself in the air. When he had been in the trees for a few seconds, and Twilight had been tempted again to get up and run, Misha Girenko re-emerged with a black bag and lowered his weapon.

His prisoners watched him approach.

'I'm glad you decided to heed my advice,' he said. 'As a priest, I find needless killing upsets me. I have been meaning to ask you about a woman in Berlin, Twilight, but I will not. What is done, is done.'

Twilight did not say anything. Which gave Cooper Brytenn a chance to re-enter the game. For more than anything now he was convinced that it was a game – a great game perhaps, but a game nonetheless. And in resigning himself to that, Brytenn relieved himself of some of the demons that had haunted him during his life.

'What now?' he asked Girenko. It was enough that he should ask this question and he was content to let it rest at that. His stomach was aching and his ankle giving more pain than he could remember since the drop that damaged it. As if all the pain had been stored up for this moment. He looked to Girenko to validate his authority with an answer now.

But Girenko seemed to be in a state of contemplation akin to prayer. Behind him, the high Caucasus mountains strained to hold back the sky, then disappeared into the clouds, while, to his left, a vaguely salty sea breeze flushed across a sharp valley slope and pushed the spring grasses forward to the beat of a high waterfall. Girenko slung the bag he carried down between his legs. 'This is what happens next, Brytenn,' he said. He spun around and looked at the colours of the gathering spring. 'I'd forgotten how beautiful this place was. You know what they call this mountain?'

'The Gravedigger,' Patrick Twilight said. 'Our friend is a Gravedigger, Cooper.'

Brytenn was happy to let the Englishman take over again. His own battle was difficult enough without wasting time on Girenko's sophistry. The priest was going to kill them all, there was no doubt about it. It was just a matter of when. Brytenn was preparing himself for death. Almost welcoming it.

'Not the highest mountain around here but very special to me and my kind,' Girenko said. 'And this year the snow has fallen on this side only,' he muttered then. 'Never mind,' he added. 'That way, as you can see, is the Black Sea. At the foot of this mountain, you will find a car and driver. He will take you to a boat. The boat will take you to Turkey. Believe me, they have already intercepted the boat you had arranged, Twilight. By the way, the car driver is Georgian, so pay him well.'

Girenko threw the bag at Brytenn.

'What you were looking for, I believe.'

Brytenn, again to assert his authority, picked it up and handed it to Twilight. Twilight opened the bag, looked inside and began to examine the contents. After a few minutes, he nodded to Brytenn. 'Vasili,' he said.

'In its entirety,' Girenko said.

'You had it all the time,' Brytenn said to Girenko.

'You had better move,' Girenko said. 'Your friend does not look as if he will last another day without attention.' He stared at Jack Summer for a second. 'With attention, who knows?' He made a sign with his hand indicating he thought Summer was a little crazy.

'And you?' Twilight asked Girenko.

Girenko looked around at the mountains again and then wiped his nose with his sleeve and sniffed. He glanced down at the bag. 'I was never here. I was executed in Paris.'

'I should have let the French kill you.'

'You had better move, Twilight, before half the Interior troops in Russia come looking for that. I reckon you have about an hour. They've blocked the road either side of the mountain, but not the section in the middle. Stupid bastards. There's an old smuggling trail that leads to the sea. You have to know it to drive there at night. It's dangerous.'

'And what will happen then?' Brytenn asked.

'They'll be waiting for us,' Olga said.

'No one will be waiting for you. I assure you,' Girenko said. 'I could have handed you over in Rostov. Look, there are reasons for this. Now, go. And take care on that path, it's dangerous, too. Sharp drop. Go single file.'

'Why did you let us go through with everything?' Brytenn said. 'When you had this all the time?'

'Because he needed a cover,' Twilight said. 'And there was a good chance he'd help wipe out what we had in the Urals.'

'A priest always kills with a heavy heart, Twilight. A Chekist kills with no heart at all.'

Twilight shook his head. 'All right, all right, keep your illusions, Misha, we'll take what we came for and leave. You can ponder your fate when you're drowning yourself in drink and women in wherever you wind up. I assume you have a way out planned?'

'I told you, Twilight, I was never here.' Girenko turned suddenly; an instinct or something else told him to do it. A single shot rang out and he fell back in the melting snow.

Cooper Brytenn scrambled over to him, examined the priest's face then looked at Twilight. 'He's dead,' he said.

Twilight knelt down beside the body and whispered a prayer into Girenko's ear. As he did, a small trickle of blood ran down Girenko's face and made a tiny arrow in the snow. And when Patrick Twilight looked in the direction the arrow was pointing he saw Anatoli Beshov standing above them, holding a rifle in the firing position.

Anatoli Beshov kicked Brytenn in the ankle. The American let out a muffled cry and saw all his efforts at dignity collapse into the snow. 'Long time, no see, Brytenn. Bet this one is a turn-up for the books. Takes a Gravedigger to pick a spot like this for a little dealing. I take it this is what we've all been looking for?' He touched the black bag but did not look inside.

Jack Summer fell forward into the snow at that moment. Olga moved to help him. 'Do it, sweetheart, and I'll blow you away, too, much as it will pain my heart. Now where's the cash?'

'There is no cash,' Brytenn said.

'There's always cash. You were buying something from this bastard. Give it to me, or I execute you here and now. There's a division of Interiors all over these mountains right now, right on your tails. Give it here, and you can have your file. You should not have left me, Brytenn, I saved your life after all.' He slammed his foot into Brytenn's ankle again. 'I'd take an hour with you, sweetheart,' he said to Olga, 'only I do not have an hour. Now give me what he gave you.' He began to search Girenko.

'He gave us that,' Twilight said, pointing to the bag. 'Stalin's Okhrana file. He was an Okhrana agent.'

'I know. I came looking for all this before, you know, during a shit cold winter in the war. Planned on selling it to Hitler. Wound up escorting a bunch of lousy Americans in German uniform out of Stalingrad because Washington did not want to be embarrassed by their capture. Misha let me down then, the bastard. Always the smart one, Misha. And too deep for his own good. Believed in things. I might have liked him but for that. That mother of his was a bitch though. Helpful, but a bitch.'

He stood up when he found nothing on Girenko, and swung around in a desperate search for clues.

'Look, I saw you all in Stalingrad, you stupid fuckers. I saw you all and I said nothing. So just give me what you gave him and we can all go our separate ways. Frankly, I have very little inclination to meet the Interiors again. Not after the last time.'

'You're open to offers then?' Twilight said.

Beshov smiled and his eyes caught the sunlight and sparkled.

'No,' Brytenn said.

Beshov kicked him again. 'Shut up, you're not my ticket out of here any more, Brytenn. So give me what I fucking want!'

'There's no money,' Brytenn insisted.

Beshov kicked his ankle again.

Olga crawled over to Brytenn. Beshov kicked her away. 'Too fucking sweet on him, sweetheart. Why not dish out some of that sweetness on the rest of us? Make your offer, Twilight.'

The sound of the dogs broke everything.

They appeared as specks against the fading sunlight, then stains on the small grasses. Beshov raised his rifle and fired three shots without hitting anything.

'Come on, Twilight, make your bloody offer. Give me what he gave you.'

But Twilight said nothing.

'You bastard!' Beshov went to turn to Twilight again, perhaps to shoot him, but Jack Summer caught his legs and upended him. Beshov pitched backward into the snow. Cooper Brytenn threw himself on top of the SS officer.

Beshov kneed Brytenn in the stomach, threw him off, then went to kick him, but Olga Sharankova caught him in the face with his rifle. He toppled back to the edge of the path, scrambling at loose stones to keep from falling over the cliff beside it.

The Interior troops behind the dogs were shooting now, single shots, wild and without a chance of hitting a target. Seeing Olga with his rifle, Beshov smiled and raised his hands.

'Kill him,' Twilight said to Olga.

'Hey, sweetheart, you wouldn't kill me?' Beshov wiped the blood from his face. 'Brytenn, tell her you owe me.'

Cooper Brytenn was trying to raise Jack Summer from the snow. 'Give me the rifle, Olga; you take Jack,' Brytenn said.

'I said to kill him,' Twilight said to Olga. He lifted the bag with the Vasili file and dusted the snow off it. 'We have to, Cooper,' he added.

Olga looked at Twilight and then at Brytenn. There were so many reasons to kill Beshov, and yet now, looking at him, almost pleading like a wounded animal, she could not do it. Beshov was animal enough to know she would not and he came at her the minute she hesitated. He came at her with enough force to knock the rifle from her hands, and hit her hard enough to stun her. He shot Twilight in the arm, knocking him sideways, while the bag with the Vasili file in it toppled over the edge of the cliff. Every one of them watched it fall and hit the loose clay below. No one except Beshov spoke.

'You stupid fuck —' The SS officer aimed the rifle at Twilight.

Cooper Brytenn shoved the point of his walking stick into Beshov with all the strength he could muster.

Anatoli Beshov's eyes looked surprised and he stared at Brytenn for a second before following the bag over the cliff. Bullets tore into the rocks and trees around them.

Twilight went to the edge of the cliff, as if he were going to jump after Beshov and the file. Brytenn pulled him back.

'Leave it!' he yelled.

Three bullets hit the snow near them and two dogs were less than a hundred metres away.

'Get out of here!' Brytenn shouted at Twilight. He grabbed Beshov's rifle and began firing back. He hit both dogs, then looked at Twilight. 'Get them out of here . . . please!'

Twilight hesitated, but the sight of what was coming at them convinced him, and he told Olga to help him with Summer.

'Brytenn,' Olga pleaded.

'I'll follow,' Brytenn said to her. 'Promise. It looks like my ankle will have to heal now, ready or not.'

Twilight grabbed Olga and the two of them lifted Summer and moved off into the cover of trees, Summer leaning on Twilight's shoulder.

Cooper Brytenn found himself some cover and took aim again. He was frightened now, and elated, and the two emotions balanced one another out. In the eye of his mind he could see men in a boat, and Swell Johnson, and he asked Johnson how he was and the usual reply came back.

Olga Sharankova was able to slide in beside him.

They did not speak.

Somewhere beneath them, Anatoli Beshov scrambled through the undergrowth ahead of the sound of the dogs. Bleeding and broken, the SS officer held tightly to the bag he carried, until he came to a stream and slid to his knees. He dropped the bag and for a while considered leaving it and saving himself, but something inside him forced him to lift it again, and he talked to himself, telling himself things he knew were untrue.

He crawled along the stream for a while, then stopped and pulled himself on to a rock. There was nothing left. Anatoli Beshov had run out of everything. Vladimir Romanovili was standing above him, surrounded by men with dogs.

'I got it,' Beshov said, pointing to the bag.

He gave it to Romanovili.

'I need medical attention,' Beshov shouted. 'Get me a doctor.'

Romanovili came closer and examined him. Then he stepped back. 'You do appear to be in some difficulty, Anatoli.'

'I've been here before. Nothing vital busted. You get them?'

'We will.'

'Come on, man, get me some help or I'll bleed to death.'

Romanovili did not speak again.

'Oh, I see,' Beshov smiled. There was such menace in his smile that some of the Interiors stepped back, too. 'You want to see if I can kill the dogs, yes? Okay, give me the gun.'

Romanovili gave the order for the dogs to be unleashed.

32

Reptiles

Lavrenti Beria took off his glasses in a fast aggressive fashion. The dacha was so far inside the woods south of Moscow that the sun had an impossible task getting through and the whole place was constantly lit by artificial light.

'This is it, then,' Beria said to Romanovili.

'As ordered.'

'You've read it?'

'Some.'

'And the people involved?'

'The search continues.'

'Call it off.'

'But there are outstanding matters.'

'Well, I suppose that's to be expected.'

Romanovili stood still for a moment, then went to salute. 'I'll go, sir.'

Beria nodded. 'I appreciate everything you have done, Vladimir. I hope you know that.'

Romanovili smiled.

Then Beria pulled a gun and shot him in the head.

✻   ✻   ✻

A few hours later a small aircraft touched down on a remote airstrip in southern Georgia. Nikita Khrushchev and two bodyguards walked across the strip to a small shack. The aircraft's engine was still running.

'Beria has it.'

Patrick Twilight came out of the shadow and took Khrushchev's hand. His other arm hung limp.

'Then Beria is Stalin's enemy,' Khrushchev replied. 'But as no one in the army or the politburo will support him, he's a fairly impotent enemy. When he's given the police portfolio again, he'll spend most of his time watching his back and Stalin will expend his energy watching Beria. A balance of terror.'

'And Berlin?' Twilight asked.

'Stalin has decided to reopen the land routes. Perhaps he has decided not to listen to Beria's advice given what's happened. Frankly, I don't think he was ever serious about Berlin, you know. He's Georgian. They don't tell their right hands what their left hands are doing.'

'Usually strangling people.'

'Always strangling people.'

AUTHOR'S NOTE

I was told this story by Jack Summer. He had been in a mental asylum since 1949. He died three days after we met. When I went to visit the grave, there was a wreath on it with a note signed: Gravedigger.

WITHDRAWN FROM STOCK